CITY OF LUST

HALF-BREED SERIES BOOK 5

DEBRA DUNBAR

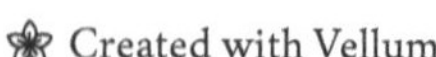 Created with Vellum

I yanked the huge purple suitcase off the conveyer belt and dragged it over to where Irix stood, reading a paper. It was in Italian, which meant I didn't understand any of it. Well, except for a few words in the caption under a large picture of an intense-looking, middle-aged man. His dark eyes seemed to stab into me, tearing through every one of my secrets, judging me and finding me lacking. If my non-existent Italian were to be trusted, I think the paper said that this man was dead. Although the caption could have just as easily said he liked the color magenta, or had found the image of Mary Magdalene in his breakfast oatmeal.

"Little help here?"

Irix reached out and pulled the bag over toward him. "Sorry. I didn't see the conveyor belt start up." He folded the paper and stuffed it into the handle of the suitcase, looking over my shoulder at the other bags going round-and-round as travelers watched with bleary eyes. "Guido Montenegro died."

I had no idea who that was. Assuming that was part of his excuse for leaving me with the luggage collection duties, I guessed it was the guy in the paper.

"Him?" I pointed to the picture.

"Yeah."

"Did you know him?" I wasn't sure whether to express condolences or curiosity. Was this guy a political figure, or someone with a closer connection?

"No. The Montenegros are a wealthy family from Bergamo. Guido Montenegro had purchased a historic villa in the Lake Como area a few years back and just completed restoration on it."

Bergamo was where the enology seminars and the apprenticeship contest were being held. Irix and I were staying in Lake Como—in Menaggio to be exact. It did seem an odd coincidence. I looked more closely at the picture. The man had dark hair that, in the grainy black-and-white photo, seemed to have the barest touch of gray. His nose was straight and long, with a beak-like hook, the lines of his face conveyed a sort of timeless quality. Maybe he was in his late thirties. Maybe he was in his forties. Maybe he was in his early fifties. It was one of those faces that blurred aging.

And those eyes.

"Kinda young to die," I observed. "Car accident?"

Irix shrugged. "It says natural causes."

Maybe this was an old photograph, before cancer had wasted him away, or heart disease had taken hold. As horrible as it sounded, I was actually kind of glad we wouldn't be running into him as we jaunted around the lake playing tourist. Something about him seemed…intimidating.

Irix pulled the handle up on the bag, shouldering both the carry-ons while I pulled a smaller suitcase behind me. He tossed the paper into the bin as we headed out the sliding glass doors into the waiting area and into the land of sharks.

Sharks, as in people desperately trying to interest us in a car service to get to our destination. Luckily I'd taken hold of this part of our adventure and had, in the face of Irix's casual insistence that he'd just steal a car, booked a rental. In record time I had the keys in hand and we were standing in front of our ride for the next two weeks.

"What is *that?*" Irix blinked at the car, one of the carry-on bags sliding off his shoulder to thunk onto the ground.

"It's a Panda. How could I resist renting a car named 'Panda'?" It was so stinking cute—tiny and bright blue with four doors and a rounded, zippy design. I loved it.

"I can't be seen driving that," he complained.

Oh the drama. Although I got the feeling he was serious. "Good thing you're not driving then." I waved the keys at him. They weren't in my hand for long.

"You're *not* driving."

"I rented the car. I'm the one who has her license on the line. You're not an authorized driver for this vehicle." I hopped up and down, trying to reach the keys that he was holding far above my head.

The incubus's eyes left the Panda, drawn to my boobs that were bouncing as I jumped. Even my bra didn't do much to hold these puppies in place when I was hopping around a parking lot.

"Steal something for yourself when we get to Menaggio," I told him. "There's nothing in this lot but Smart Cars, Minis, and Fiats. And I *am* driving the Panda."

Irix forced his eyes away from my boobs so he could look around the lot. Then he sighed.

"All right." He dropped the keys into my palm. "We're both going to die. I'm too young to die. For an incubus to meet his end in an auto accident involving a tiny European car and a tourist bus is embarrassing. It's so undignified."

"We're not going to die," I assured him. "I'm not Nyalla."

My changeling stepsister was legendary for her lack of driving skill. It probably didn't help that the first time she'd ever seen a car was at the age of nineteen. Although in a few short years she'd managed to master computer usage, so perhaps that wasn't a valid excuse for her poor driving ability.

Irix was right. We did almost die. Less than ten miles out of Milan I pulled over, rubbed my shaking and sweating hands on my jeans, and let Irix take the wheel. He was a natural, squeezing between buildings and oncoming cars with inches to spare, shouting at other motorists in a flood of Italian, and occasionally Demon. I navigated using my phone, and within a few hours we were pulling up to an iron gate that led to a stone-paved courtyard.

A woman waved, pushed a button, and the gate slid open with a whisper. I craned my neck, trying to catch a glimpse of the house I'd rented online.

Correction, villa.

From the road, all I could see was a tall, gray stone wall that butted up against a narrow sidewalk, the stone house behind it covered in ivy and tall, thin, black-shuttered windows. The courtyard was barely big enough for two cars, even tiny ones like the Panda. The house was to the left, more stone and ivy and shutters, to the right, another tall stone wall. A small path led from the courtyard, I assumed toward the lake.

And the landscaping was gorgeous, a gardener's dream of chestnuts and platanos, jasmine, gardenias, and magnolias. There was a careless order to the trees and bushes, as if God himself had been their gardener and He'd exercised carefree abandon in their placement. Wild, a perfect complement to the old stone and ivy.

The woman stood by the black iron-banded doors of the house, her short bob a stylish platinum on top, dark on the underneath. Her bright green eyes sparkled with a warm welcome as she approached us. She grabbed Irix first, shooting out a stream of Italian as she kissed his one cheek, then the other. As she walked around the car to do the same to me, I caught Irix eyeing her ass.

Men. Sex demons. They always had a one-track mind, although she was totally hot in a cosmopolitan kind of way.

"Amber! I'm Gianna," she announced in English with a faint Italian accent. "Welcome to Menaggio, to Lake Como. Let me show you around the villa and help you get settled in."

I'd expected a lock box combination and a three-ring binder with a list of rental instructions, but this personal welcome made me glad I'd instinctively selected this rental out of the hundreds listed.

Gianna took us down the little pathway that led to a small promontory with a low stone fence that overlooked the lake, a wooden bench strategically placed on the lush grass. From there, the path opened into a huge lawn that separated the villa from the lake. There was a long wooden table with four chairs for al fresco dining, on a mosaic of brick and stone that created a beautiful patio area.

"Those all open up." Gianna pointed to the row of six shutters behind the table. On either side of the patio were two narrow shuttered entrances, brick steps leading up to the doors. Accenting it all was neatly manicured ivy. "And the balcony there is off the main bedroom, so you have many ways to enjoy the view of the lake and mountains."

I'd barely had time to take it in before she led us around to the side and I found myself transfixed. There was a small step down to another lawn with an herb garden, more ivy-accented stone and shuttered windows, and the most beautiful covered breezeway I'd ever seen.

"Oh!" That was about the extent of my verbal skills as I

walked forward to the vines, climbing roses that bloomed bright red as they twined up the stone pillars. The back of the breezeway was the other side of the tall stone wall we'd seen from the street, covered with ivy and vines. There were little café tables, cushioned chairs, and an adorable wooden swing. A door at one end of the breezeway clearly lead out to the street side. At the other end of the breezeway was the side of the villa, with four stone steps leading up to one iron-banded door, right next to them a ground-level door that had row upon row of metal studs in the wood. Above that door was a marble carving of St. George, slaying a dragon.

"Never forget," Gianna whispered, touching the carving as if the scene depicted were of particular importance. Was she a religious woman? I'd heard the St. George story as a metaphor for good overcoming evil, for the defeat of Satan by those of a pure and holy heart.

Either way, I snapped a picture and texted it to Sam, thinking the actual Ha-Satan, the Iblis, might get a laugh out of the carving. Sure enough, my phone beeped seconds later.

Bite me. I'd kick that George guy's ass.

I chuckled, sticking the phone back into my pocket.

Once inside, she gave us a fast tour around the lower floor, then took us up to the three bedrooms upstairs. Irix put our bags in the biggest, then went over to open the shutters to a breathtaking view of the lake. He pushed the mullioned windows open, letting in the gentle, cool breeze and the sounds of the lake slapping against the stone caissons. Then we headed back downstairs where Gianna showed us a binder with her contact information as well as suggestions on boat rentals and activities in the area.

"What are your plans while here on vacation?" Gianna's green eyes danced over Irix, then me, then back to Irix. "Shopping? Festivals? Boating on the lake?"

"All of the above," I told her. "I've got some seminars I need to attend, some study, and an exam to complete for an apprenticeship, but I hope to get in as much sightseeing as possible."

"Amber is a botanist." There was such pride in Irix's voice that I felt myself blush. "We might tour some of the villas so she can wax poetic about all the flowers and trees."

"Oh, you must come see Villa Sommariva!" Gianna clapped her hands together. "It's been in my family for hundreds of years. We have sixteen acres of gardens."

That did sound intriguing, although sixteen acres of begonias were what was running through my mind right now. How could I politely decline to see what was probably an amateur attempt at recreating Versailles?

"My cousin, Eduardo, has a dozen gardeners to maintain the grounds. The Himalayan rhododendrons are over a hundred and fifty years old and some of them are nearly ten feet tall."

That was a whole lot more impressive than sixteen acres of weeds and begonias. "Oh wow, that's amazing."

She smiled. "I'll have Daniela come by to see you. My cousin Eduardo is elderly and deep in his Melancholy, so he seldom leaves his lair. As his heir, Daniela manages the family affairs."

Clearly there was something lost in translation there. What the heck was a Melancholy? Was that depression? A mental illness so severe that he couldn't leave his room? And lair? I vowed that from now on I was going to call my bedroom a lair. As in, once Gianna left, I intended on dragging Irix up to my lair.

"I'd love that. Thank you." The idea of eyeballing century-old rhododendrons was almost as appealing as the whole Irix-in-my-lair one.

"I'm not guaranteeing she'll allow you a tour." Gianna waved a finger at me in warning. "This is our private home, our family's treasure. We do not usually allow outsiders to see behind our gates."

I nodded. I'd need to convince this cousin of hers that I was worthy of viewing their house and gardens, of experiencing something that had been a private part of their family for generations.

We walked Gianna out where she showed us how to activate the big gates to the courtyard and set the security system for the house, then waved as she backed her tiny red car out and drove off down the street.

When the tall iron gates shut with a clang, I realized that I'd never asked Gianna her cousin's contact information. I guess she'd call me, or stop by if she was open to the idea of a tour.

"Shall we go in?" Irix dangled the villa keys in front of my face.

I took them and unlocked the narrow doors off the parking area. They were heavy and thick, swinging on huge iron hinges. We'd rushed through so Gianna could show us the basics, but now I got to truly take in the beauty of what would be our home for the next week.

The décor was an eclectic mix of new and old. Oriental rugs covered terracotta floors. The modern sofas were a distressed leather with plump cream and gold throw pillows. The fireplace against one wall had a patterned tile inset and brass andirons. The chandeliers were old with heavy, rounded glass ornamentation so different from the faceted ones on the chandeliers back home. And the walls...they were covered with wallpaper—fabric wallpaper. It was burgundy in a damask pattern. I felt like I should be sprawled across the sofa, my feet on the coffee table, a lit cigar in one hand and a brandy snifter in the other, watching the flames dance in the fireplace.

Arms encircled my waist. "We so need to fuck in here," Irix whispered in my ear. And suddenly my cigar-and-brandy fantasy took a very different turn.

"Leather couch," I murmured in reply. "Easier clean-up than the one at the winery trailer."

That poor couch. It wasn't in great shape when I'd arrived, and I'd done my best to try to clean all the bodily fluids off of it before I left, but I'm pretty sure they'd ended up burning it.

"I was thinking over there. I could bend you over the staircase banister and take you from behind."

"Behind, or *behind*?" I asked, because Irix was a bit of an ass-man. Or ass-demon as it might be.

"Hmm, can I keep my options open on that one?"

"Of course." I turned to give him a quick kiss, then went over to open the shutters. The windows looked out over the little patio area and lawn with Lake Como in the background. A haze had settled over the mountains, rain likely moving in. Oh, if it rained I was so having a fire in this fireplace. And I was definitely sending Irix out for brandy and cigars.

"Amber! Check out this kitchen."

I followed Irix's voice past a small dining room that seemed to double as a study. The kitchen was huge, nearly the size of the living room, with a fireplace big enough to roast an ox, complete with an iron spit and a huge fire-blackened kettle on a hook. There was a modern stove, a refrigerator, and a big farm-style copper sink, but clearly this fireplace was still in use.

"Could be fun," Irix teased, pointing at the fireplace.

No, it wouldn't be fun. Irix was a better cook than I was. I specialized in suburban staples such as seven-bean dip, crab dip, those little hot dogs rolled up in crescent dough. If I was cooking over an open fire, it was marshmallows on a stick. Besides, anything we cooked in this ginormous fireplace would probably feed half the town of Menaggio, not just the two of us.

"Uh, maybe we can nix that idea and just eat out most of the time?"

"What, and miss cooking in this incredible fireplace?"

"There's no dishwasher," I countered. "You cook it, then you're hand washing every spoon, plate, and that hundred-pound cast-iron witch's cauldron."

He grimaced. "Eating out sounds better and better."

There was a small pantry off the kitchen, as well as a half-bath. Heading back to the living room, I made my way up the winding marble stairs to the upper floor. Three small bedrooms overlooked the avenue, side gardens, and parking area, with narrow low beds across from ornate wardrobes. In between them was a bathroom with a claw-foot tub and tiny shower off to the side. The master suite where Irix had deposited our luggage took up half of the upstairs, with a bed that could easily sleep four, a huge wardrobe, a sitting area, and a little secretary-style desk. The walls had the same silk wallpaper as downstairs, although this room was in varying shades of deep green. The accents were cream and silver, and instead of terracotta, the bedroom had a marble mosaic floor with interlocking circles in white, tan, rose, and gray.

I went over and opened the doors and shutters to the balcony, with its wrought iron railing and little café table with two chairs, and breathed in the cool air coming off the lake. I was so going to sit out here in my pajamas tomorrow morning with my espresso and a book.

"I like this place." I turned to see Irix admiring the room. "You might have terrible taste in rental cars, but I'm putting you in charge of where we stay from now on."

It wasn't easy picking out a villa from just the photos online. It had taken me a while to find what I thought would be the perfect place. I was thrilled that Irix approved.

"It reminds me a lot of my home back in New Orleans," Irix commented.

I totally understood what he meant. This villa was low with larger rooms and nary a wood floor in sight where Irix's house was a three story narrow rowhouse with high fences and a small wandering garden of a yard. But there was a similar feel to them. Maybe it was the ornate iron fencing, or the silk wallpaper, or the mix of old and new. Maybe it was that aura of centuries gone by. Or maybe the Frenchman who'd originally built Irix's house shared some design aesthetics with these Italians. Either way, this villa felt like home.

"Shall we try out the bed?" Irix's arms came around me once more and he pulled my back against his front, where his hard-on pressed against the upper part of my ass.

"I thought you wanted to bend me over the banister?" I turned to face him, snaking my arms around his neck.

His golden-brown eyes heated. He leaned to kiss me, then looked past me out to the view of the lake, the mountains, the clouds rolling in from the north. "There's a banister here."

Yeah, a thin metal railing and a drop onto a stone patio. But the exhibitionist in me loved the idea of having sex out on this balcony, where anyone on the lake could see us. And the view...

"I'm game."

He grinned, then bent his head to kiss me. His hands sneaked under the hem of my shirt, lifting it and tickling the sensitive skin of my sides. I jerked, squeaking into his mouth. He chuckled, deepening our kiss, and moving his hands up to unsnap the front my bra.

We separated, Irix stepping back to lift my shirt over my head and slide my bra down my arms. With one hand, he twisted the bra around my wrists, pushing my arms down so my back arched. Then he bent his head to my breasts, his tongue rasping against my nipple.

This was new. We'd enjoyed some rough sex before, but not like this. The bra was practically cutting into my wrists, Irix's grip so tight that I knew there was no way I could get my hands free. His other hand unsnapped my jeans and yanked them down, pushing me back a few steps so that I felt the cold iron of the railing against my bare ass. He pressed against me, his mouth rough on my breasts, and I felt the iron of the railing give slightly.

An instinctive fear shivered through me. I couldn't move my arms. I was on the verge of going over the balcony railing, or through it if it gave way. The cold metal bit into my skin. My shoulders ached, my wrists burned. I whimpered as Irix gently bit one of my nipples, tugging it into his mouth.

His hand left my hip and I heard his pants unsnap and the rasp of his zipper. Then he kicked my legs apart, one hand twisting the bra around my wrists tighter while the other swiped through my wet folds then hooked around my thigh, lifting me slightly up and angling my hips. Now I was completely helpless, on the tip-toes of one foot, the delicate metal railing the only thing keeping me from a long fall—well, the railing and Irix's firm grip on my leg and wrists.

He trailed a line of kisses and not-so-gentle bites up my chest and neck, then leaned his forehead against mine as he positioned himself at my entrance and drove forward right as the first drops of rain began to fall.

The railing groaned. The skies opened up, drenching us instantly. I gasped, giggling at the thought of us pressed against the railing, having sex in the pouring rain. He chuckled in reply, tongue darting out to lick a drop of water from my lip. His skin was so warm, slick and wet, his hair dripping onto my shoulders. I felt the long slide of him as he pulled his hips away, then once more he drove forward.

Every nerve in my body came alive at the feel of him. Eyes on mine, he began to move, stroking deep and gradually increasing his rhythm. I could do nothing but grow soft and willing against him, watching the gold sparks flickering in his eyes, feeling his breath against my lips, relishing the feel of him as he filled me.

Irix's breathing changed, growing faster and heavier, the railing making an alarming squealing noise as he slammed into me. I didn't care. Everything was tightening inside me, like a coiled spring. If this damned railing gave way, I only hoped I came before we hit the ground.

"Don't stop," I gasped. "Please don't stop."

He growled, his movements frantic, his fingers digging into my thigh as he lifted me higher. I shattered, crying out every nerve ending pulsing as I tightened around him. He did the same, pausing deep inside me as he peaked, his eyes never leaving mine. I felt him pour every bit of himself into me, not holding back, his stored sexual energy spooling into me with every pulse of his cock.

This was more than sex, more than his sharing energy. It was so much more. I felt something shift between us, felt as if any slim barriers that remained separating the two of us had been shattered. There was something so open in Irix's gold eyes, so giving, and so vulnerable.

"I love you," he whispered, still inside of me.

His hand loosened on the bra and I felt it slide from my wrists. Bringing my arms forward, I gripped his sodden shirt with one hand, bringing the other one up to tangle in his wet hair. I watched him, watched his eyes as I traced the edge of the cowlick on his forehead. I wanted to stay here always, him inside of me, his warm body pressed against mine as the rain drenched us. I wanted this to be forever.

"I love you, too," I told him. "For all of eternity, until my very last breath, I will love you, Irix."

Something sparkled in his eyes, something that wasn't the usual demon-gold, something that looked a lot like tears.

CHAPTER 2

*I*rix had ordered food from the café across the street, then started up a fire downstairs while I was warming up in the shower. I didn't bother to dress, bundling my wet hair on top of my head and wrapping myself in a soft blanket to curl up on the leather sofa in front of the fire. Outside was gray, thunder in the distance as rain continued to pour from the sky.

I'd never felt so content, so happy, so satisfied. I was in this beautiful, snug villa listening to the rain, watching the fire, snuggled in a blanket. I heard the door open, and smelled something amazing.

"Dinner has arrived," Irix said. He put a box on the coffee table and began unpacking. There were several containers, a bottle of wine, and a carafe of coffee. And dishes. I was pretty sure the kitchen had dishes, so I shot Irix a raised-eyebrow look.

"Evidently the café across the street is used to supplying the villa owners with food, and does the same for guests. We just put the dishes in the box and leave them outside the door under the overhang, and they'll collect them. We can even have pastries, fruit, and espresso delivered in the morning if we want."

This. Was. Heaven. I was so glad I'd taken a chance on this apprenticeship opportunity and booked this vacation. It was an experience, and I wanted my life to be full of experiences like this.

Irix opened a container and spooned a huge helping of a pasta dish onto a plate.

"What the heck is that?" I'd expected some kind of spaghetti noodle and marinara sauce, but these noodles were short, broad, and thick. They were an odd taupe color, and rather than a sauce, they seemed to be coated in a pale cheese. It all smelled amazing, but the colors reminded me of the gray rain outside our windows.

"Pizzocheri," Irix said. "It's a local staple, a sort of hearty pasta that these Italians have been eating for generations. The noodles are made with buckwheat flour, hence the unusual color. And the sauce is like a thick fondue. It's fontina cheese with grappa instead of wine, garlic, butter, and swiss chard. The owner of the café says that it's the perfect meal for a rainy evening, although he claims that Italians tend to eat heavy food like this as their afternoon meal, then have a light, late supper."

I dug in and was surprised at how rich and filling the pasta was compared to the marinara-style I was used to eating at home. I finished off my serving, then nibbled on some pickled vegetables and cured meat, cradling my glass of wine while Irix stored the leftovers in the fridge and rinsed the dishes to send back across the street.

The rain continued, the gray sky darkening as the sun began to set. Without a word, Irix tended the fire, then sat on the couch, pulling me over so I was lying against him, both of us looking out the doors to the patio and the lake beyond.

"Cigars and cognac?" he murmured in my ear as I finished

my wine. "Or do you want some of that espresso the café sent over in the thermos?"

"Right now I just want to stay here in your arms. After it's full-dark, let's break into the cognac and cigars. My internal clock is kinda screwed up with the time change, and as enticing as espresso sounds, I'm afraid I won't be able to sleep at all if I have a cup."

Irix scooted me up tighter against him, my butt pressed against his crotch, his legs spread out and intertwined with mine. There was something magic about us curled up together while the rain beat a slow rhythm on the roof and windows. Irix's warm breath stirred the hair at the top of my head, his fingers gently stroking my stomach and hips under the blanket. The rain muted to a gentle mist as the sky darkened to night, the crackling of the fire rising to a crescendo in its absence.

Irix kissed the top of my head, then gently set me aside to get up. I shivered at the lack of his warmth against my back. Then I rose and, still wrapped in my blanket, I opened the tall French doors leading out to the patio, breathing in the cool night air that carried the scents from the herb garden, as well as the roses, into the house. Off in the distance, I saw a pair of shadows flit like giant ravens across the hazy, partially obscured moon. A fast-moving cloud, no doubt, coming off the mountains. The wind picked up and I shivered, thinking how the temperature had really dropped from the heat of the day.

"You opened the doors? Kinda defeats the purpose of the fire," Irix teased as he handed me the two snifters of cognac. I held them while he trimmed the ends from the cigars.

"No, the purpose of the fire is ambiance and romance, not necessarily warmth, although I'm sure I'll be glad of that later. I just wanted the fresh air."

Irix lit one of the cigars and handed it to me, trading it for one of the snifters. "I could get used to this, you know—jetting around the globe by your side, enjoying human civilization and the beauty that this world has to offer."

"So what's stopping us?" I asked. Irix had enough money to do this sort of thing. Although I didn't, I knew he'd be happy to foot the bill.

He stood next to me, our shoulders touching. Cigar smoke curled up into the night air, the brandy sparkling from the firelight behind us.

"Nothing. We could travel for a few years, or decades, or centuries until you felt the need to put your degree and botany talents to good use. Or we could put down roots somewhere and just make sure we take frequent vacations."

I eyed him, wondering where this was going. He knew I wanted a career, that I had an urge to do something heroic for the world, starting with something heroic for a company or a municipality or a local park service. The idea of spending my life traveling was an intoxicating one, but I knew I'd soon find that sort of life shallow. I needed a deeper meaning, a purpose, otherwise these amazing experiences would just begin to feel flat.

Did Irix feel differently? He was an incubus, and sex demons loved a carefree existence. Was this his way of pointing out to me that as much in love as we were, our paths were going to eventually diverge. I'd want more than endless travel and new experiences, and he'd feel weighted down by my need to save the world one plant at a time.

"Well, if I manage to get this apprenticeship, I'll be here in Italy for the next few years. We could take a year and travel after that, in between the apprenticeship and the next job. If I don't get it, we could probably spend a few months jetting around before I wanted to start work with Jordan down in New Orleans. I don't know how much vacation time I'd get, but we could always plan something big every year at the least."

He nodded, but suddenly he felt very far away.

"Do you still want that? Us moving in together in New Orleans? I could always find an apartment–"

"I want you with me. Whether that's in Italy, or New Orleans, or a rusted trailer in a vineyard in California. I want you with me."

That was reassuring, especially because with the way he'd said it, it seemed like a vow.

"I want to be with you, too," I replied.

We were silent a few minutes, sipping the cognac and smoking our cigars, when Irix suddenly spoke up. "Do you *really* want kids? I mean, demon children are very difficult to raise, as I've said before."

I caught my breath. "My whole life I thought I was human. I always saw myself getting married and having kids as well as having a rewarding career. I'm adjusting to the changes I've needed to make in those hopes and dreams, but it's hard to give up the one about having kids. I think that's the toughest dream for me to let go of."

He took a big gulp of the cognac. "It would be difficult to juggle a career and raise little demons, even if we hire a dwarven nanny to help. We wouldn't be as free to travel or stay out late. And we'd have to take care of our need for sexual energy in a way that wouldn't bring human child services down on our heads."

I winced, envisioning trying to explain to a social worker why Irix and I were out all night at an orgy. But we'd have a dwarven nanny to babysit. That should help.

"What if our child tries to seduce the kids in Kindergarten?" he continued, "or the fourth grade teacher, or gets caught masturbating in the park playground at age eight, or gets mad and sets the grocery store on fire because we won't get him the cereal he wants?"

"We'd have to homeschool," I countered. "And be very careful. Didn't you say dwarves are skilled at keeping those kind of behaviors under control?"

He was right. This was going to be impossible. I wanted to continue to live as much like a human as I could, but would that be fair to Irix? And would that be fair to a child who would be three-quarters demon? Or a dwarven nanny who needed to basically be there twenty-four seven because Irix and I couldn't manage our own child.

I took a deep breath. "Let's table that one. Honestly, I'm not ready for children right now. Maybe we don't have kids. I might be okay with that. Right now I don't want to completely rule it out. I don't want to agree that we're not going to, only to decide in a few years, or decades, or centuries that I really do want to have a baby."

"In a few decades or centuries, things might be different," Irix added. "And it's not just you who might want a child later on. Demons often go through periods in their lives where they feel an incredibly strong urge to create offspring. In a few centuries, it might be me begging you for a baby."

"So…maybe? Shall we agree on maybe and that either one of us can bring the topic up again if we feel the need?"

Irix nodded and shot me a relieved smile. "Agreed."

We stood in companionable silence for a few moments, then I turned to Irix. "So what should we get into tomorrow? I don't have to be at the seminar until Monday, so maybe we could do a few tourist things. And, of course, we'll need to scout around for some sexual partners."

Irix smiled. "I thought we'd tour a few villas, then head out at night after dinner to a bar. There's a big hotel the next town over where we could probably pick up some tourists without any problems."

That sounded fine with me. And hopefully language wouldn't be a barrier, or I'd need to have Irix around to translate for me.

"I've got some other plans for later in the week if you get a break from your seminar stuff," Irix continued. "I want us to go up through the mountains into Switzerland one day, and take a boat out on the lake another day."

"I want to explore the towns a bit, and do a little shopping in Bellagio," I told him. Although everything would need to fit in around the seminar schedules and the apprenticeship testing. As much as I wanted to enjoy a vacation, that was the real reason for this trip.

Irix crinkled his nose with dismay at my mention of shopping. "While you're looking at shoes and scarves and purses, I might go see if I can score a few quickies." He reached out and smoothed my hair. "If I know you, you'll get busy and run low on energy, then need to expend everything you have saving a hibiscus garden or something. I have to make sure I have enough energy to share."

I should have been insulted, but I'd grown used to Irix nagging me about how I needed to spend more time gathering sexual energy. And he'd gotten used to sharing his with me. What had once been an area of friction between us was now a sort of fond teasing. Even though he was right and I really did need to put more consistent effort into picking up sexual partners, I knew that he loved to share. It was his way of taking care of me, of showing his love. And energy that came from Irix was especially potent and sweet.

"I swear to you I will bang at least two tourists tomorrow." I held my hand up as if I were swearing a vow. "And I will exercise judicious restraint in healing hibiscus gardens and other plant life."

He laughed. "Deal. Do I get to pick the tourists?"

Irix loved being involved in my conquests. "If you want to, you can even watch. Or participate."

He grinned. "If the gentlemen are so inclined. I know how picky you are and I don't want to limit your selection pool even further by insisting on only those who want to add a guy into a threesome, or who don't mind someone watching."

"Maybe we can just have a party-orgy and save some time," I teased.

He looked around the room. "I wouldn't want to do that here and risk upsetting our hostess. If we have time later in the week, we can rent a hotel suite somewhere and bring a dozen people up to party."

It sounded fun, but not as much fun as it would be just spending a week one-on-one with Irix, without having to worry about finding other sexual partners or running low on energy.

Irix sat down his snifter and wrapped his arms around me, my back against his chest. "We don't need to hunt every night. I know how you hate it."

I didn't. Not really. When I'd first found out I was a half-succubus, I hated that I needed to basically spend my life siphoning sexual energy from others, that I'd have to become what humans would consider a slut, that even if I found a great human guy and married, I could never be faithful to him. But I'd fallen in love with Irix, and with him this all seemed normal. I still wanted him all to myself at times, but the fact that he went out and had sex with others didn't bother me. In fact, I thought the times we'd picked up swingers, or had orgies, or threesomes to be some of the most intimate, exciting sex we'd experienced. It was fun. And it was the sort of fun I could only have with Irix as my husband.

Well, not husband because demons didn't marry. Partner?

Mate? Lover-for-possibly-thousands-of-years? I wasn't sure what to call us.

I leaned my head back against him. "Tonight it will just be us. No heading out later to pick anyone up. Just you and me making love all over this amazing house, then sleeping all night long in our bed together, waking up side-by-side. Tomorrow, we'll hunt, but tonight is for you and me."

He kissed the top of my head. "That sounds perfect."

We stood like that, finishing our cigars and our drinks. Then closed the doors to the patio, shutting out the world to devote the rest of the night to each other.

CHAPTER 3

A light breeze blew over Lake Como, stirring my hair and rustling the scalloped edges of the awnings over the little café that was conveniently right across the street from our villa. Actually, the door at the end of our breezeway opened into a small patio area that was also claimed by the café, full of little round tables and excruciatingly uncomfortable metal chairs.

I figured the metal chairs were to discourage visitors from sipping their espresso too long, whiling the day away, transfixed by the choppy waves of the lake.

Choppy was a mild word for the silver-tipped waves. The only other place I'd seen waves this size on an inland body of water was in the Great Lakes. That alone gave me an indication of the size of the glacier lake in front of me. And the water was, as Sam would have said, colder than a witch's tit. I had no idea how the paddle boarders managed. I guess the frigid waters were an incentive to stay upright.

A woman slid into the chair opposite me, her dark hair to her shoulders, eyes shaded by sunglasses. She was curvy, but moved with an energy and grace, plopping her designer handbag on the chair beside her as she skillfully set a double espresso onto the table top. I stared at her a moment, wondering if sharing tables was a custom in Italy, and if so, why she'd chosen to share mine rather than take one of the four empty ones next to us.

"I'm Daniela Sommariva," she announced.

The name clicked. "I'm Amber Lowry. Oh my gosh, you're the cousin Gianna said she'd ask about the villa tour. I'm dying to get into your gardens."

That sounded like a euphemism for something naughty, and my effusive statement probably wasn't helping my case. But the woman spoke English with an American accent, so maybe she was used to weird American manners.

Her eyes crinkled at the corners. "We don't normally open our home up to tours, but Gianna was quite taken with the both of you. Besides, treasures lose their shine when they only have a few to appreciate them. The admiration of others is part of their value, don't you think?"

I didn't have anything that I'd consider a treasure. Well, except for Irix, I guess, and the admiration of others was part of his being a sex demon.

"When do you think we could come for the tour?" I had the seminar all day tomorrow, but hopefully she could squeeze something in either today or in the evenings later this week.

"Today in the late morning, perhaps? My father isn't well, but a short tour should be okay. And we could possibly have a drink and a light lunch afterward depending on time."

I nodded. "That would be awesome. Can we bring something?"

"Oh no, that's not at all necessary. You and your boyfriend are here on vacation! Honestly, I will enjoy the company, and especially enjoy showing off our home."

"It's been in your family for long?"

She smiled and sipped her espresso. "For nearly a thousand years. My cousins own some of the more modern, neighboring villas, but Villa Sommarilla with its gardens and artwork has always gone to the eldest child in our family."

"Are you a large family?" I asked, a bit envious. "I grew up with just the one brother, although I have a sister that I only met a few years back. I've got an uncle on my dad's side, and two aunts on my mothers, but they don't live near us, so I didn't grow up with a big family, playing with cousins or any of that."

"We have never been able to have more than two children. One is far more common with us. There are only sixteen in my family including my cousins. I'm my father's only child, so I envy you growing up with a brother."

How sad that their family had such fertility issues. It reminded me of what Nyalla had told me of the elves back home. They also struggled to have children.

It also made me think back to Irix's and my conversation last night. Would I be able to have children if we decided we wanted them? My mother had to turn to a sex demon to become pregnant with me. I was assuming that Irix would have the ability to do the same as my demon parent and override any infertility issues I might have inherited from my elven mother.

"Do you have children?" I asked Daniela. Gianna had mentioned that her cousin was living in the villa with her father, but hadn't mentioned any kids.

She looked down at her espresso. "I have a son. He is my life, the most important person in the world to me. My husband died...well, he died when our son was a baby and I will never remarry, so Sergio will be my only child. If I didn't have him, I'm not sure I would have survived my husband's death."

That was heartbreaking, but also romantic in a tragic sort

of way. The thought that her love had been so perfect that she'd never find another to take his place, that her son was all she had of that perfect union…it brought tears to my eyes.

"I don't have any children," I told her, since we seemed to be sharing these personal things. "Irix and I have discussed it, but we're not sure if kids are in our future or not. There are…issues we'd need to face having children. They'd require some additional care and special schooling, and we're not ready. I don't know if we'll ever be ready, but I hope so."

I realized after I'd finished my little speech that it sounded as if Irix and I had recessive genetic conditions that meant we'd have a high likelihood of having a handicapped child. Which was kind of true, if "handicapped" also included being able to call lightning down on a convenience store.

Daniela smiled sympathetically. "I hope you do have a child, and that he or she is perfect in every way. Sergio brings me great joy. I look forward to the day he marries and brings his bride to the villa, and hopefully fills the rooms once more with the sound of babies."

"I hope so, too."

She sipped the last of her espresso and rose, pulling a card from her designer bag and handing it to me. It was cream cardstock with embossed lettering telling me the address of the villa below an ornate coat of arms that looked like two wyverns up on back legs, boxing with their front, wings tucked in toward their backs.

"Eleven o'clock? That way we can spend a few hours in the gardens and enjoy a late lunch while father naps."

"We won't be disturbing him, will we?" I knew she said she was longing for visitors, but Gianna had mentioned her father's melancholy, which I assumed was severe depression.

"Not at all. He sleeps mostly, although if he is having a good day, he may want to join us for lunch."

"That would be lovely," I told her, shaking her extended

hand. "Thank you so much, Ms. Sommariva. I really appreciate the opportunity to see your villa and gardens."

"Daniela, please. And the pleasure is all mine," she responded.

I watched her make her way through the maze of tables and chairs in the café, thinking once more of her being a widow at such a young age. Daniela looked to be around forty, and had that immaculately groomed, subtle, but expensively clothed appearance that seemed the norm with European women. I felt shabby in my jeans and T-shirt, my hair a tangle of gold knotted up on top of my head. Maybe a shopping trip to Bellagio *would* be a good idea because I suddenly had an urge to update my wardrobe.

It wasn't until I'd headed back through the door into the courtyard of our own villa that I realized Daniela's last name was Sommariva, the same as their villa and, no doubt, the same as her father's. She hadn't taken her husband's last name. It seemed odd, because Daniela had given me the impression of a conventional woman who valued tradition above all else. Was her family name so prominent that giving it up would have been unheard of? Even with the love she'd clearly had for her husband, she'd kept her family name. Huh.

I chuckled as I climbed the steps to our bedroom. Maybe Daniela's husband had taken her last name instead. Now *that* would have been a surprise.

CHAPTER 4

"Wow." I said as Irix pulled our tiny car into a small off-street parking area.

"I agree," he replied.

Villa Sommariva was in Cadenabbia, which was the next town over from where we were staying. The winding road hugged the lake, leaving only narrow strips of tree-lined walkways, marinas, and the occasional restaurant or floating pool between it and the water. The land rose steeply on the other side of the road, leaving the residents to live on a switchback of drives and terraced lawns. Villa Sommariva was no exception, only on a grander scale than the other homes. We parked, buzzed in at the gate, then began to climb.

The first level above the parking area held a huge fountain with camellias and crushed stone pathways. The second level had a long row of arches filled with citrus trees. Lemons, limes, oranges, and grapefruits budded on the thick green vines, and I gaped, wondering how they wintered these trees which wouldn't survive a hard frost.

29

The next level showcased an enormous variety of roses, and a stone wall that cleverly hid some storage areas for gardening supplies. Climbing the broad marble steps, we reached the paved courtyard on the same level as the villa's front door. I turned around to look over the thick, carved stone barrier and caught my breath at the view. We were high enough up that the town and the road practically vanished, swallowed up with the beauty of the landscaping in the terraces we'd just climbed, and the stunning blue of the lake. The white caps twinkled in the sunlight, and from here the lake seemed enormous, promontories jutting out like fingers of green reaching toward the water. And in the distance were the snow-topped mountains, the southern edge of the Alps.

"Welcome."

I felt a bit embarrassed that we'd been standing by her front door, staring at the view without knocking to announce our arrival, but Daniela's voice carried only pride and slight amusement. Of course, she'd known we were on our way up as we'd buzzed in at the gate.

"Irix, this is Daniela Sommariva." I introduced him, noting that our host's eyes did a slow, appreciative tour of my boyfriend.

He took her hand and kissed it, and Daniela seemed charmed by his old-fashioned gallantry. Then he pulled her close and kissed each of her cheeks and I saw her blush.

Oh, that dog. I hid a grin, wondering if our host's proclamation that she'd never marry again extended to a lifetime of chastity. I doubted it. There was no reason for a woman her age to deny herself the occasional physical pleasure. Plus, Irix was tough to resist when he got that gleam in his dark gold eyes.

She reluctantly removed herself from Irix's grasp and

turned to me with a bright smile, doing the air-kiss on each of my cheeks.

"Where should we start?" she asked us. "Do you have any questions about the terraces? Should we head for the azaleas? The rhododendrons? The ferns?"

Irix shot me a glance that let me know I was the one in charge here, that this tour was all about me and my passion for gardening. Later we'd, no doubt, get to indulge in Irix's passions, but right now, we were going to spend a few hours talking about plants.

And I adored that Irix was willing to spend a few hours talking about plants. So many guys I'd dated would have left me to do this tour on my own while they sat in some local bar, but that was Irix, wanting to be by my side, taking joy in whatever I took joy in.

"I was admiring your citrus grove on the way up," I told Daniela. "Mom has a tiny lemon tree at home and has to drag it inside every year for the winter. How do you keep the frost from killing them off?"

"We cover them during a hard frost, which is where the arches are handy, as opposed to just having them planted in rows like a traditional grove. Plus, the weather here isn't as harsh as you'd think. Snow only stays for a few days before it melts, and much of the winter is above freezing. It's another story in the higher elevations, but around the lake here, winters tend to be mild."

She motioned us on and I walked by her side while Irix followed. The entirety of the land around the villa was one enormous garden with winding paths throughout. There were Persian Ironwoods, Austrian Pines, Holly and Magnolia. There was Bell Heather, Watson's Breath, a gorgeous Tasso Yew with its thick ribbed bark. We walked past a dense breezeway of azaleas that looked to be over ten feet tall. I ran my hand along the verdant leaves on their sharp, thin branches and imagined how this would look in the spring—a wall of flowers shedding their brightly colored petals across the stone pathway.

"This is a special place," Daniela told me as we rounded a corner to a bit of rocky land that jutted out from the gardens, a tiny gazebo was ringed with stone benches for intimate seating, the whole thing overlooking the lake below. Clematis wound up the columns of the gazebo, bright flowers in white and purple making this a setting that I could imagine hosting many an exchange of wedding vows.

"Very romantic," I told Daniela. Then I looked back at Irix, expecting to see him with that naughty expression that told me he was thinking the same thing I was—that this would be an ideal location to make love.

Instead he was fidgeting, his one hand fisted in his pants pocket as he looked out over the water. "Yes. Very romantic."

"Nico proposed to me here," Daniela said, her eyes dreamy. "It's a spot for lovers to sneak away and steal a few moments together. I expected him to kiss me, but instead he got down on one knee and asked me to marry him." She looked over at me and grinned. "Then, when I said 'yes', he kissed me. Quite a lot of kissing, actually."

I ran my hand over one of the stone benches, wondering how many lovers had sat here, hand-in-hand. "Did you and your husband live here in the villa, or did you return here after he passed away? Or when your father became ill?"

She smiled fondly. "I've always lived here. Nico moved in when we were married and we had a suite up on the third floor, complete with a nursery when I had Sergio. It's too big a house for one man, even if my father tends to be suspicious of almost everyone. Besides, he needed me. Father began his decline when my mother passed away." Sadness swept like a shadow across her face. "We're not meant to be alone, and we only love once, only commit ourselves to one person in our lifetime. When they die…well, it's hard to go on."

I reached out and took Irix's hand, glad that we'd have so much longer together than humans did. Neither of us was sure whether I'd live as long as him, but thousands of years was better than losing the love of your life after only a few decades together, then having to live those thousands of years alone. And in Daniela's case, she most likely didn't even have a decade with her husband. It was so unfair. That one-soul mate concept seemed romantic, but in her case, I wished she was open to finding a second chance at love. She was too young to face half her life alone except for an ailing father and a son who would eventually marry and go on about his own life.

"Come," She forced a smile. "There's another lovely section that I want you to see, but first I must show you the grotto."

The grotto was tiny with two entrances. Icy water dripped down on us from the gray ceiling, and streamed down the rocky sides. I hated it, and couldn't figure out why our host seemed so completely enchanted with what was essentially a small, cold, dark, damp cave.

"This was where I spent a good deal of my childhood," Daniela told us, laughing. "I wanted to live in this grotto. We have an enormous villa and these beautiful gardens, but somehow this little place felt like home to me. Maybe because everything else was my father's treasure, his pride and joy, where here in this grotto I could bring my little toys and trinkets and pretend this spot was my very own."

Okaaaay. I understood the need for youngsters, especially girls it seemed, to "play house", to pretend to have their very own domicile with their own things around them, but for most children that was a room in the basement or attic, or a converted garden shed out back, not a cave that dripped cold water on your head.

I didn't want to point out how very weird this was, so I made appropriate compliments about the horrible spot, and rejoiced when Daniela led us back into the sunshine and down another path, past the giant rhododendrons to a spot where the temperature dropped nearly five degrees, and the sounds of a gurgling brook filled my ears.

"This is our Valle Delle Felici," Daniela announced. "Unlike the citrus trees, these ferns can't survive even our mild winters." She motioned to the fronds that carpeted the ground of the small forest. "They are actually in pots. The gardeners dig them up each fall and take every one of them to the greenhouses until late spring when they are replanted once more."

I blinked in surprise. "But there are hundreds of them! Every single fern?"

"Every single one. My great-grandfather wanted this to be a cool forest paradise, complete with ferns, and unfortunately the ones he liked the most were from New Zealand and very sensitive to cold."

"Fortunately he had the money to employ sixteen gardeners and build half a dozen greenhouses," Irix commented wryly.

"Absolutely! It wouldn't do to have something so dear to you be lost through an excess of frugality," Daniela replied. "Whenever we acquire something, whether that be a villa, a piece of artwork, or additions to our gardens, we commit to ensuring they are well taken care of and retain every bit of the beauty that enchanted us and made us want to possess them."

We rested for a bit, admiring the towering chestnut trees and the stream that cascaded down the forest hillside, creating little waterfalls at each stone-step. Then we climbed the packed-dirt pathway alongside the stream and veered to the left, past a row of small-leaved limes.

"Tiglio selvatico," I murmured, stroking the bark.

"Yes," Daniela shot me an appreciative glance. "And because you're a botanist, you'll especially love this tree here on our right."

I frowned at the tree, what appeared to be a redwood surrounded by camphors and ginkgos with their fan-like leaves. There were other redwoods nearby—the size of which I'd only seen in California—but this one was different...odd.

"It's a Metasequoia," Daniela announced with a small smile.

I gasped and reached out to touch the tree, marveling at its structure and peculiar genetic make-up. This tree, an extremely rare Dawn Redwood, was from China. It had been thought to be extinct until a tiny grove was found in the mid-nineteen-forties.

"And this plant over here was germinated from one of two seeds found frozen in ice."

"Silene Stenophylla." Wow. This was a plant we'd thought lost to history, one only possible through today's science. I wasn't even sure the elves, with their talents in the plant kingdom, could have resurrected those seeds and made them grow and flourish.

It made me wonder. Elves such as the ones working in the vineyards in California, had skills that would be much in demand in the human world, but humans had abilities of their own. Their science and technology made things possible that elves couldn't imagine. Magic was an amazing thing, but seeing this ancient, long-dead plant brought to life made me realize that elves would be very foolish to think themselves the superior race.

"I can't believe you have this," I told her, still stroking the bark of the Metasequoia tree. I loved this thing. If I could have magically spirited it home to have for my own, I would have.

As if she sensed my less-than-honest thoughts, Daniela shot me a narrow-eyed glance. "My family adores every living thing in this garden. Although we each have our own preference in regards to our favorites, we would never let any of our treasures go, not for all the money in the world."

I smiled reassuringly. "I believe you. And trust me, if I had this tree in my garden, I would defend it with my life as well. There are some things that are too precious to risk falling into irreverent hands."

She smiled serenely. "Exactly. And now, I want to show you some of our newer additions."

We made our way along the winding pathways through patches of annuals and groves of sweetgum with their buckyball seeds littering the pathway. Daniela pointed out a few of her cousins' houses visible between the thick stand of trees, then we climbed through a tall bamboo forest to a Zen sand garden with pitted statuary I was sure were not reproductions.

The bamboo forest ended and we strolled past a huge concrete water tank that looked like an industrial-sized pool.

"What's that?" I pointed, thinking that perhaps the tank was used for irrigation, although this didn't seem a particularly arid landscape.

"Fish." Daniela grinned. "Father adores trout and is a bit of a glutton when it comes to them. We stock the tank and the gardeners ensure the fish are fed and the water clean and clear. When father has a craving for trout, which is a pretty frequent occurrence, one of the house servants comes down with a net and takes what we need."

I was also fond of trout, and it warmed my heart to think that an ill, elderly man had people who cared enough for him that they made sure they had his favorite food freshly available.

"There was a time when he would fish for himself," she added, her smile fading. "But now…well, at least he still has his appetite even if he seldom leaves the house anymore."

I felt for her father, unable to do many of the things he loved. It made me wonder how I would age. Would I grow physically weaker, my mind wandering and forgetting? Times like this I wished I knew some elves well enough to ask them about their elderly populations.

"Up this way is our newest addition," Daniela said, walking backwards as she talked to us. "I added on an extra four acres to our land uphill and am putting in an olive grove. I've always wanted one, and Sergio is supervising the installation as his first project in the family holdings."

There was a clear difference between the older, well-established gardens we'd just toured and the land Daniela had purchased recently. That area was hot, the sun beating down on a sapling-covered landscape. There was an old stone building that must have belonged to the previous owners, now being converted into what appeared to be a tenant house for servants or gardeners. The terraced land was planted with squat, young olive trees, irrigation systems in place. We walked along the rows, sweating profusely as we made our way along the virgin grove. The trees were healthy and obviously well cared for. Daniela meant what she said about taking the best care of their treasures.

We were silent as we headed back down, past Oleanders and monkshood to the rear of the villa.

"Thank you so much for sharing this with us," I told our host in a hushed, reverential tone. "This truly is one of the most impressive gardens I've ever toured."

She beamed. "Please come around to the side patio and I'll go in to ask the servants to bring out lunch."

We walked around the corner of the fifteenth-century Baroque-style home to a huge patio overlooking the top of the citrus grove and the lake beyond. And standing there was an elderly man—an elderly man who was very clearly *not* a servant.

CHAPTER 5

Beside him was a young man—tall with sun-streaked hair and a lanky build. The pair turned to us, and I could see the resemblance between them as well as our hostess.

"Papa." Daniela's tone was both motherly and respectful... and slightly scolding. "You should be in bed. Sergio, what are you doing letting your grandfather wander around outside like this?"

The boy chuckled. "He wanted to see how the lemons were coming along. There is no stopping him. All I can do is make sure he doesn't fall over the railing."

The older man wheezed, leaning on his cane. The other hand was withered and twisted, the skin covered with scar tissue that appeared to have come from a third-degree burn a very long time ago. A similar band of scar tissue twisted like a streak of lightning down his face, bisecting his dark, glittering eyes and sloping to touch the corner of his lips.

"I'm not going to fall over the railing, boy. And I'm done being in bed." With an abrupt, jerky twist of his head, he turned those glittering eyes on me and Irix. "Who are these two? Are they reds? Blues? Greens?" His eyes narrowed, his breath catching as though those colors might be a good thing or a bad thing. I wondered if he'd been in some sort of war or conflict and he was reliving those days, remembering the colors of the soldiers' uniforms.

"No, Papa." There was a river of pain in Daniela's two words.

His daughter. I eyed Daniela curiously, wondering how old her father had been when he married her mother, when he'd had her. The guy looked ninety, and she was maybe in her late thirties or early forties? It happened. And maybe this Melancholy, which I'd begun to think might be an Italian euphemism for Alzheimer's, was aging him prematurely.

"Are they here to kill us?" He demanded. "Or finally let us return home?" There was a note of hope in his voice, as if either prospect would be welcome.

"Amber and Irix are tourists who are renting Villa Sella from Gianna," she replied. "I brought them here so they could admire the gardens."

The old man's eyes narrowed. "They haven't stolen anything?"

She sighed. "No, Papa. You'd know if they'd stolen anything. Amber is a botanist and has fallen in love with your gardens."

His chest puffed out and he grinned, the side of his mouth without the scar rising noticeably higher than the other, giving him a charming, lopsided smile. "The Himalayan rhododendrons?"

"Are absolutely stunning, Mr. Sommariva," I told him. "I only wish I had been here earlier in the summer to see them in bloom."

"The azaleas, too," Sergio added. "Although you'd need to come in late April or early May to see them at their prime."

I could imagine. The shrubs were huge, thriving in the

acidic soil here and growing to an unheard-of size. "The fern valley with the waterfall is also lovely. It's the perfect place to sit with a book and enjoy some cool shade."

The older man nodded. "Although the gardeners used to complain that we needed to remove the ferns to the greenhouse each winter so that they wouldn't perish in the frost. They don't complain anymore. Not since I ate one of them."

Daniela and her son exchanged a quick panicked look, then laughed awkwardly. I smiled to let them know I hadn't taken the man seriously. He was charming, but crazy. That was okay. I could do crazy.

The older Mr. Sommariva spun around, surprisingly agile in spite of his age and the cane. "Amber, let me show you my artwork. Daniela, have you shown this nice couple the artwork? You can't steal anything though. Thieves will be eaten."

I snorted. It was like the *Trespassers Will Be Shot* signs back home. All this obsession with cannibalism made me wonder if the patriarch of this family had gone through a time of starvation. Probably not. Daniela had said this royal-sized villa had been in their family for hundreds of years. That didn't mesh well with the poor-and-starving theory.

He was just crazy. And charming.

"And please call me Eduardo," he said as he extended his elbow toward me.

I took his arm, casting Irix a quick grin over my shoulder. He winked and followed us, Daniela trailing behind, the whole time trying to coax her father into retiring back to his room. The man, who honestly did not seem to need that cane, led us back around the rear of the villa and in through a huge set of French doors. The first thing I saw upon entering the house was a pair of asses. And not of the equine persuasion.

It was the rear-view of an enormous statue, placed on a

pedestal at the height so that two gorgeous marble posteriors were right at my eye-level. One was clearly female from the gentle slope and the soft curves of waist and back. The other male, with the sort of tight, round ass-cheeks that made me drool. Muscular legs. Muscular back. Muscular shoulders.

And, holy shit, that ass. Whoever the sculptor had been, he clearly knew what a man's ideal body was supposed to look like in minute, gorgeous detail.

I was so turned on. And I couldn't help but look back at Irix, because he had an ass like that, and I'd enjoyed many an hour ogling it, many a night smacking my hands down on that that tight flesh and gripping tight, holding on as he drove himself into me.

"Nice, huh?" The old man grinned and winked. "Venus has got the best butt ever. My wife had a rear end like that."

"And I'm out of here before I hear more about my grand-mother than I ever wanted," Sergio said.

"Join us for lunch in a bit," Daniela told her son as he headed back outside.

Meanwhile, the elder Mr. Sommariva was still sighing over the back end of the sculpture in front of us. "Yes, Sophia had an amazing figure. A woman's posterior is one of the most beautiful sights in the world."

Irix made a hum noise in agreement, and I turned again to look at Venus's ass. It was okay. Nothing to write home about, but I was seldom attracted to women. There had been a few exceptions, and staring at the gentle curves of the sculpture made me think of Kai, and wish that we were still an item.

Polyamory. That's what Irix had called it. We sex demons, even me as a half-demon/half-elf, had human one-night-stands whose energy fueled us. Then we had those we loved, who touched our heart and soul as well as inspired devotion within our bodies. Then there were those, like Irix, that were as the very air we breathed and essential to our continued existence.

Didn't mean that I didn't suffer when those I loved made other choices that meant we could no longer share passion together. But Kai and I were still friends, and there was always a chance we'd be together in that way again some-time. And if not…well, at least we still could love each other platonically.

"Mars has quite the fine ass, too," Irix mentioned.

Daniela's father stiffened, shooting my demon lover a suspicious glance. "Yes. I guess. If you like that sort of thing."

"Oh, I do like that sort of thing."

Irix was so wicked at times. It made me love him even more. "Reminds me of Harkel's ass," I told him.

He pursed his lips and tilted his head. "Harkel's ass is not as round, but I do see the similarities."

Eduardo made a disgusted noise and led us around to the front of the artwork where I couldn't help but snicker.

"Okay, now I'm thinking this doesn't look like Harkel at all." I pointed at what was now eye-level on the sculpture.

Irix nodded. "Harkel would be hanging far below that fig leaf. It's entirely inadequate to cover *his* manhood. As beauti-fully as the sculptor portrayed Mars's ass, I'm afraid he sold the god quite short when it came to his genitals."

The old man sputtered. "It's neoclassicism. The artist wasn't about to indulge in vulgar exaggeration of sexual organs."

"I'm on board with that," I commented. "But why cover up something so beautiful with a leaf? No matter the size, I have no doubt that what's under that contrived modesty piece is more than adequate and worthy of our admiration."

Eduardo puffed up his chest and sent me a smoldering glance. "You are so right. I protested the need for the leaf, even though I wanted an accurate depiction of body size.

This was a remarkable artist, and unfortunately we came to an impasse on this issue. I loved the statue, and compromised on the fig leaf as it was commonplace in sculpture at the time."

It was, and I felt a bit guilty for teasing this man so. He clearly wasn't a prude, although he might possibly have some homophobic tendencies. And it was a gorgeous sculpture, even with the fig leaf slapped over poor Mars's penis.

The room was far more than just one sculpture, although the Mars/Venus piece took center stage in the middle, lit to strategic advantage by the row of French doors and huge glass transoms that transformed the entire rear of the room into one large-paned window. Lining the top of the walls, around the ceiling was a frieze that had me staring open-mouthed. It looked to be from the Napoleonic era in the early nineteenth century, still neoclassical in theme showing the advance of Alexander the Great and all of his military might.

"That's a whole lot of stallions," I commented. "Didn't Alexander the Great believe in using mares in his army? Or geldings?"

Eduardo snorted. "There is no use for geldings. If someone cannot properly ride a stallion, then they should walk. Although I have had many mares who were equally spirited and deserving of being immortalized in artwork." He looked at the frieze with a critical eye. "I never noticed the gender of the horses before. If I had, I would have told the artist to put mares in his work. Perhaps even a likeness of my Strilliana, who was my very favorite horse when I was but a boy."

He still had my hand tightly tucked against his body in the crook of his arm, so I squeezed his bicep in agreement. "I had a favorite mare from when I was young too, although I rode lots of geldings and stallions as well. We didn't have much money, so my brother Wyatt and I would sneak over to the neighbor's farm and ride their horses bareback. I'm sure they knew, but they turned a blind eye to our activities. I fell in love with a sweet dapple gray named Meredith. She's still in the pasture next to my mom's house, although she's not sound and can no longer be ridden. When I'm home, I go over with a pocket full of carrots and she comes running."

"A loyal horse is a wonderful treasure," he commented sadly. "If only they didn't die."

Yeah. Horses. Humans, friends and family. His words conjured up the bleak fears I'd had since finding out I wasn't human. My brother, Nyalla, my mother, and all of my human friends, would die long before me. And that would be far worse than losing a beloved horse or dog.

The man led me into the next room, and again I saw that the artwork was the focus, with a few small seating areas off to the side, strategically placed for optimal viewing of the artwork. This villa was the oddest home I'd ever toured. It seemed more a museum than a private residence.

"We've changed the exterior colors of the villa from pink to yellow depending on what style trends have been, but the interiors have remained relatively untouched since their redesign four hundred years ago," he told me. We paused before another sculpture that was prominently placed in the center of this room. "Here is my favorite piece of art of all I have in the villa."

I agreed with Mr. Sommariva. This was the most beautiful thing I'd seen so far, possibly surpassing even the Dawn Redwood and the other stunning plants and trees in the gardens. It was a sculpture of Eros and Psyche. She was being lifted in his arms as he knelt, his wings outstretched to raise her up. Her face was lifted toward his. It captured that split second before a kiss, that moment when the world seems to stand still. And knowing the story of those ill-fated lovers made this sculpture all the more poignant.

He was the son of Mars and Venus. She was his wife, killed because she had been filled with doubt and mistrusted him, looking upon his face in the daylight as she'd promised not to do. With his beloved dead, Eros was overcome with grief. His sorrowful kiss in some legends resurrected her, and in others was simply a goodbye to a love that was forever lost.

I hoped this sculpture depicted the former, because the latter was too tragic for me to bear. We all had doubts. I'd had my doubts with Irix, had moments when I hadn't trusted him or that his love for me was true. And I thanked the heavens every day that those moments of doubt I'd had hadn't ended in either my death or the destruction of our relationship.

Daniela's father led me around the room, discussing the various paintings and smaller sculptures, then we went into yet another room, equally museum-like in its set up. Were all the rooms like this? Did a few of them have sofas, coffee tables, entertainment systems with big-screen televisions and surround sound? I hoped the bedrooms upstairs weren't as austere as this, otherwise I could completely understand Daniela's odd fascination with the grotto as a potential home.

We paused before a large painting, and suddenly Mr. Sommariva's voice faded to a pleasant background hum. As much as I adored the statuary, something about this caught my eye. *The Last Kiss.* Romeo had one foot on the windowsill, one foot on the step as he leaned toward Juliet, his arm around her waist. Far from a passive participant, she leaned eagerly into his embrace, one hand on his arm and the other arm curling around his neck. Their mouths touched, a shared breath, eyes only for each other.

Ah, young love. And in the shaded background stood the priest from the play, not interfering, not condemning, but not approving either. There was a wariness about him, a tension in his body as he observed the two lovers' embrace. It was as if he knew the tragedy that was about to unfold.

"We only give our love once." Eduardo Sommariva's voice broke into my thoughts. "And it always ends in tragedy. Always. Watching our beloved mates die, feeling the emptiness of their loss with each and every breath is often more than we can bear."

He was such a romantic. I saw the tears in his dark eyes—eyes that had softened as he'd looked upon the painting. From what Daniela had said, her mother had died a very long time ago, but clearly the pain was as fresh as that horrible day. I couldn't help but hug him close, noticing over his shoulder that Daniela's eyes were bleak, stark as she stared at the painting, her mouth a tight line. She'd lost a loved one, too, a husband who had died leaving her with an infant son. Such a tragedy that they both had suffered a catastrophic loss. I released Mr. Sommariva, and as I stepped back, I felt him squeeze my ass.

Okay. So loving only once didn't mean you couldn't feel up a pretty woman who was comforting you in your sorrow. Good to know.

We went from room to room on the lower floor, looking at sculptures and paintings, marble mosaic floors and friezes, antique furniture, and an insanely voluminous collection of lithographs. The whole time, Eduardo clung to my hand as if he were a suitor and I a noble lady. Irix followed, clearly amused, while Daniela hovered around her father, fussing occasionally that he was going to tire himself out and that he should be resting.

By the time we'd come back around to the room with the Venus and Mars statue, it became clear that Daniela was right. Her father was clearly fatigued, stumbling as we walked, and occasionally losing track of what he was saying mid-conversation. He sighed as we stood near the door to the rear patio, rubbing the scarred hand over this thinning hair, his shoulders beginning to droop.

"Please go back to bed, Father," Daniela pleaded. "I will have one of the servants take a tray up to you for lunch."

He turned to me. "I wanted to have lunch with you. It's been a long time since I've enjoyed the company of a beautiful woman. Sophia died so long ago, and you remind me of her with your golden hair and your blue eyes. Being with you makes me remember her."

I patted his hand. "If you like, I can come back another time when you're well-rested and we can have lunch then."

As long as it was okay with his daughter, that is. And as long as he didn't get the idea that my coming over for lunch meant that I'd be adjourning to his bedroom afterward. Yes, I was a half-succubus, but I drew the line at siphoning sexual energy off men who were of an age that they were likely to die while we were in the act.

He nodded and leaned down to kiss my cheek, finally releasing me. A servant appeared as if by magic and took Mr. Sommariva by the arm, gently leading him toward the elevator by the stairwell as we said our goodbyes.

"Your father is very nice," I told Daniela. "And he has an amazing collection of artwork. I don't think I've seen this many high-quality sculptures and paintings outside of a museum."

She smiled fondly after the man. "His treasures. Thank you both so much for humoring him. He truly enjoyed showing them to you."

"The pleasure was ours," Irix replied.

By the time we went back to the side patio overlooking the lake, the servants were already setting up plates of food on a long table. They served us our first course—pasta with a creamy garlic sauce and pancetta.

"Oh this is amazing," I told her. "One of the best things about being in Italy is the food. We've got Italian restaurants back home, but few have much beyond lasagna and spaghetti with a marinara sauce."

"What's your favorite so far?" Daniela asked, as I dug in. "Which of our foods do you like the best?"

I thought for a second. "I haven't been here long enough to try much, but I really do enjoy the pastas. My favorite is probably pene pesto rosso," I told her. "I love the mixture of basil with the red peppers, and the thick pasta." Although this dish with pancetta was very good as well.

Daniela blinked in surprise, then slapped her hand over her mouth as she began to laugh. Even Irix chuckled.

"What?"

"I like pene, too," Daniela replied in a teasing voice. "Although not with the pesto or rosso."

"Ah, a purist," Irix commented. "I'll admit that I'm rather fond of pene myself, although not as much as Amber is. Honestly, I prefer fica myself."

Daniela was nearly rolling off her seat with laughter by this point.

"What?" I demanded. "What's wrong with liking pasta?"

"You have to pronounce both n's in the word," Irix said, still grinning. "Penne-. Otherwise you're telling someone that you enjoy penis."

"With pesto and red peppers." Daniela laughed.

I could take a joke, and had no problem laughing at my own mistakes. "Well I *do* like penis. And if I can put honey or whipped cream, or chocolate sauce on one, then I don't see any reason I can't put pesto on one as well."

"True." Irix chuckled

"So what's a fica?" I asked them. "I'm assuming that's pussy?"

Daniela chuckled. "Fico is fig, but fica is slang for vagina. So…yes."

I laughed again, determined that I needed to try harder in pronouncing the few words I did know in Italian, and thankful that Daniela's son hadn't been present to hear my slip-up. He didn't look to be more than eighteen or twenty, but somehow he seemed far younger than my twenty-two.

The second course was smoked trout with capers and a lemon butter sauce, and a side of roasted cauliflower, and blackberry tarts afterward. It was heartier than I'd expected for a "light lunch", but I remembered Irix saying that Italians liked to eat their main meal at noon with a light repast for supper.

With our "light meal" we had wine that seemed to come from a bottomless bottle. Daniela was constantly waving a server over to refill our glasses, and I felt a bit tipsy by the time they were clearing away the plates. Servers. I needed servers. And cooks. And someone who would vacuum and do laundry. I wasn't fond of housework, and sitting at a table, chatting while someone else prepared and put food onto my plate was heavenly. Although I wasn't sure how I'd feel about having a bunch of people constantly in my house. It would be bad enough them seeing my underwear while doing my laundry, what if they realized what Irix and I did in our spare time? What if they found out that we had sex with other people, picked up random strangers each night and did incredibly kinky things with them? These things might be commonplace for sex demons, but not to humans. I'd been brought up human, and although I had accepted, and even embraced, my succubus half, I still felt uncomfortable with the idea of friends and neighbors and co-workers and even housekeeping staff knowing.

Sergio walked out of the house as we were sipping our espresso. He loped across the patio with a casual confidence. His dark blond hair flopped over his tanned forehead as he bent down to kiss his mother's cheek.

"Sorry I missed lunch," he said with a charming smile toward Irix and me.

"Busy texting your friends?" Daniela asked, her voice carrying the edge of a scold to it.

"No, busy supervising the pruning of the olive trees we put in last fall." His smile remained, telling me that he was both used to his mother's scolding and immune to it. "Although I confess there were a few texts while that was going on."

"Well, make sure you get leftovers from the kitchen. You're too skinny. You need to eat more," his mother fussed.

He rolled his eyes. "I promise I'll eat something." Then he turned to us, that infectious grin still in place. "Did you enjoy the artwork as much as the gardens?"

"I did," Irix commented. "But I'm not sure about Amber. She's a botanist, and there's more beauty in trees and flowers for her than in anything man could create himself."

"That's not true," I argued. "Some of those paintings took my breath away, as did the sculptures. I really appreciate that your grandfather took the time to show them to me."

Sergio laughed. "Oh, Nonno would never pass up the opportunity to show his treasures to a beautiful woman. Be careful, though. He might just want to add you to his collection of precious things."

"I might have something to say about that," Irix commented dryly.

Daniela laughed awkwardly. "Now Sergio, your grandfather doesn't do such things."

"Not anymore." His eyes strayed toward the lake, then the mountains beyond. "Although I'm sure if he could acquire a harem of beautiful women to live in the villa, he would."

"Me, too," Irix said. "A harem of beautiful women in a villa sounds like an ideal life to me."

"Join us for coffee, Sergio." Daniela pulled out a chair.

"No," He never broke his stare out onto the lake. "I'm meeting some friends and have to get going. I just wanted to say my goodbyes to Amber and Irix, and to let you know I won't be back until late."

Daniela's expression sharpened. "Who are you meeting?"

Sergio sighed. "Just some friends. Bernard is coming up from Milan for the day and I thought we'd go out. I planned on taking the boat out tonight with him and a few other friends as well."

"I need to meet any girls first, Sergio," Daniela warned. "Do not betray my trust on this. And I want you back before midnight."

He frowned. "Mom. I'm eighteen. You were engaged at my age."

"No girls," she insisted. "And home before midnight. I mean it."

"Fine." He turned to us, shaking Irix's hand and kissing me on the cheek. "I hope to see you both around. Everyone does a party and bar hop with their boats on the weekend, so if you're still here and interested, you could join my friends and me." He shot his mother a wicked glance. "That is, if you don't mind me and my young friends, and if my mother allows Amber to actually step foot on our boat. As you heard, she has a strict, 'no women' policy."

"Sergio, that's not what I meant," Daniela said, but he'd already turned and was heading down the steps toward the waterfront, whistling cheerfully.

"Boys," Irix commented. "They are quite the handful, aren't they?"

"I'm sure you gave your mother just as much trouble." Daniela sighed. "Sergio is such a good boy, but he's of an age where urges are strong. I don't want him to wind up with the wrong girl. There are many out there who might take advantage of his youth and his hormones."

"There are many who might want to live in a villa like this," Irix added.

She smiled. "To my father, this villa and the gardens are his greatest treasure. I love and cherish them as well, but to me, *Sergio* is my greatest treasure. I know one day I will hand him into the care of another, but I want to make sure she's the right woman."

There were many cultures where arranged marriages were the norm, and those where parental approval was vital before either party felt free to exchange vows. I wasn't one to judge. And besides, Sergio was far too young to be thinking of a happily-ever-after, no matter how young his mother was when she became engaged. Young, fun, sexy-times, yes. Marriage, no.

"We have only one love," Daniela said, looking out over the lake much the same as her son had done. "I just want to make sure that Sergio doesn't give his heart foolishly, because for him, there will only be one woman."

CHAPTER 6

"**I**'ve got an idea." Irix caged me in, his hands on the armrests of my chair. Grinning, he leaned forward and planted a quick kiss on the tip of my nose. "It's the best idea ever."

I stuck a notecard in my book and shut it. "Tell me this best idea ever."

He could suggest we go dumpster diving at this point and I'd be game. After four years of college, here I was studying again when I really wanted to go explore. The morning at Villa Sommariva hadn't been enough adventure, enough vacation, and I could barely concentrate on *The Science of Wine, Fifth Edition.*

"First, you have to see this." Irix pulled me out of the chair. I plopped the book onto a table and followed him from the breezeway across the lawn.

"See what? Your cock? Because you know I *always* want to see that."

"Well if you're a very good girl, actually if you're a really *bad* girl, you'll definitely get to see that. But in the meantime…voila!"

54

I stood at the stone wall that separated us from the lake and looked. The view was stunning, but I got the idea that wasn't what Irix meant.

"No *here*, silly elf-girl. Down here."

I pivoted and looked over the edge of the wall. There were stone steps leading downward, along with heavy iron ladder rungs embedded into the stone. Jutting out from the rock was a tall, thick stone wall that formed a private spot of lake. It was a marina for the villa, a place to dock several boats and to come and go by the lake. And expertly tied to one of the moorings was a thin, stylish, cigar boat. It looked fast, dangerous, expensive. And it hadn't been there this morning.

"Did you steal that?"

Irix made a "tsk" sound. "I thought you preferred not to know about my methods of acquisition."

"You're right. Forget I asked. Should I get my swimsuit?"

"Not this time. We're going to see another villa. I just discovered that following Guido Montenegro's death, his estate has opened the villa for tours. It's the first time anyone besides the family and employees has seen it since his renovations. And once the new owner takes residence, I doubt it will be open to the public again."

As much as I hated to celebrate anyone's death, Guido Montenegro's had coincided perfectly with our visit. Two villas in one day. That was much more exciting than spending the afternoon studying all the varieties of yeast strains and their impact on residual sugar in grape varietals.

"Let's go."

I felt as if we were escaping the villa like in a James Bond movie as Irix helped me down to the narrow stone landing. Then he climbed down to the boat and waited, groping my ass as I hopped off the last of the metal rungs. The boat swayed and Irix steadied me until I got my balance, then I sat while he untied the moorings and started the engine with a roar.

Irix piloted a boat like he drove. We tore across the lake, wind whipping my hair into a snarl of knots and bringing tears to my eyes even with my sunglasses on. The boat rose and crashed down as it flew along, creating a spray of icy-cold droplets that occasionally blew back onto us. I squealed every time, shocked at how cold the lake water was in August. Swimming was clearly not for the faint of heart when it came to Lake Como.

We curved in a wide turn to avoid nailing a smaller craft with our wake and a promontory came into view.

"Villa Montenegro was originally owned by a Cardinal." Irix slowed the boat and pointed at a huge marble statue, that was indeed of a cardinal, at the top of the marina wall. There were other statuary of what looked to be monks, then a ton of half-naked neoclassical-style men and women. Of course, the Cardinal was in the most prominent position, and his statue was taller than the others.

"I'm assuming the Cardinal was from a very well-known family?" I asked.

"Weren't they all?" Irix steered the boat into the marina, and eased it to the dock. "This was originally a monastery, but after the Cardinal passed away, it was sold into private ownership. The house was built around the monastery, but it fell into disrepair. When Guido Montenegro bought it, the place was pretty much a ruin."

I was excited to see what the man had done to restore the villa. Hopefully whoever owned it now would continue to give it the same loving care as the late owner.

I held the wheel while Irix hopped out and tied our boat in, reaching out a hand to help me onto the stone ledge, then up the stairs to a narrow strip of lawn and hedges that separated an ancient building from the lake. In some ways it reminded me of a larger version of the villa Irix and I had rented, with gray stone and ivy, but that was where the similarities ended. We were in a small one-building villa tucked in between the lake waters and a sweet little town, where Villa Montenegro was a series of buildings on a steep rocky slope, its terraced gardens filled with rough and hearty plants that were perfectly matched to the exposed environment and brutal, rocky soil.

It made me think of survival, of carving out a bit of paradise in a hostile surrounding. I loved it and I hadn't even stepped foot in the villa yet.

We went through a gate and quickly saw that we were not the only ones taking advantage of this opportunity to see the villa. There was a second dock, and several boat taxis were ferrying people from other areas of the lake.

"The only way to access the villa is by the water?" I asked Irix.

A voice spoke from behind us. "Actually there is road access, but the town is through a mile of forest and steep elevations. Getting here by road from Menaggio or Cadenabbia would take an hour, where by boat the journey can be made in minutes." I turned around and saw a small woman with salt-and-pepper hair and a beak of a nose. "Of course, by air is the quickest method of travel."

"There's a helipad here?" It wouldn't have surprised me. A wealthy guy eccentric enough to buy an old monastery-turned-villa could also want his own personal helicopter. And it would have to be a helicopter, because this rocky, steep property wasn't suitable for any plane besides a jump-jet.

"Oh no." The woman laughed. "Mr. Montenegro didn't put in a helipad. He did, however, make significant improvements to the house. Are you here for a tour?"

This woman seemed to personally know the late Mr.

Montenegro. I would so much rather have a guided tour from someone who could give us the background on the property and renovations than just wander around on our own.

"We would love to take a tour, but haven't arranged for one," Irix told her. "Is it possible for us to sign up for one at this late notice?"

She looked at Irix, her eyes warming in appreciation as they did a slow tour of his body. Then she glanced at her watch. "I have half an hour until the next group. I can give you a quick private tour, if you like."

Irix smiled, and suddenly the sexual tension was thick enough to cut with a knife. Well. I knew who was probably getting laid this afternoon.

"We would love that. If it's no trouble, that is."

She beamed. "No trouble at all. I'm Ilaria Montenegro."

I blinked in surprise. "You're related to the late Guido Montenegro?"

"I am a distant cousin. I worked as his assistant, helping him with the renovations." She reached out and ran her fingers across the spikey leaves of a yucca plant on a raised garden bed. "He was a younger son, never married, never had children. His passion was traveling the world, visiting every continent, climbing the tallest mountains. This villa served as a showcase for all the mementos of his travels. It's his personal museum, the ideal place to house all his treasures."

These Italians and their treasures. I exchanged a private smile with Irix as we followed Ilaria up endless sets of stairs to tiny narrow terraces of gardens, far more wild and rocky than the ones we'd seen earlier this day. The building closest to the lake, where we'd come in up the steps of the private marina, was the old monastery, complete with a bell tower. The house itself was built as a series of steps, each section almost one story above the one before it. We climbed the stairs along the outside of the villa until I was gasping for breath. How these people went up and down these stairs all day long was beyond me. After a few weeks of living here, I would either drop dead of cardiac arrest, or have some really killer legs.

"This is the section of the villa where we will start the inside part of the tour," Ilaria said with a mischievous smile that made her look twenty years younger.

We paused before a giant set of arches that connected two buildings. The arches created an open-air courtyard where there was a view of the lake from either side, down far below the rocky sides of the promontory.

And that view was stunning. I wandered through the arches to the front terrace, peering down over the carved stone banister to a broad lawn below, then to the lake beyond. To my left was a pathway that branched off, one fork climbing upward to a stand-alone building with walls of paned glass, then past that to garages and what I assumed must be the road. The other fork led downward to a charming, round stone building with a slate roof.

"What's that?" I asked Ilaria, pointing to the round building.

"It used to be an ice house, but it's now Guido's final home."

"It's a tomb?" I was astonished. What an amazing place to be buried.

"Yes. It was his wish to always be here, surrounded by all his beloved possessions and the home he loved."

"How is the new owner going to feel about having Guido Montenegro's grave in the old ice house?" Irix asked. "I'm assuming the villa is being sold?"

Ilaria's eyes widened in shock. "We would never sell our family treasures. As Guido had no children of his own, he was free to will his estate to any member of our family. His niece, Bianca, is the new owner."

The woman turned her gaze down toward the ice house/tomb, and I saw a girl emerge, her waist-length black hair glinting with burgundy highlights in the sun. She wiped a hand across her eyes, then looked up to the sky a moment before making her way up the stairs toward the rear part of the property. She had the sort of face that graced a million Renaissance paintings—a pale oval with softly rounded cheeks, a smooth jaw, and a classical nose. Bianca. She looked like she should still be in high school, yet here she was, the heiress to a huge villa.

"Will she live here?" I couldn't imagine this would be an ideal home for a young girl.

"Eventually. She spent a lot of time here visiting her uncle. I saw her every weekend for the last six months." Ilaria sighed. "Her grandmother will act as trustee until she's of an age to assume control of her finances. Bianca will inherit from her as well, as her only grandchild. She's the Montenegro heiress."

There was a hint of wistful envy in Ilaria's voice, but the woman seemed fond of her young cousin, and proud of the fact that the girl would be the one who carried on their family fortune into the future.

"Well I'm grateful she is allowing the public access, even if it's just for today." Irix took in the villa on the stepped, rocky promontory, the naturalistic landscape, the breathtaking view from every direction. "This is amazing. So different than the other villas."

It was as if Guido Montenegro had taken a monastery and melded it into the land, made it part of its surroundings. Instead of conquering this rocky promontory, the villa was a symbiotic piece of it. It was like he'd taken the stone structures and turned them into a glorious, open-air cave, merging the sky and the sea and the stone. Compared to the artwork and perfectly manicured gardens of Villa Sommariva, this was a wild thing of nature and man. Two incredibly different styles of home, two different ideas of beauty. And although the elf in me adored Villa Sommariva, the succubus in me was in rapture over Villa Montenegro.

We continued our tour, mindful that Ilaria had another group she'd need to attend to shortly. The building on the far side of the arches was a sort of library with maps. Yes, an entire room full of maps—some modern, some ancient. They were displayed in cases, stored carefully in custom-made shelves, and one was spread across the table, the travels of the former owner clearly marked in a spider's web of inter-connected red lines.

The room on the other side of the arches was a traditional library with floor-to-ceiling shelves in a dark-stained oak, the books the same eclectic mix of old and new as the maps in the opposite room. These appeared to be stand-alone buildings, not even sharing a common wall with the house on the lower terraces, but Ilaria's eyes danced as she put a finger to her mouth and pulled on a shelf. It swung outward, revealing a hidden spiral staircase.

"It goes under the garden and into the larger portion of the villa," she told us.

"That has got to be the most bad-ass thing I've ever seen in my life," I told Irix, wondering if we could possibly do something like this at his New Orleans house. Probably not. The garden wouldn't be big enough to accommodate a separate building, and being so close to sea level would mean the underground passage would be under water.

"They had to tunnel through solid rock to put this in." Irix nodded appreciatively as we descended down the well-lit staircase and through a narrow passage. "Of course they had to do that for the foundations in original building, too."

Ilaria nodded. "Yes, although putting in the tunnel was tricky. Guido couldn't use explosives or anything that might vibrate and damage the foundation of the villa or the original monastery. It took a very gentle hand to dig this passageway."

"Why?" I asked. "I mean, this is super cool, and I personally think everyone should have a secret passageway, but why go to all that trouble to put it in?"

Ilaria turned, and I saw the grim set of her mouth. "Our family is not from here. Some believe that we don't belong here at all, that we are encroaching on territory that is not ours, stealing what belongs to others by our mere presence. It would be foolish not to have a secret means of moving through the villa, of escape."

Um, I could completely understand that sort of caution back when Italy was a series of tiny fiefdoms, or city-states, but now? Unless she was making an oblique reference to violent political factions or the mafia? Had Guido Montenegro been involved in organized crime? If so, then I began to wonder about the "natural causes" of his death.

"This passageway isn't so secret if you're giving tours of it," Irix commented dryly.

She swung open a door that led into a small study. When she closed the door, it was absolutely undetectable, seamlessly merging into the wall.

"Guido Montenegro is out of reach of any enemy now," she told us. "And who would harm a young girl?"

There was something uneasy in her voice. Was she was worried that there were indeed people who would harm a young girl? I assumed that there were more escape routes than this one which would now be known by everyone for a hundred miles of Lake Como. If the worst happened, enemies would be searching this tunnel, while Bianca escaped through another. A vision of that young woman, with her long dark hair came to mind. I hoped that Guido

Montenegro had just been a paranoid man, and not that her family was involved in activities that might put her at risk.

The villa was a winding maze of rooms. As Ilaria showed us through them, we'd come to the center floor of the far building. Our guide took us upstairs to see the top floor, then down to the lower. Then we went down another short set of stairs to the middle section of the second building in the villa. It was a cascading, interconnected series of structures, and I would have been completely lost if not for our guide.

"There's central air and heat, and even an elevator in one section," Ilaria told us. My mind was whirring with the ornate silk and velvet wallpaper and rock crystal chandeliers in each room, the marble mosaic tiles on the floor, even a smoking room that carried the lingering aroma of pipe tobacco, the beautiful items that covered every inch of every surface in this house.

Guido Montenegro had completely gutted the dilapidated stone villa and cleverly constructed a luxurious home. It might have melded into its surroundings on the outside, but inside the villa was a rich man's paradise.

But the architecture and interior design were nothing compared to the vast array of collectables that filled the numerous shelves and display cases. The villa was one part home, one part museum, and as we moved from room to room, I got the idea the museum portion had quickly been overshadowing the home portion. There were hundreds of walrus tusk figurines, hundreds of glass paintings, hundreds of vases and bowls, of books and maps and documents and tapestries.

By the third room I was gobsmacked. Every square inch of this place was covered. There were walls of shelves and display cases, all filled with collectables. Furniture, vases, paintings, wall coverings, every single item had obviously been carefully chosen, loved by a man who took great pride and comfort in his vast array of collections. What Eduardo Sommariva had done with paintings and sculptures and trees and shrubs, Guido Montenegro had done with figurines and other items he'd brought back from his travels.

Treasures. Way too many for my taste, but now I understood why Daniela, and Ilaria, had referred to them as such.

CHAPTER 7

*I*laria left us to our own meanderings with an apology and a quick look at her watch, I noticed her eyes lingered warmly on Irix as she headed off to her next tour, leaving us in a breakfast room that was part of the old church in the original monastery section of the villa.

"Guido Montenegro was a hoarder," I whispered to Irix with a grin. "A really, really rich hoarder."

"I've never seen so much stuff in my life," Irix commented. "Look, there are *more* glass paintings. What is that, two, three hundred?"

I giggled. "At least. It's not a house, it's a museum full of *treasures.*"

But it *was* magnificent. The outside of the house and monastery had been perfectly restored, and so had the gardens, but inside amid all the carefully displayed valuables were modern conveniences. It was an odd mix of rugged, museum, and home, and somehow it worked. I loved it. In some ways, I loved it more than Villa Sommariva. Well, except for the gardens. Guido Montenegro had his maps and

65

glass paintings, and the Sommarivas had their azaleas and rhododendrons.

It was in the dressing room off the main bedroom that I saw it, a tiny notch in the patterned ceiling that caught my eye. I looked around to make sure no one else would see me, then pulled over a chair and climbed on it to stick my fingers in the notch.

"What are you doing?" Irix hissed. "Don't get us kicked out. And don't screw up my chances of getting it on with Ilaria later. That woman has some serious energy going on. I doubt she's had sex in the last five to ten years. I want her."

"Oh hush. She'll just kick me out and drag you off to the bell tower to ravish. I see the way she's been eying you." My fingers depressed a tiny button and the ceiling panel sprung open, a leather rope ladder dropping down. I bit back a squeal. "Found another secret passageway. Irix, this is the coolest thing ever. I want secret passageways in my house."

"So you can escape your enemies?" He joked, hopping up on the chair behind me to look up through the trap door. "You'd have to crawl through this and it's pretty narrow. It's clean, though. I'll bet it leads up to the bell tower."

"The bell tower where you're gonna get some Ilaria action later," I teased.

We heard the scuff of a footstep in the bedroom behind us and scrambled to shove the ladder back into the passageway, clicking shut the trap door and scooting the chair back just as a group of tourists entered.

My heart was racing, and I was sure I looked absolutely guilty of something as Irix grabbed my hand and yanked me out of the room. I started giggling halfway down the stairs and by the time we'd made it out to the patio, both of us were laughing.

"Bad elf," Irix scolded. "We almost got caught."

"Nah, we could have snuck up through the passageway

and hid," I told him, wondering at the sudden role reversal. Irix was normally the one pushing the boundaries and breaking the rules where I was the one having a panic attack over getting caught. How funny.

"Ilaria would have heard us. I get the feeling that very little gets by that woman. And there are security people milling around, too. I'm pretty sure if someone tried to lift so much as a paperclip, they'd find themselves strip-searched and tossed in the lake."

I suddenly wondered if the villa had a dungeon. Ugh. "But we didn't steal anything," I countered. "Or break anything."

"Yeah, but I'm sure Ilaria knows we found that passageway. You're lucky you're not swimming for Cadenabbia right now," he teased.

Thankfully no one confronted us or firmly suggested we leave. We wandered the lower gardens some more before climbing upward to where a huge glass-enclosed pavilion sat, overlooking the entire villa and grounds. Irix was acting weird again, like he had been back at Villa Sommariva, fidgeting and looking around as if he were searching for something.

"Do you have to go to the bathroom?" I'd always figured demons were pretty good at holding it, but maybe he'd had a lot of water before we'd come out.

"No. Yes. I mean, I need to go check something out for a moment. Meet you down by the arches? Give me ten minutes, then be there, the front part that overlooks the north side of the lake and the ice-house tomb."

Weirdo. Just admit he had to pee, for crying out loud. "Okay."

I watched him walk away, then continued climbing. The pavilion was pretty. The view breathtaking, and as I circled the building to return to the steps downward, I saw a narrow path. It was partially hidden by boxwoods, but clearly it was a pathway that had been in some use.

This place was full of secrets—hidden passageways where the residents could escape down through the house and monastery to the private dock far below, tiny, out of the way spots with little benches and romantic views, shielded from sight by stone and clever landscaping. I was sure this was another, and as I came out onto a stone grotto carved into the side of the cliff face, I realized I was right.

I also realized that I wasn't the only one who'd discovered the hidden path. There in the grotto locked in a passionate embrace were a young couple. His hand was braced against the stone, his other arm around her shoulder, drawing her close. She, far from a passive participant, had one arm around his waist, the other encircling his neck, pulling him tight against her.

And holy smokes, what a kiss. I bit back a smile and carefully edged backward, trying to move as slowly as possible so I wouldn't disturb the two lovebirds.

He ran a hand through her long, dark hair and it fanned out, catching the sunlight and shimmering with highlights of burgundy. It was Bianca Montenegro, naughty girl, making out with some lover. I wondered if, during her many visits to her uncle's villa, she'd met a local boy. If so, no wonder she had been here every weekend. Would her uncle's death put a temporary hold on this young romance? I doubted she'd be as free to come and go now that there was no uncle to visit, but perhaps her grandmother would bring her during winter break. Or she could concoct some reason to visit Ilaria, who I'm sure would remain as a family caretaker.

There was something so appealing about young love. I smiled, lingering more than was polite. Just as I was about to turn around and retrace my steps, the two separated from their embrace and I saw the face of the young man that Bianca had been smooching.

It was Sergio Sommariva.

Oh my. It seemed his mother, Daniela, had been right in her fears that her son was not spending the afternoon with friends as he'd said. Now his longing glance across the lake made sense. It was all so very romantic, this stolen moment in a beautiful grotto overlooking the water. And as worried as Daniela was about her son falling in love with the wrong sort of girl, she needn't have been concerned. Sergio was heir to his grandfather's obviously wealthy estate. Bianca had just inherited a fortune of her own. They were perfectly suited from a financial perspective. And the look of adoration on both their faces as they stared longingly into each other's eyes and murmured soft affection was making me melt.

There was another reason Daniela shouldn't have worried. Bianca might be a suitable match for her son, but it wouldn't last. The woman could say all she wanted about true love and soul mates and bonding only once in their lifetimes, but young love like this burned hot and fast and typically was over by the time both parties went off to college. I'd been there, and as much as I'd thought that high school boyfriend was the person I was destined to be with for the rest of my life, he wasn't. I'd had a lot of growing up to do, and so had he, and looking back, we never would have made it in the long term—even if I had been human.

I was only twenty-two. And I knew Irix felt the same about me, that I was like these two in front of me—that I was too young to know a lasting sort of love. But he was wrong. Irix was it for me. There would be others I'd love in my life, like Kai and Harkel, but the fullness of my heart would always belong to Irix.

So I was completely cognizant of the irony of me, at

twenty-two, looking at these two and thinking their obvious love would quickly flame out.

Whether I was right, or Daniela was and her son had just found the love of his life at the age of eighteen, watching the two lovers was still a joy. They kissed again, and I smiled, using all of my elven skills to silently edge back down the trail and make my way to the arches to meet Irix.

I stood on the broad terrace, the picturesque arches in the background, before me the deep green of the lawn and the beauty of Lake Como. There wasn't a bad view on this villa's property. I'd loved the stately splendor of Villa Sommariva with the eclectic acres and acres of gardens, but this seemed more wild and verdant, as if it were a part of the rock and land rather than a decoration, a jewel, upon it.

And the lake… Sunlight lit on broad, black rippled waves, like reflections of dancing light on polished marble, like a lake of molten obsidian.

"Romantic?" Irix's arms came around me. I felt his chin against the top of my head.

"Very romantic."

It seemed like a tremor ran through him, like he was hovering on the edge of something. And then it was gone. I felt him breathe a soft laugh against my hair.

"Wanna fuck?" I teased. Well, I wasn't completely teasing, although there were quite a lot of tourists walking about this afternoon. I didn't mind a public display of extreme affection, but I wasn't sure they'd appreciate the two of us screwing up against the side of the building.

"No. I want. I mean, yes, always, but right now…" He pulled away and for a second I wondered what the heck was going on. I'd never heard him so nervous.

I turned around and nearly crashed into him. Which would have been funny since he was down on one knee and his head was level with my crotch.

Down on one knee. Everything spun, the villa the shrubberies, the scenic view of the lake. Irix's face blurred and for a second I thought I was going to pass out.

"Is this the right way to do it?" he asked. "Because Darci said this was the right way to do it, that humans, and especially you, put great value in the method of presentation. But you don't look very happy. You look like you might throw up."

We were drawing a crowd. I didn't care. "Ask me," I choked out. "Ask me before I puke."

He dug in his pocket, muttering something about Darci not telling him vomit was a possible outcome, then pulled out a velvet-covered box. With a flick, he opened the lid and extended it toward me.

"Amber Shania Lowry. You are and will always be the most important being in my life. I love you, and I want to be with you forever. I have been informed by your best friend that part of loving you forever means that I must pledge myself to you in a religious building in front of the deity of your choice and what will most likely be hundreds of friends, relatives and acquaintances while I'm wearing a tuxedo. I want to do this very much, because I want everyone to know that you're my forever. And most importantly I want *you* to know. I don't want you to ever doubt how I feel about you."

"Ask me." My stomach rolled. I gritted my teeth to keep the contents in place. Now was not a time to spew lunch all over my soon-to-be fiancé and the beautiful ring he'd picked out for me.

Irix's eyes widened with alarm. "Amber Shania Lowry, will you marry me?"

I burst into tears.

"Is that 'yes' crying or 'no' crying?"

Poor Irix sounded as if he were two breaths from a panic attack. "Yes, yes," I sobbed.

The crowd erupted with cheers and shouts. Irix jumped to his feet, yanking me into his arms and kissing me. It was one of those hard, desperate kisses, as if he'd thought he'd never see me again.

"For fuck's sake, Amber. You nearly gave me a heart attack here. Are human engagements always this nerve-racking?"

I wiped my eyes on my arm. "I don't know; I've never been engaged before."

Irix growled. It was a low, possessive sound that made me wonder if we could get away with fucking right now up against the building in front of all these people.

"You better not have been engaged before. Otherwise, I'd have to hunt him down and kill him."

Silly demon. He had no problem with me having sex with random strangers for energy, had no problem sharing my love with Kai or Harkel, but he drew the line at someone putting a ring on my finger.

Actually, I got it, because that was where I drew the line, too. And speaking of ring.

"Go ahead. Make it official." I held my hand out and wiggled my ring finger at him. He pulled it from the box and slid it on. It fit perfectly, a huge emerald-cut ruby with a frame of tiny diamonds and a platinum band.

"I wanted to ask you at Villa Sommariva, in the gardens among the plants that you love so much, but that darned

Daniela woman wouldn't go away." He looked around. "Although this isn't as private as I wanted it to be either."

"The setting makes up for it," I told him, kissing him again.

We broke apart and needed to accept the gushing congratulations of a dozen people, some of them talking excitedly in Italian or German, others telling Irix he was a very lucky man in heavily accented English while patting him on the shoulder. I stood, cradled against him, thanking everyone and showing all the women my ring as they waved their hands around, and kissed my cheeks.

Then I looked over and saw Bianca, alone this time, standing just under one of the arches. Her pale skin was flushed, dark eyes glittering with excitement, and I knew that she was dreaming of a romantic proposal of her own. I hoped she got it. And suddenly I found myself wishing that her and Sergio's young love was the sort that weathered the test of time. And then I thought what a lovely bride she'd make, her dark hair and eyes a contrast in the white dress.

White dress. Hmmm. Should I do white? Or a non-traditional color? A half-succubus wearing white to her wedding would be rather funny.

Oh, I couldn't wait to make wedding plans. The guest list, the cake, the band, the attendants and their dresses, the flowers. Would Leethu walk me down the aisle? With my human mother on the other side of me? Of course Darci would be my maid of honor, and then Nyalla as a bridesmaid, but who else? Kai? Harkel on Irix's side? Jordan? Sam? Maybe not Sam. I'd definitely want her there, but asking her to be a bridesmaid might be tempting fate a bit too much. The church—wait, could Irix go inside a church without lightning striking or something? Maybe we'd need to have an outdoor wedding.

"I love you," he said, kissing the top of my head, then

bending down to plant a feather-light kiss on my lips. He didn't have to say it; it was right there in his eyes. Actually no, he *did* have to say it because I liked hearing it.

"I love you, too," I replied. The crowd sighed. Then they began to drift away to give us our privacy, still glancing over at us every now and then with sappy smiles.

"Did I do it right?" Irix held my hands, turning the ring with one finger.

"Perfect." I'd never expected this. And I was deliriously happy. "But in the spirit of full disclosure, I do need to tell you that I was briefly engaged to William Pickett while in the first grade. I believe it had something to do with joint custody of a scooter," I teased him.

The corner of Irix's mouth twitched upward, and there was the dimple I so loved. "William Pickett is a dead man."

"William Pickett came out his sophomore year in high school and he is currently dating a guy named Dennis."

His eyes danced. "Well then William Pickett gets to live."

CHAPTER 9

The drive to Bergamo for day one of my seminar had me regretting my decision to stay in the Lake Como area. It was two hours in rush hour traffic. I was biting my nails, worried I'd be late and that it would give me a black mark on my score. I was worried I'd squash the Panda against the side of a building trying to get down a narrow alley with a tour bus coming the opposite direction at fifty miles an hour. I was worried I'd get lost and find myself in the south of France, frantically trying to ask directions via tourist sign -language and very loud English.

I wasn't late, I didn't get lost, and I didn't wreck the Panda, but I did have a few close calls. I arrived in Bergamo just in time, driving up the long hill past row after row of vineyards to turn down a driveway toward a set of iron gates and a giant, sprawling house to park and dash in the door just as the clock tower chimed the hour.

Castle Abbondio wasn't what I expected when I thought of "castle", at least from the front entrance. The house was built in the fourteenth century around a tower fortress that had been erected a century before to protect this critical area between two of the then-decentralized Italian city-states. Instead of the fort-like structure I was used to in the States, or the four-towered gothic hodge-podge of horror movies, Castle Abbondio was elegant in an understated gothic way.

I'd bounced the Panda up the drive with its fist-sized stones cemented into the pavement, making me wonder how Italian cars managed to keep their shocks intact for more than a year, then parked beside a row of other tiny cars. Then I hopped out, dashing through the gates to where everyone was standing around what seemed to be a registration table.

With quick efficiency, I had my nametag and a binder full of information, and was heading toward the dining room where we were to have our first presentation. I hoped they'd have coffee.

They did. And croissants. I sat to scarf one down and eyeballed my fellow participants who were doing the same to me. There were ten of us—seven guys and three women including me. Two men were in their forties. One was wearing a suit with a bow tie, the other khaki shorts with Crocs. The other five guys and the two women were roughly my age. One of the women came up to me with a tentative smile and extended her hand, greeting me in Italian.

She was pretty, with a curly mess of auburn hair and gray eyes so dark that at first I'd thought they were brown. And the only thing I'd understood of her greeting was that her name was Eva. I stood and shook her hand then introduced myself in English, once again lamenting that I seemed to have no skill at all in learning other languages.

"Thank God, another American!" she exclaimed cheerfully. "I was getting worried that I'd be the only one. We're surrounded by Italians and French I'll have you know. Well, except for Celio and Eskel. I'm surprised there isn't an Aussie here. Or someone from South America. I mean, did they really need three Italian dudes? Or three from France?

Although Marta is pretty cool. She can stay, but we need to swap those other guys out and get more diversity in here."

We were all white, so I was assuming she was speaking in terms of nationality when it came to diversity. Still, I was thrilled to meet another American. I stuffed down the rest of my croissant and picked up my binder to relocate next to Eva's seat, but she waved at the heavy tome.

"Oh leave that. We're heading out to the vineyard this morning. No sense in lugging a big book around."

She was right. A man came in and instructed us in both Italian and in English to bring only something to take notes with and come with him as we were to tour the vineyards first.

I was in heaven. Stuffed into a golf cart with a dark-haired guy from Spain named Celio, as well as Eva and Marta, we rode all over the three hundred acres of vines discussing rootstock, pruning cycles, row spacing, netting and bird control, and spraying for pests. Then the vineyard manager went into an hour-long discussion of phylloxera and other blights and how they affected both yield and grape quality. I'd just come off an internship where I'd been exposed to just about every grapevine blight known to mankind, so I stood and smiled serenely while the others furiously took notes. I was so going to get this apprentice-ship. I *knew* this stuff. It was in my very flesh and bones. When it came to things like optimal phosphorous and nitrogen levels in the soil, how best to protect against downy mildew, and what temperature conditions at which point in the growing cycle produced grapes with the highest sugar content, I was in-the-know.

We returned to the castle for a quick break with more coffee and pastries while the presenter set up for a lecture on what looked to be the steps of winemaking and the anatomy of a grape from his poster board charts. The break was over far too quickly, and we all took our seats, croissants still in hand, to listen to the sommelier discuss the vintnering process at the castle winery, as well as the styles of wines they produced.

I felt a moment's pang of regret that Irix would be hanging around Lake Como, trying to pick up and score with as many men and women as he could, while I was here, relaxing and listening to the history of this beautiful winery while I drank espresso and ate pastries that melted in my mouth. He was an incubus. He need to feed. And in spite of the fact that this was a workday for the majority of the Italians, I knew he'd find good hunting while I was learning about varietals, yeasts, weather conditions and how everything all combined together into perfect harmony to create an ideal wine.

I needed to feed as well, and I was completely aware that I'd neglected this for two days. I'm pretty sure Irix would have been pissed off and scolding me, except for the fact that we were newly engaged and he was happy to let me take a break and use his energy instead.

Newly engaged. The seminar speaker faded into the background as I looked down at my ring. It was beautiful. And it was new enough that I was fully aware of its weight on my finger, reminding me that Irix was mine, and I was his, and we were about to be married, just like humans.

I'd spent my life dreaming of my wedding, just like every young girl, and then I'd mourned the fact that it would never happen. But Irix was giving this to me. He didn't understand my need for this. He certainly didn't need it. But I did, and he loved me, so he was willing to go through with a bizarre human ritual and stand in a church and pledge himself to me in front of a God he didn't believe in.

I really hoped he didn't catch on fire or anything.

The sommelier finished up and a middle-aged German

man named Leo took the presenter's block. After a basic introduction to the process of fermentation, Leo suddenly became a chemist and the slides turned into an incomprehensible scribble of molecular formulas. It wasn't that Leo's drawing skills were bad, it was that I was a botanist, and this was even more gibberish than the foreign languages murmured in the background. I tried to copy them as fast as I could, too embarrassed to be seen snapping pictures with my phone, but well aware I was going to need to look all of these up later.

Non-fermentable sugars. Something about how they can be added during barrel aging. I knew that some grape varieties had higher sugar content, and that the percentage of fructose to glucose increased as the fruit became overripe, but all this stuff about Xylose, Arabinos, and Rhamnose was new. I could feel the sugars in the grapes. I could feel the differences between them, but outside of the basics, I didn't know what they were called or which was which. And I certainly didn't know about the impact of fructose levels on the time to ferment, or how they played a part in a stuck fermentation.

Bladder presses to keep from breaking the grape seeds and avoid lending an overly bitter taste to the wine. Exposure of must to grape skins and how that related to type, style, and the balance between color and off flavors. Leo promised to tell us all about different naturally occurring enzymes and the role they played in breaking down sugars as well as the finer points of color, flavor, and aroma after lunch.

The confidence I'd had in the vineyard was long gone. For the first time in my life, something was hard. I'd soared through school. I'd been thrilled at winning the internship at DiMarche. I was smart, capable, a talented half-elf who'd wowed everyone she'd ever worked with.

And I was in way over my head. The only thing keeping me from fleeing after lunch and never coming back was the thought of how mortifying it would be to face Irix and tell him that I'd failed.

I'd never failed before. Never. This was going to be the most difficult thing I'd ever done, but I was determined that I wouldn't fail at this.

I pushed my chair back and headed to the kitchen for lunch, realizing with a sinking heart that I probably *would* fail. But at least I'd fail knowing that I gave it my best.

By our afternoon break my mind was whirling with all the facts the presenters had thrown at us. Phenolic compounds like the anthocyanins found in skins and how they affected color depending on the specific pH of the wine. Esters like the norisoprenoids that were desirable in Chardonnay, Syrah, and pinot noir, and the mercaptans which were undesirable in everything, giving the wine a rotten-cabbage aroma. How Polyphenols bind to proteins, and all the different small and large polymers. Methox-pryazines. Mercaptans. Carboxylic acid. Monoethyl succi-nate. Butyl esters.

Yeah. I was on the edge of tears.

Okay, some of it wasn't so bad. The presentation on regional specific varietals was intriguing, especially the type of Muscat grape that only grew in this region, and its applications. The current enologist had made a lovely dry red Moscato as well as a grappa, from the spent grapes, and one element of our final test would be to come up with a recipe that would use this year's harvest and possibly other estate-grown grapes. We'd be judged on our reasons for our recipe along with our knowledge of grapes and wine and production. That, in addition to an exam—both written and oral, would determine who would be offered the two-year apprenticeship at the winery with their enologist.

It was an incredible opportunity. These apprenticeship contests only came around once every five years and admission to the seminar was by invitation only. I was still excited at the prospect, even after the barrage of chemistry this afternoon.

I could do this. That was the affirmation, the pep talk that I kept reciting in my head even as I panicked over this afternoon's lecture. I kept reminding myself that I had the edge, because I was a half-elf. I could sense flavors and chemical structures in the wines and plants that were beyond human abilities.

I could win this. Maybe. If I studied hard, came up with a good recipe, and if all the other attendees dropped out and went home, I could win this.

As I chatted with Eva and the other participants, my already weakened confidence faltered and sank. Every one of the others came from families of enologists or winery owners and they had all been creating wine recipes and working in both wineries and vineyards since they were children. They told their stories, then turned to me, expectantly.

"I...uh, well, I'm a botanist. I just graduated from college this year and finished a summer internship at DiMarche Winery."

"They're huge," a blond guy named Eskel said. "How long has your family been with them?"

"They're not. I got the internship through an application process. I grew up in Maryland, and the internship was the first time I'd even been in California." First time I'd ever been at a winery either, aside from those weekend things with bands and tastings.

"Ah. So your family owns one of the smaller wineries? There are some amazing boutique wines coming out of the east coast lately," Eva said.

"No, my family isn't involved in vintnering," I confessed, wondering whether to tell them about my human mother who'd been a homemaker and a bookkeeper, and my human father who'd been a construction superintendent, or freak them all out by telling them about my elven and succubus parents. "I'm a botanist and I became interested in all this through my internship."

All this. Sheesh, I sounded like an idiot.

"So you have no experience at all except for a few months this past summer sterilizing tanks, pulling weeds, and conducting pre-scripted wine tastings for drunken tourists?" Celio sneered. I winced, remembering that his family owned a small specialty wine operation in Northern Spain, and that he'd spent the last three years as a sommelier in France.

"No, not really. But I have a deep understanding of plants and their chemical structure and how that plays out in the final product."

Lame. Even if I did confess to my half-elven parentage and wow them with my special abilities, I still came across as an inexperienced fool who'd luckily stumbled into this opportunity. I saw the look on their faces, including Eva's. They were all wondering what strings my family had pulled to get me here—or who I'd screwed to get this opportunity.

I was so outclassed. I had no chance of winning this, but it was an honor to even have been invited. I don't know what clout Matthieu had here, but clearly somebody *had* pulled some strings for me to be included. Winning would be an incredible long shot. Heck, even passing these exams would be an incredible long shot, but I *was* thrilled to be here, learning and making contacts that would be useful if I decided I wanted to continue a career in the wine industry as opposed to the non-profit work with Jordan in New Orleans.

At least, that's what I kept telling myself. In reality, it stung not being the big fish in the little pond. It was embarrassing having the others look at me as if I were the weak link that didn't even belong here. And what was worse was they were right. I didn't belong here. Half-elf or not, I just wasn't prepared for this sort of thing, and I'd been an arrogant fool to think myself so.

"Well, that's one less person that we need to worry about," Celio laughed, turning his back to me. "Clearly there won't be any competition from this one. I'll bet she can't even tell a Chardonnay from a Riesling."

I flushed. Yes, I could tell a Chardonnay from a Riesling, but he was right about the rest. I wasn't really a contender for this apprenticeship. I was going to lose. But Celio's dismissive tone and derision made me stiffen my spine. I was determined that I wouldn't humiliate myself. I'd show this jerk that an inexperienced unknown from the U.S. could score just as high on the exams as any of them.

And I was determined that no matter what happened, no matter if I had to study all day and night, I was going to beat Celio. Asshole.

We'd tasted two of the winery's signature wines at break and were on a tour of the castle when I saw a young woman standing off to the side, her black hair pulled back into a braid. She had the face that graced a million Renaissance paintings—a pale oval with softly rounded cheeks, a smooth jaw, and a classical nose. She turned to me and I felt a stab of recognition.

Holy crap. Bianca. This was the girl from Villa Montenegro, the one who'd been kissing Daniela's son in the gardens. I'd assumed she was a local, that her parents lived only a few towns over. Visiting her uncle on weekends suddenly took on a whole new meaning when she lived two hours away.

Unless she was visiting here as well? No, it was Monday. She'd be in school today. Except she wasn't in school today. I was dying of curiosity, so I made my way through the crowd toward her.

"Hi. I saw you at Villa Montenegro yesterday."

The girl started, turning dark brown eyes to mine. "Oh! You're the woman who got engaged in front of the arches overlooking the lake." She sighed. "That was so romantic. I hope that Ser—I hope that someday I get a proposal like that."

Her eyes drifted down to my ring and I lifted my hand so she could admire my newest, and most beloved, piece of jewelry.

"You're fiancé is very handsome, too." She giggled. "Every woman at the villa yesterday was envisioning herself with him. I'm sure many husbands got lucky last night because of your man."

"Yes, Irix turns female, and male, heads everywhere he goes." I smiled at her, thinking again that she was so classically beautiful. "Your cousin, Ilaria, gave us a quick tour. She told us you inherited the villa from your uncle?"

Her face shadowed. "I would rather have him than all of his treasures. Uncle Guido was the only one who…really understood me."

What had she meant to say?

"I'm sorry for your loss. We read in the paper that he had died unexpectedly. Heart attack?"

That was being nosy. But before I could retract the question, she answered it.

"No. He–"

She looked around, and her jaw set with determination.

"I'm tired of secrets. He was murdered. We have enemies, and his villa is in their territory. They warned him not to purchase it, not to trespass on what they consider theirs, but he thought these centuries-old feuds needed to end. He thought if he showed them he wanted to live beside them in peace, they would leave him alone. They didn't. And now he is dead."

I caught my breath at her honesty, wondering how much of this organized crime ugliness was commonplace in Italian lives, outside the view of tourists.

"Aren't you scared? Won't they target you as well? Maybe you should sell."

Something fierce flared deep in her dark eyes, and her chin lifted. "I will never give up my Uncle Guido's treasures, nor will I sell the home that he still guards with his remains. And if those beasts try to take me on, they will be sorry. I want peace, but I will not hesitate to defend myself or protect what is mine. If they come at me, I will return their attack tenfold. I will meet fire with fire."

Holy cow this young woman should run for office. What a rousing speech.

"Why aren't you there now?" I asked gently.

She blushed deep red. "Castle Abbondio belongs to my grandmother. She wanted me to come home for the week or to Milan with my great-uncle to make sure I was safe. Grandmother worried that Ilaria wasn't strong enough to protect me, especially when she is busy with the tours and with settling the estate. She said she will allow me to return only when she or my great-uncle, Marcus, are able to be with me."

Poor thing. I doubted her grandmother or her great-uncle would be as indulgent as Uncle Guido had been, and she'd have few opportunities for smooching in the grotto with Daniela's son.

"And why aren't you in school? Does the school year start later in the fall here than it does in the States?"

She smiled at that. "I had tutors when I was young, but now all of my lessons are online. Once I complete the day's assignments, I'm free to do as I wish."

Ah, the life of the rich and somewhat-famous.

I notice the other attendees beginning to head back in and put out my hand, wanting to introduce myself. I'd probably never see this girl again.

"I'm Amber Lowry. Obviously from the U.S. Obviously staying in Lake Como with my now fiancé, Irix, and driving up here for the enology seminars."

She took my hand. "Bianca Montenegro. You're trying for the apprenticeship? Does your family own one of the big California vineyards? Is your father or mother an enologist there?"

Not this again. This was where I completely humiliated myself. "No. I just graduated with a botany degree, and did a summer internship at DiMarche."

Her smile said it all. I had not the slightest chance of winning this thing. "Oh. How interesting."

I needed to get back, but I wanted to confess something first. "I'm kind of embarrassed to tell you this, but I saw you at the villa yesterday, before Irix proposed to me. I saw you down in the grotto with Sergio Sommariva."

Her eyes widened and she shot a finger to her mouth. "You know him? You *know* him?" she squeaked in alarm. "They'll kill me. Grandmother will lock me in my room. And Sergio…my family will kill him as well. No one can know this. No one."

Such drama. I didn't know what to do to convince her that every teenager had done this sort of thing. I stepped closer to her. "Don't worry, I won't tell anyone. I won't say anything to his mother either."

"No!" she hissed, her eyes wild with panic. Before I could take another breath, she'd grabbed my arm and pulled me from the kitchen into a small room. "Please. Not another word while you are at the castle, or when you are near Lake Como. We have very good hearing and no one must know of this—both of our lives depend on it. My family hates the Sommarivas and they hate us. It is a blood feud. They're the ones who killed my uncle. They don't want us in their territory, imagine how they would feel if they knew what I was doing with one of their sons, with the heir to their family fortune?"

Daniela's family was into organized crime? They were the ones who'd killed Guido Montenegro? What hornet's nest had I landed in?

"Grandmother and my Great-Uncle Marcus will lock me away to keep me safe," she told me. "And his mother will do the same to Sergio. There will be blood and death—more death than we've already had. More death than is already coming to our door."

Was this just a combination of teenage drama and temperamental Latin histrionics, or was she serious? "So… your family and their family are rival Mafia clans?"

She rolled her eyes. "Don't be ridiculous. Stupid human gang-families. If they didn't amuse us so, we would crush them like bugs and eat them. No, we are enemies. We've been enemies since we were all exiled to this land. Although, I think, maybe we were not so friendly before either."

Sounded like organized crime to me. Maybe with a little Game of Thrones mixed in. "All right, all right." I patted the air in front of me, trying to calm her down. For all her insistence on being quiet, her voice had risen quite loud toward the end of her dramatic statement. "As someone who is all about love—well, all about sex—I've got to ask, how did you meet Sergio if your families hate each other?"

She looked around, pulling me farther toward the back wall of the house. There was a pretty view through the old leaded-glass windows of the courtyard and the tower, but I didn't want to be distracted from what I was sure was a really juicy love story.

"My Uncle Guido purchased Villa Montenegro years ago and set to work restoring it. The family thought he was crazy buying a house in Sommariva territory. It is like…giving them the finger, no? Grandmother told Uncle Guido he was on his own, that we would not defend him if he was attacked, and for months there was nothing. I wanted so much to see it." She bit her lip, giving me a doe-eyed look. "I've never left our territory. With my grandmother as the head of our family, and me her only grandchild, this castle and all the properties in Milan would be my jewels, my treasures. I was the heir, above all of my cousins. It is my responsibility to stay here or in Milan and to begin to bond with what will eventually be mine, but instead I wanted to see more of the world, just like Uncle Guido did."

An heiress who was born into duties and responsibilities she never wanted. Or perhaps would want once she was allowed to go out and sow some oats and see the world a bit. "So Villa Montenegro seemed a good place to start."

She nodded. "It is not too far from Milan or Bergamo, and my Uncle Guido would be there to protect me. I mean, I can protect myself," she puffed out her chest, which was quite perky. "I know how to defend myself against attack, but it felt safe to start where I had family."

I completely understood. Good girl. Next step: college in Paris.

"At first glance I was enthralled with Villa Montenegro, and my uncle often invited me there. He has always been fond of me. He had never fallen in love and married, so I was his little one. I was the child he'd never have. I was his heir."

She brushed a hand over wet eyes, sniffing. "I know some cousins were jealous, but how can I be to blame if Uncle Guido loved me enough to entrust me with his treasure after his death? I was not to blame for that."

No, she wasn't. And all this made me wonder what familial jealousy had to do with the rivalry between the Montenegros and the Sommarivas.

"After a few months of visiting, I began to venture to places outside the villa," she continued, "always careful to keep watch for our enemies. One day I was not so careful, and a boy saw me and followed me. When he cornered me in a quiet street, I knew right away who he was and was scared. But he told me not to be frightened, that he'd been watching me and that I was the most beautiful girl he'd ever seen." She blushed a lovely shade of rose. "He asked for one kiss, just one kiss to carry with him for the rest of his life."

Damn, these Italians had game. Even the teenage ones.

"One kiss became many. And many kisses became... more." Her blush this time was closer to magenta.

Oh, they were totally doing it. Like monkeys. Like only horny teenagers could.

"I know how that goes," I reassured her. Yep, I knew exactly how that went. "So what do you plan to do? Confess to your grandmother? Run away and elope?"

Yikes, what was I saying? Hopefully she wouldn't take the last as a suggestion. I'd hate to be the one responsible for a European-style amber alert.

"I cannot tell my grandmother. I cannot tell anyone." Her shoulders slumped. "I don't know what we're going to do. I tried to break things off last year, but I couldn't stay away. Even now I long to be with him. And I know he feels the same."

"Maybe your grandmother won't be as angry as you think." I completely understood the whole "our families hate each other" thing, but this wasn't Romeo and Juliet. This was the twenty-first century. Kids dated people that parents weren't exactly thrilled about all the time, and no one got killed. Maybe she was wrong about Guido being murdered. And even if she was right, I couldn't imagine that either family would stoop to killing teenagers, to killing children.

"I don't know." Bianca sighed. "Sergio wants us to elope, but we cannot run away. He will inherit their family fortunes as will I. Neither of us can be far from what will be our treasure. We have responsibilities. We have ties that keep us here and keep us connected to our families. There is no way we can run away together."

"But you're both eighteen, aren't you?" I waited for her nod. "Outside of you having Villa Montenegro, there is no immediate inheritance for you to manage. Even if Sergio's grandfather passes away, his mother is young and in good health. I'm assuming the same is true with your grandmother. Neither of you will be inheriting these responsibilities for decades. You could elope, or at the very least run off and spend some time seeing if this romance is really something worth rocking your family feud for, and be back in plenty of time to learn how to run the family businesses."

"Even if we could manage to be apart from our treasures, they will find us," she said with sorrow. "We won't be able to hide. Where would we go? How would we take care of ourselves? I've only lived at home, with my family to support me, and so has Sergio."

"But doesn't your recent inheritance solve those problems? I mean, except for Sergio's and your entailment, or whatever. You could sell Villa Montenegro and elope with Sergio. With the money from the sale, you could both live comfortably until you finished your education and got your careers off the ground."

She caught her breath. "I cannot sell Villa Montenegro.

Ever. I love it. I have bonded with it. It is my treasure and I will not willingly hand it over to another until the day I die."

Holy shit, the drama.

"Okay, I get it. Keep the villa and manage it from afar. Maybe lease it out or something. And maybe you and Sergio can abdicate your larger inheritances in favor of a cousin."

She frowned and typed the word into her phone, paling when she saw the translation. "Oh, that cannot happen. The Sommariva treasures are his when his grandfather and mother pass away. He has already bonded with them. He would never be able to leave them for long. So you see, even though he wants to elope, we both know that we would need to return within a year at most. And then there would be blood and death."

Again with the blood and death. And these two families had an unhealthy attachment to things.

"Is there a distant relative, a family friend, any kind of friend that you can confide in who can help? Someone who could help smooth things over between your grandmother and Sergio's mom?"

She shook her head slowly, then her eyes lit up. "You!"

Oh no. Not me. "Uh, I'm an American. And I just met you. And I'm thinking helping the two of you to run away might be illegal, like aiding and abetting or something. There has to be someone else."

"There is no one else." Her eyes filled with tears. "And we are in *love*!" she wailed. So much for being quiet so the others didn't hear.

I took a deep breath, wondering how much of the last lecture of the day I'd just missed. "Okay, let me think about things. I'll talk to you tomorrow. In the meantime, don't do anything crazy."

She threw herself into my arms. "Thank you, Amber. Thank you."

I sighed, hugging her back and wondering how the heck I was going to help her and Sergio. Because I had to help them. Two warring families. Two young people in love. It was just like Romeo and Juliet.

Except I hoped this story didn't end in tragedy.

CHAPTER 11

I plopped the eighty pounds of binders onto the coffee table and slid myself into a chair, resting my head on the cushion and wondering if I could possibly squeeze in a nap. I was beat. The drive. The info-dump at the seminar. The emotion-laden talk with Bianca. The drive back, which wasn't any easier than the drive there.

The sun was dipping low on the horizon. I hadn't eaten supper. And I hadn't satisfied my succubus needs in three days because I'd been too busy the day of our flight, then I'd wanted that first night alone with Irix, then it seemed weird to go have sex with other men right after I'd gotten engaged. But I couldn't keep sponging off Irix. I needed to go out and get laid. Although this sofa was very comfortable, and I wasn't looking forward to the early morning drive tomorrow as it was.

Maybe I could just stick a sign on the door that said "come in and fuck me—no charge". I could just lay here on the sofa. Except I didn't think a nearly passed-out partner would gain me much in the way of siphoned sexual energy. There were very few guys with that kind of kink, but I wasn't sure those were the kind of guys I wanted to be having sex with anyway.

With a groan I got to my feet and staggered up the stairs, hoping a shower and maybe a pot of coffee would revive me. I was wrapped in a towel in front of the closet, trying to decide what to wear when Irix came in.

The guy practically crackled with energy.

"Whoa. Someone had a good day," I teased.

"I hung out at a hotel a few towns over for breakfast and managed to get three tourists between seven and noon, then a shopkeeper on her lunch break, then a guy who runs a boat taxi service, then a tour guide." Irix grinned. "This place is amazing. I swear you can just walk down the street, crook your finger, and be naked in a bed five minutes later."

"I hope it's that easy, because I'm exhausted." I yanked a tank top and a pair of jeans out of the closet, deciding that I was just going casual tonight. "Quick light dinner with me? Then I'll probably find a bar somewhere."

Then I'd dash back here to the villa and desperately try to study all this biochemistry stuff so I didn't fall even farther behind tomorrow. Of course that would leave me with about four hours of sleep before I needed to get up and face the rush-hour traffic once more.

"Just screw the waiter." Irix wrapped his arms around me and kissed my cheek. "Or stay here. I'll order in from the café. You can eat in bed, get to sleep early, and be refreshed for tomorrow."

I looked that tired. Even Irix could tell, although he was more perceptive than most. "I can't. I need to find at least one sexual partner tonight. I didn't have time this morning. The commute is insane, and I'm half afraid to have sex with any of the attendees. Not that I have time to do that. Or that I'd even be able to work up any kind of pheromones. After listening to the chemical structure of wines for five hours, I don't think any of the guys there could get it up anyway, half-succubus or not."

"You'd be surprised. I'm sure any guy who is at that seminar is probably turned on by the chemical structure of wine. And they've most likely been eyeing you all day. You'll need to do a couple of them before you leave, just to make them happy."

"Maybe on the last day. Where should I go tonight? You've spent the day checking everything out. Where's a spot where I can find a sexual partner with the least amount of time and effort? Someone who wants a quickie in the elevator, so I can get it done, study, and get to sleep at a decent hour."

He flicked my nose. "With that attitude it's going to take you all night. Normally, I'd be scolding you and telling you to get out there, but I know how hard you've been working today. Plus, this is kind of my fault. I'm the one who wanted us to stay in Lake Como. I didn't realize it was quite so long of a commute for you."

I leaned against him. "How about we do that waterfront restaurant in Cadenabbia, scoot down the street to a bar, and I'll find someone there? Once I get some food in me, I'm sure I'll be in a better mood to be picking up men. Although I need to warn you that I'll be bringing flash cards to study during dinner."

He hugged me close. "Then study. We'll order a couple of different wines for you to analyze during dinner. And I'm sure you can find someone for quick sex. If I can manage three tourists before lunchtime, you should be able to find one of them who wants to do it behind the counter of the gelato shop, or on the rooftop terrace of the hotel. Just one, so you can get some sleep tonight. I'll share my energy with you to make up the difference. I've got plenty to spare."

"I feel guilty when you do that," I complained. Actually I

loved it when I shared his energy—loved the feeling of closeness and caring I got when Irix poured it all into me. But I wasn't a child, and I needed to take care of my basic needs on my own and not be relying on him all the time.

"Tomorrow night you can pick three or four guys up. Just find one tonight so you don't feel like a mooch, and I'll do the rest."

I smiled. "Okay."

I grabbed the notecards out of my binder and we walked, hand-in-hand, along the lakefront path through Menaggio and into Cadenabbia. Villa Sommariva was only another ten minutes to the south, but we'd halted just past a plaza, in an area with hotels and everything a tourist could want, along with bars, dining, and shops selling silk scarves next to Lake Como refrigerator magnets.

Irix led me down to a little place overlooking the lake and the mountains in the distance. It was sandwiched between the road and an amazing floating pool. The breeze coming off the water was lovely, and the soft lighting and guitar music gave it an intimate ambiance.

I spread out my notecards, and asked Irix to quiz me as the food came out. Everything we were served was on a stick aside from a few bowls of couscous, pickled vegetables, and chilled salads that were family-style on our long table. I ate lamb, chicken, beef, sausage, and enormous shrimp, all slid from a lethal-looking metal skewer onto my plate. And just when I felt I could eat no more, the staff came by with grilled pineapple—also on a stick.

"Here." Irix moved his glass of wine over to me. I'd already sampled three and was feeling pretty buzzed right now, but the more practice I got at detecting these components and describing them appropriately, the better I'd do on these exams.

I swirled it around the glass and eyed the color, tilting it and holding it up to better see it. The lighting in here was romantic, but not the best for detecting subtle color differences in wine, even with my elven vision.

"Red, but it's more mahogany than ruby. It's got some brown notes, so it's either aged more than a few years, or oxidized." I closed my eyes and remembered the talk earlier today about anthocyanins found in the skin of grapes, about how they were water soluble pigments that reacted with the tannins in wine and faded over time. So this was an older wine, maybe ten years or so I was guessing. That, or it had a shitty cork and air had gotten in the bottle. Only taste would tell.

But first, I gave it another swirl, noting the way it streaked down the side of the glass and making an educated guess about residual sugar. Then I shoved my nose into the top of the glass and inhaled.

"Spicy. Black pepper. Cloves. Dark cherries. Oak…no, more like charred oak. Vanilla."

Irix sat across from me, completely stoic, not revealing a thing. I sipped the wine, swishing it around, then swallowing it because spitting out wine in the middle of a restaurant was a sin, no matter how tipsy I was getting.

"Smooth, soft, almost buttery mouthfeel. Dry. Peppery bite, with cherry and vanilla, and a smoky aftertaste." I pursed my lips and threw a Hail Mary. "2007 Sonoma Coast California Pinot Noir."

I could tell by Irix's expression that I was wrong, but the presence of a young man at our table forestalled his correction.

"Irix and Amber!"

I looked up and saw Sergio smiling down at us. The smile was nervous, the look in his eyes a bit apprehensive. Ah. He'd spoken to Bianca and she'd told him of our conversation. And now he'd hunted us down to make sure we didn't spill the beans and let everyone know about their illicit relationship. He needn't have worried. I'd been so busy worrying about flavonols and esters that I hadn't even told Irix yet.

Irix greeted him warmly, standing and shaking his hand, then inviting him to sit. He did, after bending over to kiss my cheek. Then his eyes landed on my left hand.

"Bianca was telling me about your ring. It really is beautiful. I was planning on getting her a diamond, but I think I'll look at rubies."

I beamed, admiring my ring once more. He and Bianca were eighteen—far too young to be thinking of engagement rings, but I wasn't going to be the grumpy twenty-two-year-old that flattened his dream.

And it was the perfect opening to address a topic that I knew was on his mind.

"I spoke with her today and the castle and she told me of the challenges you both face. I'm sorry."

His expression darkened. "My mother would never approve, and neither would her grandmother. I know our love is doomed, but I can't imagine my life without her. I'd sooner die. I'd rather leave every bit of treasure behind and live with the pain of losing it all than suffer the worse pain of losing her."

Irix quickly caught up with the conversation. "Maybe in time, both of your families will come to accept your love for each other?"

I read between the words. Either the families would eventually accept it, or in time their love would fade and they'd both find other people to love—people who were probably more acceptable to their families.

Sergio shook his head, his smile sad. "I doubt it. Our families have been at war with each other for a thousand years, since before we owned Villa Sommariva, before the first stones on the tower that was to become Castle

Abbondio were even laid. A feud that long-standing doesn't end one day just because two young people are in love."

"I told Bianca I'd think of something, that I'd try to help you both if I could," I told Sergio with an apologetic glance to Irix.

"The only solution I can think of is for us to run away, but now that Bianca has inherited Villa Montenegro, I'm not sure if she can. It's one thing to withstand the pain of leaving a treasure that has been promised to you, but another entirely to bear the agony of leaving a treasure you have actually held in your hands. If Guido had not died, I'm sure Bianca and I would be on our way to Paris right now. But as it is…"

It seemed the only solution left was to somehow convince the adults of both these families that a young romance wasn't something to go to war over. Easier said than done.

"Let me know if you think of anything I can do to help," I told him.

"Me as well," Irix added. He gestured toward one of the seats. "Join us. Amber is tasting different wines and trying to determine what they are."

"Very unsuccessfully," I told Sergio. "Obviously I got this one here very, very wrong."

"I can't tonight, but maybe I'll join you another evening." Sergio reached over to pick up the glass of wine swirling it around in the light then drinking it down.

"Very nice. 2006 Bordeaux region Cabernet Sauvignon." Then with a smile and a bow, he headed off while I stared at his retreating back.

"He's right. It was a 2006 Bordeaux region Cabernet Sauvignon," Irix told me.

Damn it all. I was so going to fail this test.

CHAPTER 12

I made it to Bergamo early the next day, which meant I had some time to chat with the other attendees as well as get pointers and tips from the presenters. Two of them were going to be the ones testing us and judging our submissions. They would be there each day, helping quiz us and in the wine-tasting segments that were starting this afternoon. There were other guest presenters who would only be there for their portion of the classes, then head back home.

One of them was the guy from yesterday—Leo Something Unpronounceable from a winery in Germany. He'd given that insanely complex speech with all the chemistry stuff as well as one about vineyards in the Rhine, and was back today to discuss the qualities that made German wines distinctive and how to recognize those in both the grape and the glass. He was in his early fifties. He was cute in a nerdy, wine-geek kinda way. And he couldn't keep his eyes off of me.

Should I? He didn't appear to be married. He wasn't too old or too young. He didn't wear socks with sandals, at least he hadn't in the last two days that I'd known him. I'd picked up a British tourist after Irix's and my dinner last night, but beyond that, I hadn't had sex with anyone but Irix since we'd arrived in Italy. Even with the energy he was sharing with me, I was starting to feel that gnawing need. That first night had been special—our first evening in Lake Como. The second night…well, we'd just gotten engaged and I wanted some one-on-one time with Irix. Last night I was exhausted and only had time for one. And I was discovering that one really wasn't enough—especially if I wasn't going to tie my sexual partners to me in any great degree.

A light tie meant they could love others, that they wouldn't be driven mad obsessing about me and the one night we shared together, but it also meant less energy over the long term. I was willing to make that trade-off, but it meant I'd need to not skip two or three nights in a row like I'd done. I wouldn't die, but as Irix had said, if I needed to do something requiring a lot of energy, like save a bayou or a pineapple farm, or feed a small town in Hel, then I was going to drain myself to death.

I couldn't keep relying on Irix to help me. I needed to take care of my own needs, and here was someone who would take hardly any effort to get into bed—or a back room, or the back seat of a car. So I smiled at him and sauntered over, trying to carry on a conversation where I knew no German and he was clearly more interested in my boobs than in anything I was trying to say.

"I'm really looking forward to your talk today," I murmured, tracing a finger down the lapel of his jacket. "Maybe after lunch we can find somewhere private and you elaborate more on the Xylose and Arabinos?"

All the guy heard was "after lunch" and "private". He nodded his head vigorously and suggested that I meet him in old tower behind the stable/carriage house, which was now a garage. People were starting to take their seats, so I agreed with a knowing, sultry glance, then turned around to see Celio glaring at me.

Crap. Did he hear that? Even if he didn't, he probably saw me standing far closer than Americans generally did to strangers or business associates, as well as saw me touching Leo's jacket.

He was Spanish. The guy knew flirting when he saw it. And this probably confirmed his theory of me sleeping my way into this event. How embarrassing. I brushed past him and heard him mutter something under his breath. I was suddenly very glad that I'd nearly failed high school Spanish and had no idea what he was calling me. Actually I had a good idea what he was calling me, and I was happy to pretend to be ignorant.

Once seated, I noticed Bianca up toward the front of the room, standing next to a woman with a beautifully tailored navy-blue pants suit, her silver and gray hair styled in a cut reminiscent of Jackie Kennedy. She had sharp, shrewd eyes as well as the sort of ageless beauty that meant she'd look the same at eighty as she did at fifty. And there was a striking resemblance between this woman and Bianca.

And the man next to them with, the one who scanned the crowd with perceptive, watchful eyes, halting when he saw me. I shivered. They were the eyes of a predator, or someone who was used to getting his way, of having his orders obeyed without question. It was as if he saw right through me, knew that I wasn't human. I stared back, more out of shock than any sort of defiance.

Then today's presenter broke the spell, telling us all to take our seats and informing us that he was pleased to introduce our hosts: Catarina Montenegro, along with her brother Marcus Montenegro and her granddaughter, Bianca Montenegro. He pronounced their names as if they were royalty, bowing and nodding as Catarina, clearly the matriarch of the family, took his place at the podium.

She spoke first in Italian, then welcomed us all in an elegant English with a vague European accent. I felt the strength of her character, her pride in her 'treasure' that she was sharing with us this week. She spoke about the winery, the extensive vineyards, and how much Castle Abbondio meant to her family.

I admired her. She was strong, a powerful figure, an astute businesswoman who clearly adored her family from the warm glances she sent toward Bianca and her brother. Bianca obviously adored her back, and even Catarina's scary-looking brother softened as she spoke about the castle, the winery, and their lands. At the end she wished us all luck in the upcoming tests, and announced she was looking forward to personally congratulating the winner. She left the podium to loud applause.

Was I the only one who saw her shoulders slump as she neared the doorway? Saw Bianca reach out a hand to take her grandmother's arm in support? Felt the sadness that came off the woman in waves? That speech…that had been an echo of a former Catarina Montenegro, one who had mustered up this ghost of her earlier self to speak on behalf of her family and their holdings. The real woman was crumbling inside. I wasn't sure if it was depression, the Melancholy that Eduardo Sommariva had, or if she had a serious illness that was causing her to waste away, but I got the feeling this woman only had years at the most to live.

One of the other presenters went first, and my heart sank when he launched into more chemistry—this time all about how acidity affects color and the pros and cons of adding citric acid as a brightener. Then he took us all down the rabbit hole of malolactic fermentation either during or after primary fermentation as opposed to adding the bacteria in the barrel.

There were so many variables in winemaking. I'd gone into this thinking it was all about the grape variety and growing conditions, but all these different yeasts and tannins and flavonols and more chemistry crap than I'd ever wanted to know about played just as much a role in the final product as the grape itself.

And somehow I was supposed to come up with a recipe and process for the vineyard's Muscat grapes in the next two days. After lunch we were to work on our tasting and study in small groups, then we'd go home with a bag of grapes and get to work. One more day of lectures, then we'd have a day of testing and presentation of our recipes. Then we'd come back on Friday for our results and the announcement of the winner.

Which wasn't going to be me.

The Italian dude left the stage, and my admirer took his place. Leo's presentation was brilliant, even though I needed to write down phonetically some of the terms he was using to look up later. I'd also noted a few phrases where he'd lapsed into German to have Irix translate for me. I needed to start taping these sessions. Actually I needed to try to learn other languages. It was so frustrating how elves could quickly and easily pick up any language they were exposed to, how demons could Own a soul and instantly be fluent in that person's language, but I lacked this talent. I more than lacked this talent. I was an idiot when it came to anything but the Americanized English I'd grown up with.

And if I ever met my sire, Leethu, I planned on having a stern word with her about this lack. She was the one who'd decided what traits I got when I was formed, and for the most part, she'd picked well. I had the things I needed to survive, a wonderful mix of elf and demon that served me well. But this was something I wished she'd thought of.

By lunchtime my back was aching and my head whirling with all the terms and new information. The other attendees were nodding thoughtfully while I was frantically scribbling in my notebook and trying not to panic. Part of me wanted to just bag the whole test thing and go have fun with Irix, to treat this as a vacation. But one look at that jerk Celio and I kept my ass in the chair and continued writing. I wouldn't give him the satisfaction. I wouldn't give up. And I'd score something respectable on the tests, even if winning wasn't in the realm of possibility.

And I'd bang that German presenter. He'd been eyeing me all during his lecture. It had been hard to look sexy and sultry while I was frantically taking notes, and very aware of Celio's hard stare, but I'd managed an encouraging smile or two. At lunch, I scarfed down a few of the turkey pinwheels and some bruschetta, and headed out to the stables-turned-garage for my quickie.

I snuck through the giant kitchen with a fireplace that looked big enough to roast an elephant, and dozens of shining copper pots hanging from the ceiling on hooks, then through a room with lemon-yellow plaster walls and a terracotta floor. The huge wooden doors swung wide on well-oiled hinges. Carefully closing them, I made my way across the cobblestone drive past the sliding doors of what used to be the stables to the old tower.

That's where I stopped and stared, my mouth agape. This was the oldest portion of the estate. The tower had been here before the house and private chapel had even been built. It was small as fortresses go, only made to hold nine or ten guards, but it was still impressive. I reached out a hand to touch the stone, marveling that I was laying my hand on something that was nearly eight hundred years old. I was a half-elf/half-succubus. I'd probably live for tens of thousands of years. In the scope of my life, this wasn't all that remarkable, but as someone who had been raised human, who'd always thought of her lifespan in terms of less-than-a-century, this was amazing.

I went through an iron-banded door and down a small hallway to a room that didn't seem sufficient for ten people to live in.

"Amazing, isn't it?" Leo asked me. "The guards took shifts. They slept above the stables. Others would stay here and cook or relax. The tower is up there, but it's not big enough for more than one or two at a time."

It was fascinating. I envisioned a time before the house was here, where humans lived here for months or years at a time, the early warning system for attack. I'd walked around yesterday and seen the old moat as well as the remains of a suspension bridge that allowed the guards to escape if needed—and to spread the news before the marauding army arrived in the city. It *was* amazing. I could close my eyes and envision the lives of the men here, the boredom, the camaraderie, the need for vigilance. And I also envisioned the fantasies of the man here with me, spooling them into my mind and making me catch my breath in anticipation.

Oh, he was a naughty man. And this was going to be so much fun.

"There's a dungeon?" I asked, pointing to the grate in the floor.

He nodded, and I sensed his blood quickening, his heart pounding. "When that metal door is closed over the top, it is absolutely dark down there. No windows. No other entrance or exit. Just stone all around, a few shelves carved into the walls, and a ledge where the prisoner could sleep."

I peered down, thinking this was going to be one of the kinkiest things I'd ever done. "How do the prisoners get down there?"

I thought of a guard tossing someone onto the stone below and winced. Having someone with broken bones, bleeding slowly out on the stone and moaning while you were trying to cook your and your coworkers' dinner, didn't sound fun. Plus, I was assuming these prisoners needed to be kept alive.

"There used to be a ladder that they'd lower down, then pull up once the prisoners were inside. Now they have metal bars embedded in the stone as a sort of ladder for people to climb up and down."

I leaned over. "And do people climb up and down?"

He walked up to me, putting his hands on my waist. "Very rarely. Most people find the dungeon to be horrifying." He nuzzled the back of my neck. "I have known the Montenegro family for many years. I've been their guest here many times. And this dungeon has always held a particular fascination for me."

I turned toward him, pressing myself against him and wrapping my arms around his hips. "Should we go down? Do you want to…down there?"

There was a certain amount of shyness and hesitation that he wanted in me, and I willingly gave it. Yeah, screwing in the dungeon sounded cool, but the part of me that had been raised as a human was screaming a warning. No one knew I was out here with him. If I climbed down first, he could shut the metal door on me and I'd be down there in total darkness until someone found me.

But they'd find me. Even if none of the seminar attendees noticed I was gone, Irix would. He'd track me back here, and set up a search party, and they'd eventually find me. That is, if I didn't manage to escape myself. I wasn't as strong as most demons, but I could blast that metal lid off with a lightning bolt. And then I'd hunt down this German prick and make him rue the day he'd locked me in a dungeon.

But that wouldn't happen. I saw his fantasies, and they had nothing to do with entombing a woman or raping and killing someone and leaving their body in a cell. He was just as nervous as I was, wanting to be gallant and go down first so he could help me down the metal rungs in the wall, but afraid that I might do what I'd just been imagining and lock him in the dungeon.

"Candles?" I slid his shirt up and ran my fingers along the sensitive flesh over his ribs. "Or dark? There will be a bit of light through the grate, so at least you can see what you're getting."

He leaned in to kiss me, slow and full of passion. Then he pulled his mouth just a breath away. "No candles. I'll go first, then I'll help you down."

"No, me first." I ran my hand around to the front of his chest then downward, hooking my fingers in his waistband and tugging. "Do you want me naked and waiting down there, or do you want to take my clothing off yourself?"

I saw him thinking of ripping my clothes off, then realizing that I had nothing to change into for the rest of the seminar. Plus, he was remembering that ripping clothing wasn't as easy as he'd thought it to be, and yanking forcefully on fabric that wouldn't give didn't portray a sexy, manly image.

"I'll be naked," I decided for him. "I'll be your prisoner and you the guard. You can do what you wish with me, force me to comply with your every demand."

I got the feeling his demands weren't going to be anything out of the ordinary. This guy's excitement was all about the location, the novelty of fucking in a dungeon. My purpose would be to make this exciting, in spite of cold uncomfortable stone and darkness. I was thinking lots of sexy talk, and lots of role play.

Leo stepped away from me and pulled the grate up on the dungeon, grunting from the effort. Even though there was a bolt and loop for a lock on the gate, it had to have been heavy, otherwise the prisoners might have been able to open it themselves.

Although now that I was staring down into the hole, I wasn't sure how they would have accomplished that. There was nothing to use to push the grate upward, and it was high enough from the floor and the ledge of the cell to make jumping and knocking it upward impossible. A very agile person could have possibly jumped up and grabbed the grate with their hands, but then their weight would have made opening it impossible.

I shivered again and climbed down the rungs, gratefully taking Leo's assistance in getting my grip and balance on the first two. Once down in the cell, I realized how bleak incarceration down here would have been. It was cold and damp and dark. The room was barely six by eight with no blankets or mattress to relieve the ache such cold stone would cause to muscles and bone. Someone had scratched something into one of the walls, but what it was I couldn't tell in this dark. It chilled me to wonder what the prisoner might have used as a carving tool.

I heard a step on the rungs and realized that I needed to get busy. Shedding my clothing, I piled it off to the side where I was sure I could find it all later. It would be horribly embarrassing for someone to discover my underwear down here, although it would probably go unnoticed for weeks. I doubted this was a regular spot for the residents. Then I remembered Daniela's fascination with the wet grotto at Villa Sommariva and chuckled. For all I knew, the Montenegros came down here all the time.

Leo hopped off the last step. The faint light from the tower room above cast dark shadows on his face and body, making him seem menacing and brutal. He was far from that, but I knew that I needed to play along. It wasn't just the energy I wanted to siphon from him, but the need to fulfill his fantasies. I wanted this. I wanted to please him, to give him an experience that he would remember for the rest of his life. It wasn't just about securing a strong viable source of energy to feed my succubus side, it was about giving him a gift of ecstasy, of a precious moment to cherish in a life that was sometimes disappointing, sometimes even heartbreaking.

I whimpered. "I can't take it down here anymore. Please let me out. I'll do anything. Please."

He walked over to me and grabbed my wrists, yanking me against him. "You can...oh sorry. Did that hurt? I'm sorry."

Oh sheesh. Spare me from nice guys with naughty fantasies. I ignored his concern and kept in character, standing on my tiptoes to trail a line of kisses down his neck. I was lucky I didn't miss, because it was so damned dark down here I couldn't even see his neck. Hopefully he could find the right hole. Although with me, it really didn't matter where he stuck it in.

"Please," I begged. "I'll do anything."

He hesitated, and I felt him waver, felt his indecision. This was too weird, too kinky. He was afraid of hurting me, afraid that I'd not enjoy this, that *he'd* not enjoy this. Did this make him a pervert? Would I later accuse him of rape, or tell the Montenegros that he accosted me and forced me?

Oh, for Pete's sake. I yanked the rest of his shirt out of his pants, and expertly unbuttoned them, easing the zipper down. Then I dropped, ignoring the cold stone grinding into my kneecaps. Sliding his pants to his ankles, I pulled his cock out of the fly of his briefs and stroked it gently, pushing the foreskin back and licking the tip. He groaned, leaning into me, his hands in my hair.

I played with him until all his fears went away and all that remained was desire. Then I worked my way up his body, unbuttoning his shirt and kissing my way up his chest and along the column of his neck to skate along his jaw and finally take his lips with my own. His hands in the meantime were busy, telling him everything about my body that his eyes couldn't see in this darkness. I felt him stiffen further against me and rocked against him, standing on tiptoes and spreading my legs to position him so he slid between my thighs.

"Take me. Anything. Just let me escape. You can have me any way you want as long as you let me out of this dungeon afterward."

He made a strangled sound deep within his throat and spun me around, placing me face-down on the stone ledge. I shoved my rear in the air, smiling as he kicked my legs apart, and guided himself up through my folds.

Then he eased into my ass. And immediately froze, uncertain what to do. I sensed his embarrassment, his coming apology, his confusion about whether it would be acceptable to screw me in the pussy after having been an inch in my ass. Was that unsanitary? Did that make him a weirdo?

I moaned and shoved my butt against him, relaxing so he went all the way in. I heard him gasp, felt his hands tighten on my hips. Then without giving him a chance to overanalyze the situation and doubt the whole thing, I set up a rhythm, bringing him in deep, then pulling away to where he was at the very edge of my entrance. Irix was an avowed ass-man. He'd taught me the joy was partially due to the novelty, the very different feel of anal versus vaginal sex, as well as the feeling of the tight ring at the very entrance.

Leo had obviously never had anal sex before, and he was excited to be doing this down in the dungeon where he'd fantasized for years about bringing a woman and having his way with her. Three strokes in and he took charge, his fingers digging into my hips as he slammed himself in, building up a frantic rhythm that had my boobs bouncing wildly and my head on the edge of hitting the wall. I pressed my hands against the stone and braced, the whole time moaning and shouting encouragement, telling him how fucking good he felt and how I was ready to come.

I wasn't, but that wasn't the point. *He* was the point. This was all about him, and as he built toward his climax, I realized that I actually *was* on the edge myself. I'd forgotten about the cold and the stone, and his fingers bruising the skin of my hips, and his cock balls-deep in my ass. This was…hot. And kinky. And cool. Wow, what fun.

When Leo shouted out his release, I followed, arching my back. Then I stood, pressing myself against him as he slid from me, wet and limp against my leg, raining kisses down my neck as his hands fondled my breasts and reached down between my legs.

Oh. God bless this sweet guy for wanting me to come again, when he was clearly spent. I edged my legs apart and leaned against him, letting him have his way and losing myself to the enjoyment of his fingers on and in me. I came again, two fingers shoved deep in my pussy, his thumb rubbing my clit while his other hand played with the nipple on my right breast and his tongue licked along my neck and collarbone.

Then I cleaned up as best as I could with my underwear, shoving them into my pocket and shimming into my clothing, well aware that I'd need to spend the rest of the day with that just-been-fucked feeling and smell. Lovely.

Actually it *was* lovely. I was ablaze with Leo's energy. I'd had a lot of fun. A dungeon. That totally had to be a bucket-list item.

Leo helped me up the rungs of the dungeon, kissing me in the tower hallway before walking me back to the house.

Once inside the room with the harp, we separated with fond words, both of us knowing that we'd never see each other again. It didn't matter. I'd given him something special. And as for him…well, he'd continue to give me something special for the rest of his life.

CHAPTER 14

The moment I'd walked back into the dining area, I realized that my absence hadn't gone unnoticed. A few of the attendees grinned at me. Eva gave me a thumbs up. Celio curled his lip and walked over as if he wanted to spit in my face.

He stopped inches from me and glared. "You can sleep with all the presenters you want, it's not going to help you win the apprenticeship."

This was one of the things I hated about being a half-succubus. Here I was trying to save some time and gain some much-needed energy, and humans either saw me as a slut, or someone who was trying to sleep her way to the top.

"That's not why…" I waved my hand, realizing that he'd never believe me. "If I get this apprenticeship, it's because of my knowledge and abilities, not because I had some fun in the back room with a presenter."

"You won't win. Typical American, come over here with no experience, no background, and think you can attend a few seminars and be better than the rest of us. 'I read a book on the plane ride over,'" he mocked. "'And I once drank a Chardonnay. I know all about wine, just ask my friends.'"

I tamped down my anger, realizing that from his view, this seemed to be the case. He didn't know I was a half-elf, and that brought special skills into the mix. Of course, even with my half-elf side, I was way outclassed here. Maybe with a few years of study I could beat these other guys, but not now. Not even if I seduced every judge in the place.

Well, maybe if I seduced every judge in the place, but that wouldn't be fair. I was only a half-demon. A full succubus might not have such hesitations about winning through dirty tricks.

Still, I wanted to show this jerk that I wasn't quite the stereotypical blonde American bimbo he took me for.

We took our seats and sat through an hour of how American oak barrels differed from European ones and how that affected the wine, then we were assigned groups and sent into the kitchen where bottles of wine with the labels covered up sat next to glasses and notecards.

We were in teams of three—and my team was me, Marta, and Celio. Of course I was in a group with Celio. Why couldn't I have gotten Eva or…or *anyone* other than Celio? Not about to be the one to complain, I gritted my teeth and headed to our assigned area. Marta had already picked up the notecards and poured two samples.

I picked up two of the glasses of wine and passed Celio one.

"White wine. Clear. Bright," he commented, swirling the wine in the glass and holding it to the light.

"No shit, Sherlock." I smirked. "It's a white wine. He's brilliant. Just give him the apprenticeship now and send the rest of us home."

Celio glared at me, but didn't reply. He stuck his nose in the glass and inhaled. I did the same with far less drama.

"Lime. Apples. A faint melon aroma and a slight tropical note. Floral."

I nodded in agreement. It smelled like wine. Clean. Crisp. Sweet but not cloying. Not overly alcoholic. I pretty much knew what varietal it was before tasting it. This was where being a half-elf and having spent the summer in a vineyard helped. I knew grapes. It was just all the other stuff that threw me.

We both drank, eyeing each other as we rolled the liquid around in our mouths. Celio spat his into the can provided for such. I didn't.

Cue all the jokes about how I swallow and don't spit.

"You're going to get really drunk by the end of this," he warned me. Which was actually a nice gesture given that he clearly didn't like me.

"No, I won't." I didn't go into how as a half-elf/half-demon it was pretty hard for me to get drunk. It happened after a couple of bottles of wine. I'd probably end up spitting it out later in the day if we were going to be sampling a few hundred of these glasses, otherwise, I was going to stick it out.

"No oak flavors. Medium acid. Medium alcohol. Fairly complex. Faint chalky notes. Lilly florals. Very dry."

"Yeah, yeah." I rolled my eyes. "It's a Riesling. Not a German, or another European vineyard. These grapes grew in a temperate climate. I'm thinking it's a California vineyard, probably Sonoma."

I was totally pulling the last one out of my ass. I was positive this was a Riesling, and equally positive it wasn't German. Beyond that, I was blindfolded, throwing a dart at a board.

A flash of doubt crossed Celio's face, then vanished. He took another sip, swished it around, then spit it out. "No, I'm thinking Australia or New Zealand."

Ugh. Their wines had a lot in common with the California ones I was more familiar with. Was I right, or Celio? I had spent the whole summer with one of the bigger Riesling producers in California. And this did taste a lot like the grapes from that region.

"So? What is your conclusion?" Marta asked. She'd been writing on her little pad, holding the notecard so we couldn't see what was written on it.

"It tastes fairly young," I observed. "Less than three years. I'm going with 2016 Sonoma Valley Riesling."

Celio squinted at the glass. "2014 Riesling…Southern Australia."

Fuck, that was specific. I held my breath while Marta consulted the card.

"2014 South Australia Riesling."

Damn it all to fucking hell! I hated this asshole. Couldn't I just once beat him at something? I didn't have to score higher than him on the test. I didn't have to beat him for the apprenticeship contest. I just wanted to get one of these tastings right and be able to rub his nose in it.

I was glaring at him, trying to think of how I could possibly blast him with lightning and get away with it, when the guy smiled.

It wasn't smug or condescending, it was a smile of relief. "I wasn't sure," he told me. "You know California wines better than I do, and I'm not as confident when it comes to non-German Rieslings. In all honesty, I was going to say Napa Valley, but I hate you and couldn't bring myself to agree with you on this one, so I went with Australia."

He hated me. Well, the feeling was mutual, even though for a second there I'd been shocked to feel something very different for this jerk. Just for a second.

"So you went against your instincts and chose something

halfway across the world from my conclusion, just to spite me?"

He grinned and I felt that very unwanted jolt of attraction again. Just for a second.

"Yes. Clearly that's my strategy from this point forward. If I'm in doubt, I'll just choose the exact opposite of what the American bimbo says."

Annnnd it was gone. I set down my wine glass and chewed on a cracker while Marta queued up the next selection.

It was a dark red, almost purple in color but edging toward mahogany. Earthy plum aromas. Smooth finish, but a tannin bite that told me…something. I eyed my notes, but didn't want to give Celio the satisfaction of having to use a cheat sheet. I sipped it, noting the firm structure of the wine, the rich flavor of plum and blackberry. It was so fruit forward that the plum flavor was the first thing on my tongue, but it wasn't overly sweet.

"2015 Argentina Malbec," I announced.

Celio snorted. "Malbec, yes. Argentina, no. It's French."

"Fuck you and the horse you rode in on, it's from Argentina," I insisted.

He blinked, clearly not understanding the first part of my sentence. "It's French, you moron."

"Argentinian, you Eurotrash snob."

"There is no way that's from Argentina," Celio scoffed. "There's too much sun in Argentina and it gives the wine a weaker structure than the French Malbecs. Then there's the tannins, not that you'd recognize tannin if it jumped out of the glass and bit your tongue. Southern France has a thinner topsoil. It equates to a deeper wine than what Argentinian wineries can manage with their soil and the climate there."

In general, yes. But in this case, no.

"You'd be right if all the Malbec wines produced in

Argentina came from the Mendoza region. The ones made in Salta are different. There's a higher degree of limestone in the soil which adds to the tannins, plus the limestone brings calcium into the mix, giving the wine additional structure and acidity. Argentina. I'd bet my life on it."

Celio snarled. "France. I'd bet my life on it."

"You're both dead," Marta drawled. "It's a 2015 Malbec, from Chile."

Damn it. I was so going to lose this apprenticeship. The only bright spot was that Celio seemed unlikely to win at this moment either.

"Amber is right about the soil in that region of Argentina, though," Marta told my nemesis. "That was a good call on her part."

I took the notecards while Celio and Marta tasted the next two wines, then Celio had his turn with the cards. I got every single tasting wrong, and Celio was a complete ass about making sure I knew how very wrong I was.

Celio had been right. After tasting four wines, I was slightly buzzed. And I had to pee. The other attendees made their way back to the seminar room to gather up their study materials and head home, while I raced to the bathroom to relieve my very full bladder. As I shimmied my pants down over my hips, I noticed that something was *not* in my pocket as I'd thought it was.

My underwear. Shit. Fuck. Damn. I could swear I'd stuck them in my pocket after using them to wipe up after my encounter with Leo. Yeah, I know that was kind of gross, but I hadn't wanted to leave them behind, and I really didn't want to put them back on. The pocket was the less gross of three gross alternatives, so that's what I'd gone with.

Gone. The operative word here. I caught my breath, wondering if they'd fallen out in the tower, or somewhere in the courtyard, or even worse, in the middle of the seminar room.

Oh, God. Everyone pretty much knew I'd been banging Leo at lunch, leaving my filthy panties around would be the nail in the coffin for any credibility I still had left. Even if a miracle occurred and I scored perfect on these tests, I'd never get the apprenticeship.

Leaving the bathroom, I retraced my steps through the seminar room, thankful that I didn't find them there. I spent a moment of panic wondering if someone had found them and picked them up, only to realize that they had to be back at the tower.

I snuck out through the double doors and past the stable, carefully making my way into the tower. Sure enough, there were my underwear, caught on the edge of the dungeon grate. Grimacing, I snatched the piece of lace up and shoved it firmly into my pants pocket. I headed out, back to the house through the room with the harp, but stopped at the kitchen door when I heard voices.

They were angry voices. I recognized one as Catarina Montenegro's voice, the other an adult male. They were both speaking in Italian. I froze, but before I could back away, I heard the name Guido Montenegro.

That was the man who'd died, Bianca's uncle and Catarina's son. She'd survived both of her children—Bianca's father who had died a long time ago from what I could tell, and Guido. I listened intently, trying to stay silent, then surprised when the conversation suddenly switched to English.

"He was murdered," the man insisted. "And we cannot let that stand."

I remembered my conversation with Bianca. She'd insisted that her Uncle Guido had been murdered. I wondered if this had to do with that organized crime feud between the Montenegros and the Sommarivas.

"He was living in their territory," Catarina countered. "I told him not to buy the villa, but he insisted, saying he'd bonded with it on sight and that it was his treasure. How could I deny him, my beloved son who'd never found his mate, never had children of his own? How could I deny him his treasure? We all knew the risks. I'm just surprised that they hadn't moved against him before now, or that they did it in such a sneaky, underhanded manner."

"It is the sneaky underhanded manner I object to the most," the man countered. "They should have sent a grievance to you or declared war, not killed Guido while he lay sleeping. That is not our way. *That* is what we should seek vengeance for. Guido should have had the chance to die like the warrior he was, and not be killed in his sleep."

"And what do you suggest we do?" Catarina asked.

"We declare war. We fight them to the death. We rid ourselves once and for all of these vermin."

I heard her laugh. "And for what? I do not want their treasures. Marcus, I have survived both my sons and my husband. I only want to rest surrounded by my treasure and wait for the chance to be reunited with my loved ones in death. The only thing in this world beyond my treasure that brings me joy anymore is Bianca. I won't risk losing her in a war, or losing any more of my family. I think it would be the end of me if Bianca would die, and I would bear the guilt for every cousin who lost their life avenging Guido's death. No. We will let this go. So far the Sommarivas have not threatened Bianca or Ilaria when they have gone to the villa. My hope is that they will let them enjoy their treasure in peace. If I sense any danger, I will forbid Bianca from going. But until then, I will not act in retaliation for Guido's death."

I heard the man make a hissing noise. "You have grown weak in your Melancholy, Catarina. Be careful lest these

Sommariva scum try to steal your treasure from you—or take Bianca from you."

She snarled, a low rumbling sound. "Have you heard anything to support that accusation? Do they plan to move against us? Because if that is so, Marcus, then we *will* prepare for war."

"No, I have not heard that," the man replied. "But I fear for Bianca's safety, given Guido's murder. Is Ilaria enough to protect her? Should we send some of our cousins with her when she wishes to go to her villa?"

There was a moment of silence before Catarina responded. "Yes. I'll tell her that she is to travel only with extra guards until we know the Sommarivas' intentions. It's been over a century since they made any move to attack us here, but the villa is technically over the edge of what they consider their territory. I agree, we would be wise to take precautions."

"I will put together a list of available escorts for Bianca," the man said, his voice smug.

I heard a rustling of fabric, the shuffling of footsteps. "What would I do without you, Marcus?" Catarina said, her voice somewhat muffled as if she were pressed against his shirt in an embrace. "I was always the stronger one of the two of us, but in my Melancholy, you have grown powerful while I've faltered and weakened."

"I'm here for you sister," he replied. "You rest and mourn, and enjoy the sunset of your life, and know that I'm here for you."

Why did that statement send a chill down my spine?

CHAPTER 15

"Someone had a good day," Irix teased, repeating the words I'd told him yesterday.

"I did. And I'm not as tired as I was last night, so get ready to go out and get our freak on."

He grinned. "So, was this a competitor? Were you wrecking his concentration to give yourself an advantage?"

My thoughts immediately went to Celio. Ugh. I wouldn't fuck that guy if he was the last human left on Earth and I was starving to death.

"It was one of the presenters. I thought I was safe because he was leaving today and not presenting again. I'd have sex with him and never see him again, so there wouldn't be any awkwardness, or him trying to follow me around or anything."

"But?" Irix raised his eyebrows.

"We got caught."

"In the act?" Irix smothered a laugh.

"No, but people clearly knew. I don't know if they saw us head out together, or noticed him making eyes at me during his presentation, or what." I felt embarrassed all over again.

"The sex was great. He wanted to do it in the dungeon, so it was super kinky and I loved it. I got this blast of energy from him, but then everyone was staring at me when I came back. These guys are my competitors who now think I'm trying to screw people to win. They probably all hate me. One hated me before, but now I think they all do." It was hard enough that I kept getting partnered with Celio. Now that everyone knew, it had turned a fun event into something horrible. I grimaced, dreading tomorrow's session. If I walked in and everyone shunned me, it was going to be hard to continue attending.

"We'll get you two or three tonight. Then you won't need to worry about hunting tomorrow. If they see this was just a one-time thing, they'll think you were just attracted to the guy, and not that you were trying to game the system with your, quite impressive, sexual skills."

Maybe. "Well, there's no sense in my worrying about this right now. I've got tonight for partying and sex, and figuring out what the hell I'm going to do about a recipe with these Muscat grapes I brought home, so let's get going and have some fun." I eyed him. "And speaking of good days…did you screw half the town this afternoon or something? Sheesh, Irix. You're looking exceptionally well-fed right now."

"Ilaria."

Oh, that's right. Today was his day to wine-dine-and-screw the lady. Hopefully there would be no awkward explanations regarding Irix's and my "open relationship'" if we ended up running into her or Bianca in the next week.

"So you were right. She hadn't had sex in a long time and was raring to go?"

"Yep. And more than that, she's not human. At least not fully human."

What the what? "Not human? Then what is she?" My mind ran through all the likely scenarios. Part demon was the most likely. Demons sometimes liked to impregnate humans, and their offspring had some demonic traits and the occasional one had minor powers. How weird that the family I assumed was into organized crime had a family member who'd been sired by a demon.

"I'm not really sure, to be honest. I'm thinking she might be half or three-quarters demon. I'm getting reptile from her, and lots of demons use reptile mixes as their first forms."

"So what, she turned into a lizard with a lion head or something when you were doing it? How do you 'get reptile' from a sixty-year-old woman while having sex with her?"

I suddenly envisioned a long tongue. Kinky.

"No. It was more of just a feeling I got when taking her energy. I've had sex with thousands of demons in my life, and I can tell the differences in energy between them as well as between theirs and human energy. Hers didn't seem exactly like demon energy, but similar, so I'm thinking she's half, or maybe three-quarters."

Cool. Or maybe not cool. "Will that be a problem?"

"No. Sex with demons, as you've just recently learned, can come with all sorts of strings attached, so there needs to be a carefully worded discussion sometime before about what sex means and if there are any lasting connections implied in the contact. If she's not a full demon, then that's not an issue." He spread his fingers and electricity arced between them. "She had a great time. I had a great time. I've got more energy than I know what to do with right now, and although I got the idea she'd be open to a repeat occurrence, she hardly seemed like the stalker type."

I was fascinated. "Are half-demons usually the stalker type? And are *you* open for a repeat occurrence?"

Irix usually wasn't. He was a one-and-done kind of incubus unless his partner was a demon and they'd agreed to a more substantial relationship. I fell into the "demon" category, thankfully, even though I was technically only a half-breed.

"Yes, half-demons tend to be the type that boil your pet rabbit and try to chain you in their basement. That's why you need to be careful. And that's why I usually don't even consider a repeat occurrence." He narrowed his eyes in thought. "I might with her, though. She seemed unusually stable for a half-breed. And she was a heck of a lot of fun to have sex with."

Good. I liked Ilaria. But what was that comment about half-breeds?

"So Ilaria is unusually stable for a half-demon?" I wrapped my arms around Irix and looked up at him, one eyebrow raised. "Am I unusually stable for a half-demon?"

He chuckled. "No. I don't think you're the type to boil pet rabbits, but if I tried to leave you, I can completely imagine you knocking me over the head with a rock and dragging me down into your basement."

I smirked. "Damned straight I would. Now come talk to me while I'm getting a shower. I've got a whole lot I need to fill you in on."

His eyebrows shot up. "Go get started. I bought some more wines for you to try to identify. I'll bring them up and you can get some studying in while you're soaping up."

I didn't have the heart to tell him I was bombing out on this whole seminar, and that the steam and smell of body wash wasn't going to help me in identifying wines. He was doing everything he could to help and support me in this, and I totally appreciated it. Besides, I wasn't going to turn down a few glasses of wine while showering.

I was just lathering up my hair when Irix's arm snuck through the curtain, a glass of wine in his hand.

"I really wanted to join you, but I don't think I can manage to pour this stuff while in the shower."

I laughed, rinsing off one hand and taking the wine. "Well, it's white. Actually the fluorescent lighting is giving it a lime-green glow, but I don't think that has anything to do with the wine itself. And I doubt I'm going to get any indication on aroma right now."

I stuck my nose in the glass, confirming that the shower smells were overpowering whatever was in the glass. Then I took a sip.

"Moscato?" I asked.

"One point for the elf-girl. I thought since you're supposed to come up with a Moscato recipe in the next thirty-six hours, a flight of them might inspire you."

I loved this guy.

Setting the glass of wine carefully on the shower ledge, I rinsed my hair, then took another sip. "Napa Valley. 2012? It doesn't taste super young, but Moscato wines don't hold up all that well after five years."

"2014, but other than that, you're right!" Irix reached a hand in for the glass and I drained the contents before handing it to him. "So what do you like about that wine? Is it something you can do with the grapes from the Montenegro vineyard?"

I thought about it a moment while I shaved my pits and nether regions.

"Well, I like the hints of peach and nectarine, but that's more a factor of the grape than the process. Although I guess I'd want to create a wine recipe that preserved those flavors as well as enhanced them."

Irix's arm came into the shower with another glass. This wine was slightly fizzy.

"Another Moscato, this one from Italy. It's not carbonated enough to be an Asti." I sipped it again. "Did you know that the floral aromas come from a chemical called linalool which is also found in mints and citrus flowers?"

"No, I did not." Irix's voice held a hint of laughter. I knew he couldn't care less about these things, but he loved my nerd-girl botanist side.

"You know, I'm thinking those grapes might make a nice Moscato d'Asti. Maybe I'll do that, but do something to make sure the orange blossom aroma is primary."

"How will you do that?" Irix poked his head in the shower. "And you still haven't identified that wine."

I wrinkled my nose. "Italian Moscato. I'm going to call it sparkling and assume it's either light by choice or that you opened it earlier today. And…2016?"

"Nice job!"

I drank down the rest of the wine, and finished my shower, thinking about my recipe. A Moscato d'Asti, highly aromatic, with an alcohol content on the low side.

Irix took my glass and set it aside as I stepped out of the shower, wrapping me in a huge soft towel.

"So what happened today at the seminar? Did that Spanish guy give you any more grief?" He rained a line of kisses across the nape of my neck and rubbed me with the towel, sliding some of that glorious sparkling energy into me as he dried me off.

"No. I mean, yes. He called me a slut in Spanish, and he also call me a bimbo, and insinuated that I was an idiot. I think he even told me I was a moron at least once."

"He's jealous." Irix gently dried my hair.

I snorted. "Hardly. The guy's family owns a vineyard. He was learning the finer points of wines while I was sucking on a pacifier and playing with teddy bears. He's been a somme-lier in Paris, for fuck's sake."

"Sounds like *you're* jealous," he teased.

"I am." I thought about that for a second. "You know, Marta is just as knowledgeable, and she doesn't make me want to grab a knife and start stabbing. I don't think it's jealousy. I think it's because he's such an ass to me. He doesn't talk to Marta that way. Or Eva. She's American and he's always very nice to her. It's me he hates, and I can't figure out why. What did I do to him?"

Irix knelt down to rub the towel up along my legs and my thoughts took a naughty detour. His obviously did as well from the way his hands were lingering.

"Was it when he caught you sneaking off with that presenter? Maybe *that's* what he's jealous of—he wanted to be the one having sex with you, not that other guy."

"Hardly. He's been that way toward me since day one. I've got no idea why the guy hates me. Maybe I remind him of an ex-girlfriend, or he hates blondes or something."

"Maybe he's been attracted to you since day one, and it pisses him off because you're the pretty blonde American girl that he feels he *shouldn't* be attracted to, or that he could never get." Irix stood up and tossed the towel on the sink, leaning over to plant a kiss on my shoulder. "Have you read his fantasies?"

No, I hadn't. I'd been so busy that first day worrying about getting lost on the drive, getting situated, jumping into the deep end of a topic I was discovering I knew very little about, that I hadn't read the fantasies of *anyone* there. Normally it was an unconscious thing, like a sort of radar that allowed me to hone in on potential sexual partners. I thought back to that day, and realized that the moment Celio had sneered at me and mocked me, I'd shut him out. I'd relaxed and picked up on Leo's interest, as well as the fantasies of a few other attendees, but I got nothing from Celio—and I was thinking that was because of *me*, not him.

"Do you really think so? Maybe he just hates me." It would suck to open myself up to his fantasies, and find out that the sexual ones were about Marta, or one of the guys, where all his thoughts concerning me were of me falling off a cliff or getting run over by a bus.

Irix shrugged. "Give it a try. At least then you'll know."

He was right. I'd open up to Celio tomorrow and see what I could discover. But there was more on my mind than an irritating seminar attendee and what I should do about my Moscato recipe.

"I overheard Catarina and Marcus talking right as I was getting ready to leave today," I told Irix. "Toward the end of their conversation they switched to English. They were discussing Guido's murder and whether to retaliate against the Sommarivas or not."

Irix frowned. "So they really do think he was murdered? It's not just Bianca coming up with wild conspiracy theories in her grief over her uncle's death?"

"They do. Catarina wants to just let it go. She doesn't want to risk any of her family in an out-and-out war between the two families, but Marcus wants to retaliate."

Irix watched me as I pulled a mini dress and some underwear from the dresser drawer. "Daniela doesn't strike me as the sort of woman who would murder a guy just for moving into her 'territory', even if they are rival families, and her father can barely walk around the house without needing to rest afterward. Why do they think the Sommarivas killed Guido?"

I slipped the dress over my head. "Because they're in the middle of a nine-hundred-year-old feud, so they blame everything on each other? It doesn't seem like the sort of thing Daniela would do, but we don't really know her."

Irix sat on the bed. "I can't imagine waiting a few years after the guy moved in to kill him, but maybe she sent him a bunch of warnings first, or maybe Guido did something that was the final straw."

"Or maybe he pissed off a human who stabbed him. Or

maybe he accidentally fell on his steak knife." I shimmied the dress into place and smoothed it down. "It's going to make things worse for Bianca and Sergio though. They're not going to let her go to the villa without a bunch of guards. No more sneaking away to see each other."

Irix laughed. "Oh you underestimate the resourcefulness of young people in love. I'm sure Bianca will be able to sneak away on a regular basis. I'm more worried about the thought that there could be an actual war between these two families. Drive by shootings, assassination attempts, conveniently set fires or car accidents? There are going to be human casualties, especially if it escalates."

I dug the mascara out of my make-up bag and thought. Would the government get involved? I remembered how difficult it was back in the States for law enforcement to police these organized crime groups. Gangs routinely killed each other, and although there might be the occasional arrest, bringing down the leaders, or the heads of the families, took decades of work and often yielded few results. It would be a shame if that sort of thing cast a shadow over such beautiful tourist areas here, or if those who were just trying to go about their normal lives got killed or had their businesses destroyed as well.

"Well, Catarina made it clear she doesn't want to retaliate, so unless the Sommarivas do something stupid like attack the Montenegros or try to kill Bianca, this should all blow over."

"What if Bianca and Sergio get caught together?" Irix asked.

"I can't imagine that would start a war if Guido's murder didn't," I replied. "There might be some yelling and threats if someone caught the two of them in bed. Depending on who catches them, Sergio might find himself with some bruises and a broken bone or two, but that's it. The worst thing I could see happening if they got caught is that the Sommarivas put down their foot on any Montenegro in their territory—which included the villa—and the Montenegros lock Bianca in her room. And take away her cell phone and internet privileges."

Irix chuckled. "Oh my. For a teenage girl, that would probably be a fate worse than death."

CHAPTER 16

The restaurant in Bellagio had café seating with little romantic lights strung across the edge of the roof and along the banister that separated it from the lake. There was someone in the plaza singing, and the sound filtered its way through the hum of conversation. I sipped my wine, picking at the last bit of veal that I was too full to eat.

Full. With delicious food, wine, and sexual energy from the jewelry store shopkeeper that had shown me the special stock he had in back, then shown me a whole lot of other things. Of course, that was nothing compared to what I'd shown him.

"You look very content." Irix's smile was warm, his eyes glinting with lighter shades of gold in the reflected light.

"I am. I'm feeling better about the tests and tastings," I told him. "Thank you for helping me with the wine samples and quizzing me with the notecards. This can't have been what you were thinking of when I asked you to come with me to Italy."

"I'll admit it wasn't, but I get a kick out of seeing you study and work so hard for something. Besides, when it's all over I've got a surprise planned for us. So Friday, when you get back from Bergamo, be ready to celebrate your winning the apprenticeship in a big way."

There was no way I was going to win this apprenticeship, but the idea of a surprise got my blood racing—especially one of Irix's surprises.

"What is it? You have to tell me. Please? Please?" I begged.

"It's a surprise," he repeated. "And no promises of blow jobs or anal sex are going to get me to reveal where we're going or what we're doing Friday afternoon and evening."

"Okay." I liked surprises. I'd also spied our waiter, who had been flirting mercilessly with me all evening, head out front supposedly for a smoke. That look he'd sent my way was just begging me to come after him and I intended to oblige.

"You'll excuse me a minute?" I scooted back my chair and inclined my head toward where my prey had headed.

"Of course. Take your time. I'll order another bottle of wine for when you return."

The waiter's attentions hadn't escaped Irix's notice and he knew exactly where I was headed.

"I won't be long. He'll want me to come back later, once he's off work so we can take it slow." I was quickly learning that most Italian men preferred romance at a leisurely pace, even when having a one-night stand. It took some adjustment from the American style of fast-hard-and-out-the-door, but I was enjoying it. It meant that I couldn't fit in quite as many sexual partners as I normally could in a day, but the quality of the energy was richer and stronger—which made up for the lack in quantity.

"Flirt a bit," Irix instructed. "And make me out to be the jealous sort. He wants to feel like he's stealing you away right under my nose."

I'd gotten that impression as well, but it was good to have confirmation from the more experienced Irix. "Will do."

I made my way through the diners, to where the man was smoking, leaning against the wall of the restaurant. He gave me a lazy smile and stubbed out the cigarette. "Are you lost, beautiful?"

I walked up. He stilled, watching me as I maneuvered myself so close I could feel the heat from his body.

"Yes. I fear I am very, very lost." Then I gripped his shirt tight in my fist and pulled him to me, kissing him with everything I had. The energy, the attraction had been significant all through dinner, but now it roared to life, intoxicating in its sweetness. I moaned into his mouth and he sprang into action, gripping my ass with both hands and pressing me against him as he dove his tongue into my mouth.

Ugh. Cigarettes. But any minor irritation at the tobacco taste was quickly overcome by his lust that was like a fire raging through me.

I pulled away, breathing heavy. "I can't. He's waiting and he'll notice I've been gone too long. I shouldn't even be here, but I just couldn't help myself."

"Amber?"

I turned around at the outraged female voice and saw Bianca. Shit. Why was it always me that got caught? Irix screws her cousin, and no one knows, but I'm the one that gets caught sneaking out with the seminar presenter and shoving my tongue down the throat of a waiter.

"Bianca! This isn't…it's not what you think." Crap. I could hardly go into a long explanation of how Irix was totally on board with this sort of thing. For one, she'd never believe me. And two, my lovely waiter friend would be a whole lot less interested if he thought I was some sort of swinger who did it with just about every guy she met.

"Bianca? What are you…oh, hi. Oh."

Sergio. Who was eyeing me and the waiter with an expression that said he just wanted to slink away and pretend he'd not seen anything.

"How could you?" Bianca snapped at me. "Engaged to such a gorgeous man who clearly adores you, who proposed to you with so much romance at the villa. How could you betray him like this just days after he pledged to love you, and only you, always. You…you…*zoccola*."

I had a pretty good idea what that might mean. There was no way out of this, so I just hung my head in supposed shame. I hated that Bianca thought so badly of me, that she and Sergio would both probably tell friends and relatives about what a *zoccola* I was. And worse, I wasn't sure my waiter friend would now be willing to have a late-night rendezvous.

Actually, yes he would, if that hard-on poking me in the ass was any indication. Crazy guy. Not only did Irix's fake jealousy turn him on, but having my indiscretions outed turned him on as well.

"Come on, Bianca." Sergio wrapped his arm around the girl's shoulder and tried to urge her on down the street. "This isn't our business."

"She is betraying her fiancé," Bianca stated, still clearly outraged. "I would never do that to you, darling. I will always be true to you."

She turned in the boy's arms to face him.

"I know." He kissed her, gentle at first, then with more passion.

Guess I wasn't the only one into public displays of affection. And this was making waiter-guy's erection even harder. A few more seconds and he'd have to go around back and beat off.

"Sergio." The word was a hiss, but it vibrated across the block. The waiter behind me caught his breath, and locals scattered, leaving tourists to stare in surprise as a curvy dark-haired woman stomped across the cobblestone street, her eyes glowing with an unnatural shade of green. As she drew near, I noticed it wasn't just the color of her eyes that was unnatural, but her pupils had elongated into a slit of black in the bright green iris.

"Mother." Sergio grabbed Bianca and pushed her behind him as he turned to face Daniela.

Shit. The scrutiny was off me and my *zoccola* ways, but I wasn't sure this was going to be any better. I doubted Daniela was going to pull out a pistol and start shooting, American gangster style, but there would clearly be a lot of yelling, and possibly some slapping going on. And this would be the end of Sergio and Bianca's young romance. She'd be banned from the area, and banned from a lot of other things once her family found out. And I had no clue what Sergio's punishment would be, but I got the idea there would be no more freedom to go hang out with friends or take the boat out and cruise for parties along the lake.

Sure enough, both Daniela and Sergio erupted in a stream of shouted Italian that I was pretty sure included a lot of very vulgar descriptions of Bianca from the red fury of her face and the outrage in Sergio's.

"Dragonessa," the waiter whispered in my ear. I got the feeling he was saying it more to himself than to me. I agreed with him though. Daniela was most definitely being a dragon of a mother right now.

She went to grab her son's arm. Sergio swung around to pull away from her grip and knocked Bianca backward. The spike of the girl's heel caught on the edge of a cobblestone and she went down, her head making an ominous crack noise as she hit the ground.

Bianca cried out. I cried out. Sergio cried out. Before I could take a step to go to the girl, her body morphed, splitting and tearing her clothes until a six-foot-long black dragon stood in the plaza.

My waiter now cried out, pushing me aside and high-tailing it down the street. The tourists did the same. Bianca-the-dragon shook her head, droplets of blood flying. She staggered a little getting her balance, then she lifted her head to the sky and roared.

Daniela shouted something and stood back, also ripping her clothing to shreds as she too morphed into a black dragon—this one twelve feet in length. Her tail swung, knocking one of the small cars on its side. Not to be undone, Sergio did the same, his black dragon form slightly larger than Bianca's and just a hair smaller than his mother's.

Was it weird that the only thing I could think of when confronted by three dragons about to fight and destroy this town, was that they'd just ripped up a whole lot of expensive designer clothing shifting form, and that they should have taken the time to strip down first?

Daniela dove forward, pushing Sergio aside with a wing while Bianca scrambled backward, still disoriented from her head blow. The larger dragon inhaled and I knew what was coming. I remembered the scars on Mr. Sommariva's face and hand and suddenly envisioned the same on Bianca's—if she survived.

"No!" I shouted. Then I did the only thing I knew how to do. Flowers shattered pots as they instantly grew to hundreds of times their normal size. Seeds slammed roots through the pavement, sprouting a veritable forest in the middle of the street. Ivy shot tendrils from the sides of buildings to wrap around Daniela, choking her and tangling her limbs and wings.

The dragon coughed back whatever she'd intended to blast out at Bianca and struggled to break free of the vines. Then taking a deep inhalation, she shot out a stream of fire so hot it crumbled all my trees and plants to ash. Bianca had made a squeaking noise, ducking low. Her quick movement, plus the fact that Daniela was hampered by thick ivy around her neck meant the blast of fire scorched the building, melting stone where it hit instead of hitting the girl.

Had Daniela meant to hit her or had she just been trying to burn the vines and instead almost incinerated Bianca? The woman had clearly been preparing for some sort of attack earlier, so I wasn't taking any chances. I summoned more energy, grabbing hold of what remained alive of my vines and trees, jolting them into renewed growth.

Before I could do more than create a few saplings, Bianca had shot back an attack of her own, a small mini fireball that missed Daniela and narrowly missed Sergio to melt a hole in the pavement. I ran forward, tightening the newly formed ivy noose around Daniela's neck and growing additional vines to help hold her in place. "Run," I shouted to Bianca.

Sergio tried to get around his mother, but she pushed him back again with her tail, which he bit. The larger dragon roared again, and I heard a click noise, as if she were about to ignite another blast of fire.

There was a screech that nearly made my ears bleed and a rush of wind that knocked me to my ass. Suddenly a huge reptilian bird appeared between the two female dragons. He was brownish-red and gold with a long, sharp, curved beak that snapped at Daniela. His leathery wings bore foot-long talons along their edges and at the ends.

Irix.

Daniela choked back the fire she'd been about launch and reared back, tearing the vines from her body. Irix advanced on her, screeching and snapping, his broad wings blocking Bianca from the larger dragon.

I heard a sob and looked to see the girl on the ground, transformed back into her human shape. She was naked and clutching her still bleeding head. On her shoulder and down one arm was a blistered burn. I ran to her, guessing that Daniela's shot hadn't entirely missed her after all.

Pulling her to her feet, I wrapped my arms around her and got her into the outdoor area of the restaurant, where I could grab a napkin and try to staunch the bleeding in her head. She held the napkin to her scalp, and I poured water over her arm, looking at the red, angry skin. It didn't look much worse than a regular burn. She'd been lucky. Dragon or not, I'd seen what that fire had done to stone and trees, and I was pretty sure a direct hit would have turned her arm to ash.

"Here." I wrapped a tablecloth around her, noticing that the staff was huddled in the kitchen, staring at her through the door.

"What is that? What is that?" She babbled, looking at the demon who was still forcing Daniela backward one step at a time.

"That's Irix. He's a demon. That's what he looks like when he's in Hel." I glanced over at the incubus, thinking he was just as sexy as a giant prehistoric bird-thing as he was in his human form.

Bianca caught her breath. "Will he kill her? Will he hurt Sergio?"

I got the idea that the last question was the most important one. "No, he won't hurt Sergio. He won't kill Daniela either. Although if she had injured me, that might have been a different story."

But I wasn't sure Irix could have killed a dragon. Daniela was big, and that fire was a pretty impressive weapon. I got the impression she was holding back, that she was just as startled to have a demon in front of her as Bianca had been. Until she knew the extent of his powers, she wouldn't want to engage him.

It was one thing to attack a young dragon, or a member of a rival dragon clan, another entirely to jump into a fight with a demon of unknown strength and abilities.

"How are you?" I asked Bianca as the girl began to shiver. She looked up at me, her eyes big.

"This ruins everything. It's all my fault. I shouldn't have come to see Sergio. I shouldn't have snuck out, but Grandmother told me she didn't want me to come to the villa without guards from now on, and I knew I might not have the chance to see him again. But now that we've been discovered…"

"Bianca!"

I turned and saw a human, and naked, Sergio dart under his mother's wing and around Irix's talons to rush toward us.

He stopped at the curb, staring at the blood-soaked rag Bianca held against her head, then at the burn on her arm.

"Sergio! Get away from her." Daniela was now in her human form, trying to get around Irix's huge wings.

Sergio's eyes blazed, his mouth narrowing into a thin line. Then he spun around and took three steps toward his mother. "You hurt her. How could you? How could you do that to my mate, to my treasure?" He spat on the ground. "I hate you. I hate you and I never want to see you again."

With a snarl he morphed into his dragon form and took to the air. Daniela cried out, shifting into her dragon form as well. Irix held her back as best as he could, but the dragon managed to evade him and leap upward into the air to chase after her son.

Irix turned, making sure there was no other dragon waiting to attack, then with a flash of light he was back into his human form.

"Are you okay?" His eyes roamed over me as he approached.

I nodded, thinking there was a whole lot of public nudity

going on tonight. Maybe I should offer Irix a tablecloth as well.

"I need to go home," Bianca told me. "I'm in danger here. I'm trespassing on their territory, and now that they know I've been with Sergio, they won't spare me because of my age like they would if they'd just found me shopping or dining here. I need to go home."

"You need to rest, heal, clean up, and get some clothes," I told her. "You can't go home like this."

She couldn't. I imagined the brutal fighting that would occur if Bianca showed up at her grandmother's house bleeding from her head with burns on her arm.

"It will take me weeks to heal this burn. I can't be away that long." Bianca looked down at her arm. "Maybe if I wrap it and wear long sleeves, they won't notice."

I helped her up. "We'll take you to our house and you can get cleaned up. I'll bandage up your arm, put some burn cream on it. Then I'll loan you some clothes to wear." I pulled the napkin away from her head, happy to see it had clotted. She'd have a big scab there for a while, but if she parted her hair on the other side, it would cover the wound.

"And I'll drive you back home to Bergamo", Irix told her. "They won't attack you as long as you're with me."

She nodded, tears glistening in her eyes. "Thank you. I…I know this will get back to my family eventually, but if I can hide from them that I was hurt, then I can claim it was all my fault. I'll tell them I was trespassing, that I fell in love with Sergio and came to see him, and hopefully that will keep them from attacking the Sommarivas."

I exchanged a knowing glance with Irix. Daniela would, no doubt, let Bianca's family know that she was never to cross into Sommariva territory again, but teenagers were ruled by their hearts. The next time, Irix wouldn't be here to protect Bianca.

And I was pretty sure that her family was going to feel the same resentment toward Sergio. They'd be equally harsh if they ever found the boy in their territory. And when that happened, the families might not be so willing to overlook the continued trespasses or the forbidden romance.

Eventually there was going to be war between these two families. It was just a matter of when.

CHAPTER 17

*T*rix and I got Bianca back to our villa wrapped in the tablecloth. Then I took her upstairs, doctored up her arm, and plopped her in a steaming hot, lavender-scented tub while I looked for clothing she could borrow.

She cried the whole time—gut wrenching sobs that brought tears to my own eyes. I left her in peace, and when she finally came out to the bedroom, wrapped in a towel, she'd stopped crying.

I patted a spot beside me on the bed. "We'll figure this out. It's going to be okay."

She choked back another sob and shook her head. "It won't. Sergio's mother will kill me if she sees me again. And if she won't, her father will." Bianca shuddered. "He's a terrifying dragon. I don't think even my grandmother could best him in a fight."

Eduardo Sommariva could barely get out of bed, let alone hunt down and murder a young girl. I had no doubt that at one time he'd been a formidable fighter, but I was pretty sure those days were long behind him.

"I know how these things work," I told Bianca. "Once

everyone calms down and Sergio has a chance to talk with his mother, she'll come around. She may never approve, but I don't think she'll actively be trying to kill you once she comes to her senses." I hoped not anyway. With a quick glance outside, I wondered if I could apply human logic to these dragons. For all I knew, they *would* kill a young woman like this, just for falling in love.

"Sergio talks about elopement, but I doubt he would ever leave. He has already bonded with his grandfather's treasure. He's the heir and he can't leave, just as I can't leave that which will be mine. This love of ours will end tragically. We will never be together, and because we are mate-bonded to each other, we will never love another."

I suddenly wondered if that was what had happened to Guido Montenegro. Had he bonded with someone who didn't return his love, meaning he spent his life alone? I knew pretty much nothing about dragons beyond what Nyalla had told me. I'd seen that young red dragon who was living at Sam's house a few times, but kept my distance.

"Well, you're safe here." I patted her shoulder. "We'll tell your family that you're visiting friends for the night. And tomorrow, we'll think of something."

She looked up at me, eyes glistening with tears. "I'm endangering you both. I should leave."

I put out a hand to keep her where she was. "Did you *see* Irix? He's a demon. He might be an incubus, but he's perfectly capable of protecting you and us from a bunch of weak, pansy-ass dragons."

That got a brief, shaky smile out of her, even though I wasn't sure of the truth in my words. Irix had startled the crap out of everyone in Bellagio with his demon form. I was pretty sure now that they knew what he was, and we no longer had the element of surprise, the dragons would get the upper hand. I got the feeling that they were powerful, smart, and there were a whole lot more of them than there were of us. I really didn't want Irix to be in a position where he had to fight the entire Sommariva clan with only little ole me and a sixteen-year-old dragon-girl as backup.

"I'm sorry I called you that name earlier," she sniffed. "I mean, I still don't like that you were about to cheat on your fiancé, but you saved my life."

Time to explain this. When I thought she was human, I was sure she'd not believe me, but a dragon, who'd just witnessed my fiancé in his demon form, would.

"Irix is a demon, an incubus, and he needs to have sex with a variety of humans to siphon off their sexual energy and tie them to him. It's his way of 'feeding'. If he doesn't do that he dies. That means that although he loves me with all his heart, he needs to have sex with other people and I need to just deal with it, or eventually embrace it."

"Um, okay." She scowled. "I would have a difficult time with that. Is that why you were kissing that waiter? Revenge?"

"No! I'm not human either. That plant thing I did isn't because I'm a witch, it's because I'm a half-elf. But the other half of me isn't human either, it's demon. I'm a half-elf/half-succubus. Which means that I have a thing for plants and, like Irix, I need to have sex with other people and siphon their sexual energy for my own use. If I don't, I'll die."

Her eyebrows shot up. "You're serious? I think that would be very hard for me, but if that is something both you and Irix need to do... How do you not get jealous? How can you stand that he cheats on you, and that you cheat on him?"

"It's not cheating. We both encourage each other to do this. And it has nothing to do with the love we have for each other."

Bianca sighed. "I don't get it, but dragons are different. We're very jealous and possessive, and we mate only once in our lifetime. I'll never understand how you can do that, but I'm sure you will never understand our attachment to our treasure either."

She was so very right. I really didn't get the whole "treasure" thing.

"Do you have a giant dinosaur bird form as well?" she asked.

I laughed. "No. Just this one, although one time when I was in Hel I was able to alter my appearance a bit. I can, however, make a clematis turn into something from a horror movie. That's my big superpower."

She giggled. "Yes, I recall you doing that exact thing."

I placed the clothing in her lap. "Get dressed. Come down and we'll get you some food and a big glass of wine, and we'll talk about how to get you home."

Her face grew serious once more. "I'll have to tell my family. Uncle Marcus will be livid. And Grandmother…"

"We'll cross that bridge when we come to it." I patted her shoulder, then went downstairs to give her some privacy.

Irix was standing on the lawn, staring over the lake with his arms crossed in front of his chest, like he was single-handedly holding back the storm.

He was. I could feel them, watching, hovering, waiting. I might not be able to see the dragons, but I could distinctly feel their presence nearby. They weren't attacking us, probably because there was a golden-eyed demon staring them all down, making it quite clear that he was going to fuck them up if they tried anything.

He was only an incubus, but even an incubus had some powers. And Irix was good at bluffing. They didn't know what he could do, what his limitations were, and they didn't want to risk losing half their family members finding out.

"Someone from the town must have called Bianca's

family, because those aren't the Sommariva dragons over on the mountains there," he told me.

"Great. I'm surprised they're not on our doorstep already," I replied.

"They're not because the Sommariva dragons are on this side of the lake. There are two of them across the street, behind our villa right now."

I shivered. Dragons to the front. Dragons to the back. And us, smack dab in the middle.

"Should we call for backup?" I asked. "Harkel?"

"If we need to," Irix said. "I don't think it's come to that yet, and I don't want to disturb him. He's busy in Southeast Asia right now. Although I'm sure if told him there was a war between two dragon families brewing, he'd drop everything and run."

I grimaced. Harkel was a warmonger. Bringing him into this conflict might do more harm than good, and Irix knew that as well as I did.

"So what should we do?" I stared out at the mountains, seeing a dark shadow move across the moon. They were fast, stealthy. If I hadn't been staring at the sky hard enough to make my eyes water, I wouldn't have seen them.

"Protect her. Tomorrow we'll get her safely back to her family, but in the meantime I'm ensuring her safety even if that means I need to stand out here and look menacing all night long."

There was a throat clearing noise behind us. Both Irix and I spun around, and I felt the tingle of electricity from him.

Gianna's eyes grew huge and she threw her hands up defensively. "I'm the messenger. I have no intention in harming the girl, nor in fighting with you."

Irix powered down but we both watched her with wary eyes. She was a Sommariva, and I wasn't sure we could trust her. Crap, she'd rented us the villa. Would we be scrounging for a hotel tomorrow morning? Would we need to leave Lake Como?

Gianna took a big breath and let it out slowly, lowering her hands. "We have no fight with you. Daniela likes you both and realizes that the events in Bellagio, as well as the revelation of her true form, was a huge shock." She turned to Irix. "You're a demon, and she understands that you would immediately act to defend your mate, as well as what appeared to be a young, injured girl. She does not blame you for your actions in the marketplace."

Irix kept his expression emotionless and didn't reply. I followed his lead, wanting this messenger to lay it all out on the table before we said a word.

"You are both welcome to stay here in Lake Como with no repercussions. As I said, we have no fight with you."

Yep, they were very concerned about how powerful Irix might be. They didn't want to piss him off, but they had too much pride to grovel. This was their compromise, and even this must have been a bitter thing to swallow.

"The girl, however, must leave by midnight. She must be out of our territory."

Irix's eyes glowed golden, and I saw Gianna flinch.

"Or?" he drawled.

She swallowed. "Please understand, we do not want to battle with you. We are unfamiliar with demons, but surely you must see what a predicament we are in. An enemy of ours has come into our territory. She has wantonly seduced one of our own—"

I snorted. "Oh, innocent little Sergio. I'm sure he'd be very angry hearing himself described as a pawn who was duped and seduced by a Delilah of a girl. Some mighty powerful dragon to inherit your family fortunes when a young girl can 'wantonly seduce' him."

Her jaw clenched. "She needs to leave by midnight or we will kill her."

"An eighteen-year-old girl," I scoffed. "You bad-ass dragons are going to lower yourself to killing a child?"

"That's assuming you can even get to her," Irix added. "Because I won't allow it. You'll need to kill me first."

"You're one demon," she countered. "I don't want to fight you, but if the head of my family commands it, I will. As will all of my brethren. Are you able to kill sixteen dragons? Because you'll need to. We will fight to the death."

"So you kill Irix, which means you'd need to kill me, then you kill the girl," I said. "And that starts a cascading chain of events. You have your family, do you think Irix and I are without family of our own? That we're not connected to other powerful demons? You'll find that seventeen of you, or however many are left after we're finished, won't be able to stand against a hoarde of demons and angels. I'm sure the Montenegros will jump in to help us as well." I took a step toward her, and bluffed. "And other dragons as well. You're not the only ones here, you know. There's a red dragon who is a close friend of my sister's, then there is another family friend, a dragon who has taken up residence in the British Museum. He's big and old, and I'm pretty sure he could make quick work of your family."

The bluff worked. Gianna paled and stepped backward. I saw the fear in her eyes and wondered how many enemies their family had made. Clearly the Montenegros weren't the only dragons who hated them.

"Please. I have nothing against this girl. She just can't be here in our territory."

"But it's not your territory. It's *human* territory, and they've granted the public access to it. Trust me, you don't want to start limiting who can come onto human land, or doing anything like what happened tonight that threatens human lives, otherwise you're going to wind up with a bunch of archangels ramming swords down your throats."

She bit her lip, and I went for the kill shot.

"If you think Saint George was your nemesis, well you really don't want to face down the archangels. Or the Iblis for that matter."

She rubbed her hands over her face. "What am I supposed to do?" she wailed. "This isn't my fight. I really don't care if this girl lives in that villa across the lake. I don't care if she eats dinner or shops in Bellagio. None of this is my treasure. Honestly, nothing beyond their villa is Daniela or her father's treasure either. They've extended their reach too far, grown unbending in their grief over the loss of their mates. It's what happens when we are forced to bond with human lovers. We always outlive them, then find our heart slowly hardening until we are facing the Melancholy. But I have no choice but to help if my family goes to war. I have no choice."

We were at a stalemate. But as I exchanged a glance with Irix, I realized that there was a glimmer of hope somewhere in all this. Gianna was surely not the only member of her family who felt this way, and I was sure there were Montenegros that were the same. If we could just get the inflexible ones to see reason... And maybe the key to that lay with Bianca and Sergio. But in the meantime, deescalating tensions was the immediate task at hand.

"She will be gone by midnight," Irix said. "If I have to fly her out of here myself, she'll be gone. But her exit must be unhindered. There will be no threat to her when she leaves, or to a member of her family who might choose to come here to escort her home. And there will be no retaliation on her for what happened tonight—that includes her property on the lake. So help me, if you or your family plot against her, I will see every last one of you in your graves."

Gianna took another step backward. "Understood.

Although if her family moves to attack us, then we have every right to defend ourselves."

Irix nodded, then with a short bow, Gianna turned and left. I admired the woman's guts to turn her back on a demon and casually stroll away.

As soon as she was gone, I threw myself into Irix's arms in a display of affection that probably wasn't in keeping with his bad-ass persona right now.

"Thank you," I told him. "I know you probably don't care about Bianca, or any of these dragons, or humans, or whatever, but I appreciate you becoming the guardian angel here."

He laughed. "Oh how you insult me, calling me a guardian angel. You do know they're the weakest of all the angelic ranks?" He snuggled me close against him. "I had to do it. It wasn't just for you. She's a child, and I felt this odd, completely unfamiliar need to protect her. It was very undemonic of me. Please don't tell anyone about it."

I kissed him. "You'll make a wonderful father."

"No, I won't. The kid will electrocute his classmates and I'll end up killing an entire SWAT team to protect him. You'll rue the day you ever talked me into siring your child."

I kissed him again, this time with as much passion as I could. "Trust me, my soon-to-be-husband, I will *never* rue the day you father my child. Never."

CHAPTER 18

Bianca came downstairs, pale and subdued. We lit a fire in the study fireplace, ordered food from the café just before they closed for the night, then sat around and drank wine after our late-night snack was done. She confirmed that the mountains across the lake held several members of her family. Her cousins were there, as well as her Great Uncle, Marcus. News had spread fast of the incident in Bellagio, and they'd come swooping down to ensure her safety and enact their revenge for any injuries she may have suffered.

Her injuries were bandaged and hidden from view. And from the firm set of her jaw, she clearly wasn't going to be telling her family about them.

"Why didn't your grandmother come?" I ask, wondering why the absence of her heir hadn't brought the matriarch of the family here.

"It's difficult for her to leave her treasure. That's how we are as we get older and in our Melancholy. It's easier for me with Villa Montenegro because I'm young and I just acquired it. Grandmother is two hundred years old. She's not only going through the Melancholy, but she's so obsessed with her treasure that she's afraid to leave it." Bianca took a sip of wine and looked down into the glass. "I don't want to be like that. Sometimes I wish I was human. I wish I could run away with Sergio and just be happy. I don't want to feel the pull of my treasure. I don't want to eventually go insane, worried that every human, that maybe even members of my family are trying to steal it from me. Sometimes I hate being a dragon."

I immediately envisioned Eduardo Sommariva, who seemed to be going through the same problems, only at a more advanced stage. It was all so tragic.

"So what are you going to do?" I asked.

Her shoulders slumped. "Go back to Castle Abbondio with my family and hope things calm down enough that in a few years I can live at Villa Montenegro without the constant threat of attack. Or maybe by then I'll be strong enough that if I'm attacked, I can defend my treasure."

"Can't you sell it? I know you said you've bonded with it, and it's your treasure, but you'll inherit your grandmother's treasure. And you're young. Maybe you can pull away enough to sell it." I frowned. "If only your uncle hadn't willed it to you."

She shook her head. "It's not just that I inherited it. Even if Uncle Guido hadn't left the villa to me, I bonded with it. I would still long to be there. I'd still feel the pull of it."

"Is Ilaria bonded to the villa as well?" Irix asked, refilling both of our wine glasses and taking a seat.

"Yes. That's why she stays and why she'll help me with it. She's just as attached to it as I am. Treasure can't belong to two, but we manage the emotions of the bond through inheritance, or family ties. It's hard. It's worse with siblings. I'm okay with Grandmother's treasure, because I know I'll inherit it, and she tolerates my occasional possessiveness of it because I'm the heir. If I had a brother or sister, we'd struggle with the concept that only one of us would gain the treasure."

"What happens then? Do you split it?" Irix eyed her intently, making me wonder where he was going with this.

She gave him an odd look. "No. That would never happen. Either the non-inheriting sibling learns to deal with their hunger, tries to be satisfied with some small treasure of their own, or they fight for the right of inheritance, or ownership. If that happens, one dies and the other takes it all. My great-great-grandfather had a sibling that he fought for the treasure. He killed him. Ilaria is a descendant of the brother's side of the family, but she didn't seem to inherit the hunger to that degree. She's satisfied just being around the treasure she bonded with. She doesn't need to feel exclusive ownership of it. Some of us are so possessive that we can't even allow other family members around our treasure, or for humans to be around it. That's when a dragon retreats to their lair, and quickly declines, eventually dying. They can't leave to go get food, and they'll kill anyone who tries to bring them food. Eventually they starve to death. It's a terrible, extreme sort of insanity of which we all have a small part."

Yikes, what an awful end. I thought about Ilaria and her love for the villa, how she could somehow manage to find satisfaction just being near there, even though it wasn't technically hers. What if she'd been different? What if she'd felt that gnawing need to possess this treasure for her own? Would she have killed Guido to obtain it? Would she have even killed Bianca to obtain it? Of course, that wasn't the case here.

Or was it? Guido had been murdered, and I just couldn't see Daniela Sommariva as the killer. But Ilaria hadn't made any move toward Bianca, and given what I'd just seen of Daniela's temper and protective instinct toward Sergio, maybe I was wrong.

"But what about your great-uncle? Marcus?" Irix asked. "He can't be very possessive about the family treasure given that his sister inherited instead of him, and it will go to you upon her death."

Irix's words suddenly reminded me of the conversation I'd overheard in the tower. Catarina had said she'd been the strong one. Maybe it wasn't that Marcus was light when it came to possessiveness of treasure, but that he had a stronger survival instinct. Why lose your life fighting your powerful sister for control of the family fortune, when you could just wait for her to decline and die, then snatch it from a young girl?

But I was probably wrong about that, too. The picture of Guido Montenegro had given me the chills. He'd seemed sinister, powerful, menacing, yet according to Bianca and Ilaria, he'd been a wonderful guy. Maybe I was misjudging Marcus as well. Yes, he'd wanted to attack the Sommarivas for Guido's murder, but it was perfectly normal to want to avenge a cousin.

"Yes, Grandmother was the eldest, so she inherited the treasure. Uncle Marcus has his own treasure, but he's also bonded to Grandmother's. As she gets further into her Melancholy, she'll refuse to allow him near her home or her lands. The same with me. It will be hard for us, not only because we'll long to be near the treasure we've bonded with, but because we'll know she's near the end of her life." Bianca looked out across the lake. "I love her. And I know Uncle Marcus loves her as well. I don't want to see her die, but we both know it's just a matter of time. A few years at most."

"I'm so sorry," I told her.

She nodded. "Grandmother sometimes says that Uncle Marcus or I are trying to steal her treasure. I'm sure she's starting to go mad. Both of us love the castle, but we love her as well. I'd never steal from her, no matter how much the vineyard or the properties call to me, and I know Uncle Marcus feels the same. Their entire life he's never made a move against her. And I know he wouldn't now."

"But you?" I asked. "In a few years his beloved sister will pass away, and a very young grand-niece will inherit. What if his need to own the family treasure grows stronger without his sister? What if he attacks you? What would happen then?"

She laughed. "I've known Uncle Marcus since I was a baby. He's our protector, our defender. He'd never hurt me."

"What if he did?" I insisted.

She smiled, clearly indulging a silly American woman who didn't understand her family and their ways. "Then I would fight him. If Uncle Marcus attacked Grandmother and won, his line would inherit, not me. I have bonded with the treasure, and I wouldn't be willing to let go of my claim on it. He'd need to kill me as well as Grandmother." She shot me an ironic smile. "And if she dies and he attacks me, I'll do my best to fight him off. I'll probably fail because he is so much older and more powerful than me, but I'll do my best."

"I hope that doesn't happen," I told her.

"It won't." Her chin lifted in defiance. "But the weird thing is that none of us knows the exact extent of Grandmother's treasure. In her Melancholy, she's acquired things and hidden them away, paranoid that someone might take them. If she died and one of my cousins were to steal those things, I wouldn't know. I'd feel their loss, knowing something was missing, but I wouldn't be positive what was gone or who took it. It could be one of my cousins. It could be some human. It could be that Grandmother hid it in Moscow and we have no idea where or how to find it."

"If your grandmother dies in the next year or two…" I thought of how I could say this. "I think you'll need allies. Whether the Sommarivas killed your uncle or not, I'm worried about you inheriting the entirety of your family's treasure without allies."

Bianca wrinkled her nose. "It would be easier for me to inherit it if Grandmother could hold off on the Melancholy and stay alive until I'm older and stronger. But if not...well, I'll need to gain allies among my cousins. It's unfortunate that I was Father's only child, and that Uncle Guido died childless, or I'd have those cousins on my side. As it is, all of my cousins are far enough removed that they are either in Uncle Marcus's line, or from farther back in our family line."

This treasure thing was a nightmare. I was beginning to be very glad I wasn't a dragon. And I was thinking of what I could do to help support her if she inherited young. Maybe I could hire some demons to protect her? Or a sorcerer? But Villa Montenegro and her grandmother's decline weren't the only issues Bianca was facing.

"What about you and Sergio?" Irix asked the question I'd been thinking.

Her mouth set in a stubborn line. "I'll keep in contact with him. We'll try to meet in neutral territories. It will be hard, because both of our families are going to be very controlling about where we go for the next few years, but we'll manage to occasionally see each other. We're bonded, and as strong as our bonds are to our treasures, what we have between us is of equal, or greater, strength. Neither of us will fall in love again. Neither of us will marry another. Neither of us will have offspring with another. Our families have managed to bond with human mates throughout the centuries, but the bond between two mated dragons is even more powerful. We will either find a way to be together, or we will forever be alone."

Or one or both of them will end up dead. Irix looked over at me and I could tell that he felt for these two young lovers. Demons tended to have very little empathy, but lately Irix had shown me he had a soft spot when it came to humans and their emotions.

"Will you help us?" She turned her big, dark eyes up to look earnestly into my own. "Will you help Sergio and me? Neither of us wants to fight any members of each other's family. We just want to be together, to share our treasures. We don't want a war. We just want to be together."

I remembered Gianna's words, and thought there were many in each of these families that wanted peace. The trouble would be convincing those who wanted otherwise to hold back and let all of this go. In Bianca's family, the instigator for war would probably be Marcus and those in his line. In Sergio's family the issue would be Daniela and her father. Maybe. I wasn't sure Mr. Sommariva would be any more of a problem than Bianca's grandmother.

"I'll do my best," I told her. Then I looked down at my cell phone. "It's getting close to your deadline. Do any of those dragons on the mountain have a pouch with a cell phone handy? Irix offered to fly you out, but personal experience tells me you'd be better off shifting into your dragon form and flying on your own with him as a winged escort."

She nodded. "I'll call Ilaria. She's most likely still in her human form at Villa Montenegro, but she can shift and fly over here to escort me back. I'll fly, that way you can have your clothes. And my scales will hide my burn until I get home."

"I'll escort you both to the border of your territory," Irix told her.

I handed her my phone, and she made the call, rattling off an emotional plea in Italian. Hanging up, she handed the phone back with a sad smile. "Ilaria will be here shortly. I'll go out to the side yard to have some privacy while I shift into my dragon form, and I'll leave your clothing on the table back there. Thank you. Thank you for protecting me in Bellagio, and for sheltering me here."

"I'll do everything I can to help you," I told her, knowing that there was most likely nothing I could do.

She went outside around to the side yard while Irix and I once more stood looking out at the lake. A dark, winged form came across the water, so low that her feet nearly touched the surface. Tilting her angle and spreading her wings wide, Ilaria landed on the very edge of the stone barrier, balancing her eight-foot-long body gracefully as she stood.

She eyed Irix, and I saw the spark of attraction there. He nodded with a smile, then stepped back. With a flash of light, he assumed his demon form at the same time Bianca came from the side yard.

They were two black dragons, and one pterodactyl-looking demon. Ilaria took flight to lead, Bianca right behind her, and Irix guarding the rear. The three flew across the lake, making a steep ascent at the mountain range in the distance before vanishing from view. I waited a few moments, staring at the reflection of the moon and stars on the lake, feeling the presence of eyes on me, and knowing that I was very vulnerable here alone.

Irix had left me here alone. And that thrilled me. There had been a time when he'd been almost smothering in his need to protect me, but here he flew off to guard a young girl, leaving me in the presence of a bunch of dragons. He trusted me, knew that I could hold my own here at least until he got back to assist. And I think he trusted them to keep to their word.

That was another fact I squirreled away. These people kept their word. Gianna had promised Irix that he and Bianca and any of her family who came to get her would have safe passage out of their territory. She promised that

Irix and I could continue to stay here, unmolested and unthreatened by the Sommariva clan. And her entire family would honor that vow.

I needed to find a way to make that character trait work for me. These dragons—or whatever they were—were possessive, territorial, and bloodthirsty, and they held a grudge for generations. But they kept their promises, and it seemed some of them did want peace.

I only had to convince the others that peace was in their best interests as well, that it would help them keep their treasures safe, help them ensure their family was safe, and honor commitments that maybe they'd forgotten they'd made through their ancestors hundreds or thousands of years ago.

I somehow had to get these two families to sit down at the table together, to break bread and come to an understanding. Because I was sure that the key to bringing them together was through Sergio and Bianca. If only I could get them to see that.

CHAPTER 19

I'm not sure whether Bianca was unable to hide her injuries, or someone who'd witnessed the fight in Bellagio told, but no sooner had Irix gotten back to our villa than the night erupted into war. Flashes of fire steamed down from the sky. I could hear explosions, the roaring of monstrous beasts, the screams of humans and the squealing of tires as those who could get out of the blast area did so.

I felt sick, wondering how many people would return to destroyed homes, how many might be injured or killed in this spat between two powerful families. And it didn't escape my notice that none of the battling dragons came near our villa. It was as if we were encased in a protective bubble that repelled them all. Even so, Irix set up guard outside in his demon form, pacing across the lawn and occasionally flying up to perch on the roof. He wouldn't interfere, but he made it very clear that he would protect me with his life.

God, I loved him.

I'd promised Bianca I'd help, although with what was going on outside, I wasn't sure there was anything I could do to ease these tensions or establish a cease fire. I'd do what I could, but right now, all I could do was stay inside this villa and wait for daylight and hopefully a chance to talk some sense into these dragons.

But to do that, I needed to know as much as I could about these beings. So while Irix stood out back making sure we didn't get caught in any not-so-friendly fire, I made a phone call.

There were two dragons, that I knew of, that lived here among the humans. One was at the British Museum for six months of the year, and the other lived with my stepsister, Nyalla. I wasn't sure if the one in England had a cell phone, so I opted for the one who lived with Nyalla.

"I'm engaged," I told her when she picked up, because there were some things more important than others.

She screamed. I screamed. We both screamed.

"When?" Nyalla demanded. "You have to tell me all about it. I want to know all the details of this proposal. All. The. Details."

"I thought I was going to throw up. We were touring a villa, and I turned around and he was down on one knee with a box in his hand. I swear Nyalla, I almost puked on him."

She giggled. "I had a feeling he had something planned. He'd called and asked for Darci's number, then he was asking me all these questions about what kind of jewelry you liked."

"It's a ruby," I told her. "Huge fucking ruby. Emerald cut with little white diamonds around it and a platinum band. I *love* it. I absolutely love it."

"I told him to pick a ruby." Nyalla sounded smug. "And emerald cut makes them look more red. Those faceted cuts always seem more pink."

"Well, I want you to be one of my bridesmaids," I told her.

She screamed. I screamed.

"We are seriously going to start planning the moment I get home. Do you think Irix can go into a church without spontaneous combustion?"

"Sam goes into churches," she told me. "She said she feels kind of icky, like there's a bunch of spiders crawling on her, but she doesn't catch on fire or anything."

Ugh. As glad as I was that Irix wasn't likely to catch on fire, I didn't want him to feel like bugs were crawling on his skin during our wedding ceremony.

"But that's Sam," Nyalla continued. "Maybe Irix will be fine. There's a bunch of churches over there. Drag him into one and see how he feels. If he catches fire, then maybe you can have an outdoor wedding."

I adored how quirky and pragmatic my stepsister was. "I hope I get to be in your wedding someday," I told her.

There was an awkward silence followed by an even more awkward laugh. "Yeah. Someday."

"Nyalla, do you have a boyfriend?" I hated to ask her this. She'd been through so many guys, and none of them seemed to work out. My heart ached for her. Nyalla was the sweetest, most wonderful person I knew and there had to be a guy out there for her. I hoped this one lasted longer than her other boyfriends had.

"Yes, but…oh, I can't tell you. I love him so much, but there are some complications we have to deal with before we let anyone know."

"Nyalla, I would never tell your secrets. But even if you don't confide in me, I hope it works out. I hope he loves you —really loves you."

"He does." There was another long silence. "He's an angel."

I felt my heart sink. "Oh not Nils again. Nyalla, please tell me it's not Nils. He was such an ass to you. I don't care how hot he is, he's a jerk. You can do better than that."

"No, not Nils. I really can't tell you, Amber. When you get

back to the States, I will, just not over the phone."

"If he breaks your heart, then Irix and I are going to fuck him up. We've got your back, girl," I promised her.

She laughed. "Trust me, if he breaks my heart, then you and Irix are the very least of his worries. But he won't. He's….he's so sweet. He's honest and kind, and he adores me."

Well then, that was what mattered. I didn't like the idea of Nyalla falling for an angel, given what I'd seen of them and her past with Nils, but I was hardly one to judge, having fallen in love with an incubus.

"And now for the other reason I called you at what is probably super early in the morning there. I've got a weird question."

Nyalla laughed. "Oh, color me surprised. What's your weird question?"

"I need to know about shapeshifter dragons."

I could tell from the brief silence that was a question she hadn't ever expected.

"Shapeshifters? I don't think dragons do that. Are you sure it's a dragon and not a demon? Lots of them look like dragons when they're in their demon form."

Nyalla would know. She'd spent most of her life in Hel, and although she'd been a slave to the elves, she'd still spent a lot of time in the company of demons. I suddenly began to wonder if she was right and that instead of dragons, Bianca and Sergio and their families had been descended from demons.

"They *say* they're dragons. And they look like dragons, when they're not looking like humans. I get the feeling they've been here a long time, and they've interbred with humans, so maybe they just *think* they're dragons. Irix had sex with one of them and he said she felt like maybe she was a half-breed."

Nyalla made a hmm noise. "I haven't known a lot of demon/human offspring, but from what I've been told they can't shapeshift. I guess it's possible though. Nephilim can shapeshift, and *their* offspring are all werewolves. Or werebears. Or werecougars. Or were-other-things."

I hadn't thought about that. Maybe these were particularly skilled demon offspring, like werewolves, only instead of shifting into a wolf form, they shifted into a dragon one.

"I don't know. They say they're dragons, and I'm inclined to believe them, but I don't want to rule out that they might be some kind of shapeshifter."

I heard the click of the door and Nyalla's footsteps on the pavement. "Hang on. I'll go see what Little Red knows. He's over by the stables catching and eating mice. They're like snacks to dragons, he tells me. I eat potato chips, and he eats mice. Isn't that gross?"

It was.

I heard her talking, then heard the young red dragon's voice on the other end. Nyalla must be holding the phone up for him because he would have poked a talon through the thing trying to hold it.

"Amber? Hi! Are you in Italy? What's it like there? Send Nyalla a picture. I've always wanted to go to Italy, especially in the northern part near the Alps. From what I've seen on the internet, it looks a lot like the mountains back home. Send me a picture. Send me lots of pictures."

"I will. I promise." Darn, I wish I had a picture of the dragons in the street in Bellagio to send him so he could see what I was talking about. Unfortunately, I'd been a bit too preoccupied to snap a cell phone pic at the time.

"Hey Little Red, I've got two groups of dragon families here who are about to burn each other to a crisp. They shapeshift into humans, which seems to be how they spend most of their time, and they interbreed with humans."

"Are you sure they're not demons?" Little Red said, repeating Nyalla's theory.

"They might be, but they're clearly not full demons, but I've never known demon/human hybrids to shapeshift. And they claim to be dragons."

"We're always dragons," he told me. "Maybe there's some magic that could make us take another form, like something a sorcerer could do, but why would we want to do that? Why would a dragon ever want to lower themselves into taking on the form of a lesser being? Ouch, Nyalla, that hurt!"

I grinned, knowing that my sister had probably punched the dragon. Only Nyalla would have the balls to punch a dragon. Or spray one with a super-powered water hose.

Maybe these two families *were* some kind of demon offspring with extra powers. Or maybe a group of dragons with amulets that never needed recharging and who didn't mind stooping to becoming a human for a great deal of their lives. Neither of those sounded all that plausible.

"Are you sure? They like hanging out in rocky structures and grottos. They collect stuff like a reality show hoarder, call it their treasure, and threaten to kill and eat anyone who would steal so much as a paperclip. They're black with bright green eyes and those long pupils like you have. And they look just like dragons when they are in that form."

"Well, everything sounds like a dragon except that they're black. There aren't any black or gray dragons. They were all killed off a thousand years ago."

A thousand years ago. Both Bianca and Daniela had said their families had been here for over nine hundred years. It gave me an idea. "Little Red, what if during the war or plague or whatever killed the black dragons off, a few of them escaped and came through a wild gate here to live among the humans?"

I heard a rustle noise, then some crunching that made me wince.

"Mmm. Brsfraska mmmsfr."

"Don't talk with your mouth full," Nyalla told him.

"Okay, okay. Sorry. I guess a few might have slipped through, but I don't think they would have lived for long. The human world is kind of nice now. Humans have lots and lots of treasures and aren't so greedy about keeping them all to themselves. And even though they have weapons, they seem to like us now more than they did back then. Back then, if one of us came here, we'd be hunted mercilessly. We couldn't so much as eat a few sheep or take some gold without a bunch of humans showing up to throw rocks at us and stab us. Humans are pretty easy to kill, but there are so many of them, even back then. A dragon has to sleep, and eventually one of them would always kill us. It wasn't safe. Not like it is now."

Yes, definitely an idea.

"Let's say some black dragons knew they were going to die if they stayed in your homeland, so they came here. And when they realized they were going to get killed by the humans, they figured out the only way to survive would be to shapeshift into a human form and pretend to be human?"

"But I don't think they *can* shapeshift," Little Red mused. "I'll have to ask one of the dragons back home. I wasn't born when the fighting that killed off the black and gray dragons began or ended, so I don't really know. I've never met one of them."

"Would the dragon in the British Museum know? The big golden one there?"

"Oh yes! He's very old. But I'm not going to go ask him. He doesn't like me. I'm not a member of his family, so he thinks I'm there to steal his treasure. Of course, he has some very nice treasure," Little Red added wistfully.

Which was exactly the reason why I was sure these dragons here in Italy were actually dragons and not some kind of demon hybrid.

"No worries, Little Red. I'll have someone else ask him."

Someone who was fairly fire-proof, and who didn't mind visiting a grumpy, territorial dragon right in his own lair.

Sam.

"Thanks Nyalla," I said into the phone.

"Anytime. And Amber? Can the bridesmaid dresses be blue or green, or maybe blue-green? G—I mean, my boyfriend really likes sea colors and I want him to think I'm beautiful in the dress."

Tears stung my eyes. "Girl, you'd be beautiful in a dime-store dress. But I'll make sure whatever we pick out knocks that angel's socks off."

* * *

"You owe me big time," Sam announced the second I picked up the phone.

"What, more bean dip? Maybe I can bring you a designer purse or scarf? A Hermès?"

"What the fuck am I supposed to do with a scarf?" she retorted. "Oh wait, yeah, bring me a scarf. Or two. One for Candy and one for Michelle. That's two Christmas presents I don't need to worry about now. Crossing those suckers off my list."

It was a small price to pay to have Sam teleport to London and brave the lair of the dragon for me. Besides, Irix had stolen a dozen of those scarves while I was busy banging the shopkeeper in Bellagio. It wasn't like I was going to wear them all, and I only had so many of my friends to give them to.

"Okay, you're on speaker phone right now. Here's Sparky.

Sparky, this is Amber. She's a half-elf/half-succubus, and she thinks she's found some of your relatives down in Italy."

"Well, not relatives exactly," I chimed in hastily, worried that I might offend the ancient dragon and he'd either refuse to talk to me or try to eat Sam. "There are some dragons down here that shapeshift into human form."

"Maybe they're humans who shapeshift into dragon form," the voice rumbled. "I can imagine that humans might desperately employ any sort of magical means to attempt a copy of one of us. Anything to try to improve their puny, stupid bodies and lives."

I winced. "They act like dragons, though. They hold territory and have treasures, and eat any human who tries to take anything of theirs. When they turn into dragons, they shoot fire out of their mouths that melts stone. There are two families who are feuding down here, but from what I can see, they're all black dragons with green eyes."

"Black dragons? They were all killed a thousand years ago in a war. Nasty creatures. They don't really get along with anyone, even members of their immediate family."

Did any dragons get along with members of their family?

"I'm wondering if a few escaped here, assumed human form to blend in with the humans so they wouldn't get killed. And I think they're interbreeding with the humans, because there aren't very many of them in each family, they pretty much threaten to kill each other on sight, and I haven't seen any hint of incest."

"It's possible, but how humiliating for them. They should have just died fighting the humans, or died in our homeland. What a horrible, degrading existence."

I was pretty sure the original dragons had died, and that the descendants didn't find this existence so horrible, but I wasn't sure.

"Black, white, green, and gray dragons all have the ability

to change form, although I cannot recall them ever doing so. Why would they want to be anything but dragon?"

"Because when they came here, the humans would have killed them had they been in their dragon form. And now it's been so long, and they've interbred with humans that human has become their primary form."

Sparky made a noise that sounded an awful lot like "ick".

"So what do I do? These two families have a blood feud. One was murdered for encroaching on another's territory. Then a young dragon from their family was caught with a young male from the other in the male's territory, and now her family is here, burning everything down."

"Well, as for the first one, getting killed is always a risk when you cross borders into what someone calls their own. Did the other family declare war in retaliation?"

"No."

"Hmm, well there you go. The trespasser was in the wrong. His family knew it, and is refusing to avenge his murder."

I remembered the conversation I'd overheard between Marcus and Catarina. They hadn't moved to avenge Guido. But the odd thing was no one was insisting Bianca sell the villa and stay away. She was the heiress. Didn't her grandmother worry that she'd be killed as well?

"How about a child? A young dragon of eighteen years inherited the property of the murdered dragon by human law, but the other family still calls it their territory. Would they kill her?"

"Not until she reached adulthood, which for us is at the human equivalent of thirty years old. But the family will probably take drastic measures to drive her away. They won't easily tolerate her presence, although we don't kill young."

Here was the big question. "It seems this young dragon girl and a young dragon boy from the other family have fallen in love and were sneaking out to see each other. She was injured when they caught her here. And although she was trying to hide her wounds from her family, I think they may have found out."

The dragon sighed. "Stupid black dragons. Normally alliances such as these are what put an end to long-running feuds. We often mate our young to heal factions and to resolve disputes in regard to territory or treasure. The fact that these two young ones are in love would make it all the easier. But black dragons are stubborn and they hold a grudge like no other. I doubt even a marriage between them will allow either side to forgive and forget."

"So what do I do? Neither young dragon wants to leave their destined treasure behind, but I think they're going to elope. The elders, on the other hand, are burning everything on this side of the lake. What do I do?"

"Get out of the way? Unless you're fireproof, that is. Black dragons will never budge. Never."

Then all hope was lost. These families would fight and destroy each other. Sergio and Bianca would have to reject each other, remaining unbonded and childless their whole lives. And this would be worse for Bianca, who would most likely need to leave behind the treasure her uncle had willed her, or face harassment and eventual death at the hands of the Sommarivas.

"Of course," Sparky mused. "They are not really black dragons anymore, are they? They have diluted their blood with that of filthy humans for many generations."

He was right. And instead of being insulted, his words gave me hope. Because unlike black dragons, humans were sentimental. And most humans had the incredible capacity to forgive and forget.

CHAPTER 20

The air smelled scorched even at six o'clock in the morning. The humans at the café across the street were somber, and afraid. I couldn't understand a word they said, but I knew that nothing like this had ever happened to them. The dragons had never before let their feud grow to the point where they rained fire down on the towns and buildings. One woman explained in heavily accented English that the Sommarivas had ensured they were safe during World Wars I and II, during all the various skirmishes the area had seen through the centuries.

The dragons had protected their treasure, and that meant they'd protected the humans and their holdings as well. The humans blamed the Montenegros, but they admitted that the Sommarivas were not completely innocent in all of this, that events had been escalating to where this sort of war was probably inevitable.

I stared out over the lake, wondering how Bianca was doing. If she knew about what had happened. The fighting last night had to have upset her terribly. Her relatives were avenging her injuries, but their retaliation put any hope of reconciliation even farther into the future—if not smashed it entirely.

I heard a chair scrape and looked up to see Daniela lowering herself into the chair across from me. I barely recognized her. Her eyes were swollen and her skin blotchy as if she'd cried for hours. Her hands shook. And an angry red burn extended from one of her ears down across her neck and the upper part of her chest. I remembered her father's hand and face, and knew she'd forever carry that scar.

"I've come to beg your forgiveness." Her voice broke, and she took a few ragged breaths before continuing. "I told Gianna to let you and Irix know that you were both safe here. This isn't your fight, and I'm so sorry you were in the middle of what happened in Bellagio. None of our family will harm you. And even if you had continued to shelter the girl, we would not have fought you or invaded the villa to get her."

"No, you would have waited outside to pounce the moment either Irix or I left, or when she went out of the villa," I replied coldly. "You threatened a young woman in a public area, endangered the humans and everyone else who was there. You hurt her, and you came very close to hurting, or possibly even killing me."

She clasped her hands in an effort to control the shaking. "I never meant to endanger you last night. I was so angry, and I truly didn't see or recognize you there. All I saw was *her*, and I knew at once that Sergio was lost to that creature, that he'd been ensnared. I lost my temper, but I promise you that I will not do that again."

"You would have killed an eighteen-year-old girl," I retorted. "You would have killed the young woman your son had pledged his heart to, his soul mate. You claim he's the most important part of your treasure, but it would have destroyed him if you'd killed Bianca."

She flinched. "You don't understand. Our families have been feuding for thousands of years. If Sergio had been found in their territory, with their daughter, his body would have been thrown on my doorstep."

I stood, throwing down some money for my espresso. "That doesn't excuse your actions. You hurt Bianca. You threatened to kill her. I don't accept your apology."

"I couldn't catch up to him last night and he never came home. I don't know where he is. They might have him. They might be torturing him or waiting to use him as leverage. I need…" She looked down at her hands on the top of the table. "You know the girl. Can you ask her if he is safe? Ask her where he is? I beg this of you as a mother who fears for her son's life."

That I couldn't deny her. "Okay. I'll ask Bianca. But I'm not asking where he is, only if he's safe and not being kept prisoner somewhere. If he's gone off to Switzerland or something, then I don't really blame him. He'll either be back when he's ready, or not, but I won't give him up to you. Not after what you did."

She nodded. "Thank you. There is one more thing I want to ask of you."

I wanted to tell her no, but curiosity got the best of me. "What?"

"I need your help. I beg of you to please help us." She stood and reached out a hand, as if she were going to stop me from leaving, then quickly jerked it back. "Please. I saw what you did to the ivy and the plants last night and…I don't know if you can help us or not, but I hope you can. Please. I'll do anything. I'll promise anything. I desperately need your help."

I wasn't inclined to help her, but I was intrigued. And honestly, my anger at her was diffusing to see her in such pain and so very upset. I wouldn't easily forgive what she'd done last night, but I'd been raised as a human, and I did forgive.

She was part human as well. And if I could leverage whatever she wanted of me into something that could benefit Bianca and Sergio, it was worth helping her.

"What do you need me to do?"

Her breath hitched as she inhaled and I realized she was on the verge of crying. "Can you come to the villa? I need you to see it. Last night we were attacked. I'm sure you heard the fighting." She looked around. "Everyone heard the fighting. They got through to the villa. They…it's our treasure. They destroyed some of our treasure. Father is devastated, and I'm barely holding together. I'm sure that Sergio is suffering as well—not just from what happened last night with that Montenegro girl, but because he's bonded to the family holdings. These treasures are to be his, and the damage to them injures and scars us worse than any physical wound."

My mind immediately went to the gardens. Those beautiful gardens that I'd admired, that I'd fallen in love with had been damaged or destroyed. Now I was the one choking back sobs at the thought.

I guess I could sympathize with these dragons and their obsessions over treasure. I was the same about plants. I'd been gutted every time those demons had damaged the grapevines in Napa Valley, I'd been physically ill at the thought of magic harming the plants and trees in the bayous and city of New Orleans, and I'd nearly killed myself trying to heal that pineapple grove in Maui. The dragons had their treasures. I had plants.

"I've got a seminar at ten in Bergamo," I told her. "That only gives me two hours before I have to leave."

"If you could just look at them and let me know if you can

help…?" She waved her hands in a helpless gesture. "If you could even heal one plant, I would be forever grateful. And so would Father. He is so distraught. I fear that this damage to his treasure might hasten his end."

I might be mad at Daniela, but the thought of Mr. Sommariva suffering did sway me. Plus, I couldn't stand the thought of what might have happened to those beautiful gardens.

"I need to let Irix know where I'm going," I told her, well aware that he'd completely lose his shit if he woke up this morning and found me gone and not in the café as the note I'd left said.

Daniela nodded. "I need to get back. Can you meet me there? If there's anything you can do, our whole family will be forever in your debt."

And that's what I was hoping. "I'll be there right away."

Irix was awake and in the shower when I came in. I was so tempted to strip down and join him, to make love with the hot spray of water on us and let all these problems wash down the drain, but instead I stood at the shower door and admired his body, waiting for him to rinse the shampoo out of his dark hair.

He smiled at me, and heat pooled down between my legs. Damn. Stupid dragons. I should be screwing my fiancé in the shower, not trying to settle an ancient family feud and help two young lovers have their happily-ever-after.

"Take off your clothes and join me," he purred.

Oh, I so wanted to do just that.

"I can't. Daniela came to see me over at the café to apologize for last night."

His lip curled in a sneer. "Did you tell her to go fuck herself?"

"No, because she was begging me and telling me she and

her family would be forever in my debt if I helped her with something."

His eyes narrowed. "I don't like this Amber. What does she want you to do?"

"The Montenegros attacked their villa last night and from what she said, I think they may have destroyed some of the gardens."

Irix caught his breath. "Oh, Amber. I'm so sorry. I know how that must make you feel. You loved those gardens."

I did. And I loved how he knew me so well that he realized how much the loss of any of those plants would hurt me.

"I think she's hoping I can heal a few of them or regrow some. I won't know until I get there. But if I can, and I do this for her and her father, they'll be in my debt."

"Amber, that doesn't necessarily mean they'll overlook a relationship between Sergio and Bianca, or be willing to let go of the fact that their rival clan attacked them last night."

"They attacked because Daniela hurt Bianca," I argued. "And remember what Gianna said? They hold true to their word. I think they're like demons when it comes to vows. And if that's the case, then I can leverage this. I'll heal what I can, get in their good graces, have them owing me a significant debt, then hopefully be able to negotiate something."

"You'd need to do the same to the Montenegros," he warned. "And they don't have a burned-up garden for you to heal. The Sommarivas killed Guido. They hurt Bianca, even though she was technically trespassing here. And there are probably centuries of injuries that we don't even know about. Growing a bunch of plants isn't going to solve this problem."

"But I have to try."

He reached out and cupped my face in his wet palm. "I know you do. And you'd go there to heal those plants even if she hadn't promised you a favor in return, because you can't stand the thought of those beautiful gardens being ruined. Do you have enough energy? Do you need more?"

I loved how he was so willing to share his energy with me to heal a bunch of plants he really didn't give a flying fig about. "I think I'll be okay. If I have to, I'll heal what I can, get more energy, then come back to do more repairs later."

It didn't escape me that a huge amount of energy I was carrying right now was given to me by Irix, and gained by him from Ilaria Montenegro. How ironic that I'd be healing Sommariva treasure using energy from one of their mortal enemies.

Irix turned off the water from the shower and I handed him a towel.

"Do you want me to go with you? Will you be safe?"

Again, I appreciated how he trusted that I could take care of myself. How far we had come that, even though he was worried, he'd let me head into the dragons' lair on my own.

"No, I want to go alone. You're a big scary powerful demon and I don't think they'd be as open if you were there. I'm a less scary half-demon who doesn't turn into a big carnivorous predatory pterodactyl, and who only seems to be able to speed-grow plants."

He wrapped the towel around his hips. "Be back in an hour or I'm storming the castle. Okay?"

I had a vision of that scene from The Princess Bride, and laughed. "Okay."

* * *

IT COULD HAVE BEEN WORSE. That's what I kept repeating to myself as I walked past the melted stone and blackened hedges of Villa Sommariva. Humans were out in force with heavy equipment to demolish what couldn't be saved and haul it away. Others scraped and polished, trimmed and treated. They all looked devastated, from the man who let me in through the gates to the one retying broken citrus trees on a newly repaired arbor.

I reached out to the lemon tree and touched it, feeling the ache of torn limbs and burned leaves. Irix was right. I didn't have enough energy to fix this. I wasn't sure I'd ever have enough energy to bring every plant in this garden back to glowing health, but I could try.

Closing my eyes, I sent my energy into the lemon tree, repairing bark and photoreceptors, regrowing leaves and limbs. I felt it come alive under my hands, vibrant and lush.

The gardener gasped. "You're one of those elves, aren't you? But where are your pointy ears?"

"Yes, I'm an elf," I replied, figuring it wouldn't be wise to have it all over northern Italy that I was a half-elf. Someday I'd feel safe in making that widely known, but for now I still worried the elves might find a way to hunt me down and kill me if they knew.

"Are you here to restore the gardens?" He looked down at his trimmers, no doubt wondering if he should just go grab a cup of coffee and come back later.

"It'll take more than me to do that, but I hope to be able to repair the most critically damaged areas. You all can replant the annuals and the olive grove, but things like centuries-old azaleas and the more rare plants need my help."

He smiled. "Thank you. I know the Sommarivas will be so grateful."

I was counting on that. But as I made my way through the gardens I didn't see any of my hosts. I conserved my energy, concentrating on the rare plants and trees as I'd told the gardener. By the time I reached the valley with the ferns, I was already beginning to feel exhausted. There was so much. And if this made me want to cry, I could imagine how Daniela and her father must feel.

Yes, Bianca had been hurt, but it was a minor injury. It wouldn't even scar. And she'd been trespassing in a place where she knew there were risks. As angry as I was at Daniela for losing her temper, none of that justified this horrible attack.

I bypassed the ferns for the moment and made my way to the gazebo overlook, running my hand along the charred wooden railing. I could see clear across the lake to the dark shapes with wings on the snow-capped mountains. They were still there. Would they attack again at night? I suddenly realized that although I might use my ability to heal these plants to get the Sommarivas to back off and declare a truce, none of that would matter if the Montenegros continued to attack.

Too bad they didn't have a bunch of gardens for me to heal in return for a favor.

But I'd need to worry about them later. For now, my priority was to get Daniela and her family on my side, and I had an idea where she might be found.

I picked my way back down the path through the tall azaleas, which had thankfully suffered minimal damage in the raid. And there, in the damp tiny grotto, sitting on the wet stone was Daniela.

"I can already feel what you've done," she said, her voice numb. "Thank you. Every little bit helps. Thank you."

I hovered, not really wanting to step in and have icy water drip on my head, but not wanting to loom over her in the doorway like this. "Come out and prioritize for me. I won't be able to heal everything today, but I can come back each day I'm in Italy and do a little more."

She stood up, and walked out into the sunshine, shaking the water from her clothes and hair. "I know we should try to hire a group of elves to come in, but Father would never allow strangers here, even if they were coming to help restore his treasure. He likes you." She smiled, and this time it reached her eyes. "He *really* likes you. So anything you can do while you're here in Lake Como will be appreciated."

"There will be a price," I warned her. It was a bit of a bluff. I'd already healed several trees and shrubs. It was agonizing for me to walk by some of these plants and not help them.

A muscle twitched in her jaw. "What is your price? I have to tell you now that I won't be able to give you any of our artwork or statuary. Perhaps some clippings off the rare plants, but nothing else. You must understand that it's physically painful for us to part with our treasure."

"You won't retaliate against the Montenegros for this attack," I told her. "And you will allow Bianca to go to and from her villa and stay there without any harassment from you or your family."

She spun about to face me. "You're joking. I'd be willing to allow that girl access to her villa as long as she stays away from Sergio because I feel bad for hurting her, and I know what it's like to be separated from my treasure, but we cannot let this attack on our home go unavenged."

"They let the death of Guido Montenegro go," I told her. "I'm pretty sure they were willing to let that slide, but the injury to Bianca was the tipping point for them."

She tilted her head, her eyebrows coming together. "What do you mean?"

"Coupled with Guido's murder, you harmed a child of theirs. If she'd been an adult trespassing, then they might have been willing to overlook that, but she's only eighteen."

"That I truly regret, but I mean Guido's death. What do you mean we murdered him? He died of natural causes. I know we're dragons, but we've been interbreeding with humans for nearly a thousand years. We've inherited some of their frailties, and with each generation our lifespan grows shorter. He was over one hundred. He had never found his mate. And he smoked. I wasn't particularly surprised when I heard he died."

Was she lying? I got the feeling that she was earnest in her belief that Guido had died of a heart attack or a stroke or something. But if Daniela hadn't killed Guido, that didn't mean one of her family hadn't.

"The Montenegros are convinced he was killed. Perhaps a member of your family murdered him and you didn't know about it?"

Her laugh was short and bitter. "Who? Sergio? Why? He would hardly be able to kill a mature dragon. Even if he had gotten lucky, he would be covered with scars from the battle. My father wouldn't leave his treasure to kill a mere trespasser unless Guido had attacked him first. And the rest? Gianna is very like her side of the family. They want peace. They want to enjoy life with their human mates, sleep among their treasures, fly across the lake and through the mountains in the dark of the night. Yes, Guido Montenegro's presence was like a splinter in our thumbs. We were constantly aware of his presence when he was at the villa, and we were always vigilant in case he were to attack or attempt to steal what is ours. But in spite of his trespass, we would *not* have struck the first blow."

I believed her. I know it was absolutely weird, but I believed her.

If they hadn't killed Guido Montenegro, then who had?

"Are you sure?" I asked. "Sometimes murders are committed by the people you'd least expect. Are mate-bonds always reciprocated? Maybe one of your cousins fell in love with the dragon across the lake, and when he spurned her, she killed him out of shame. Or maybe there was a member of your family who had secretly bonded with the villa as their treasure and couldn't stand the thought of another dragon, especially one from a rival family, taking possession of what they thought of as their own."

She bit her lip. "I just can't see it. Most of my cousins are very non-aggressive. You'd need to walk into their house and try to rip the treasure from their hands before they would even think of shifting to their dragon form, let alone trying to burn you to ash. The only ones who feel the dragon so strongly are my father and I. I'm not even sure Sergio is as possessive as we are." Her eyes grew soft and a smile curved her lips. "He is so like his father. Gentle. Kind. Loving. Stubborn. The only thing Nico was ever possessive about was me. From the moment we met, he was determined to make me his own. It amused me to see a human so bold and forward—amused and flattered me. He sent me flowers and little gifts. He sang to me. He would surprise me with special trips and weekends that were meticulously planned and thought out. His devotion won my heart and within weeks my dragon was determined to make him mine. I'd hoped that we would have decades together. I'd hoped for possibly the gift of another child. But one rainy night, his car…"

I felt her pain. It was like a knife twisting in my stomach. If that had been Irix, I don't know how I would have gone on. But she had Sergio, her greatest treasure, the one reminder she had of the man, the mate, she'd loved.

"Do it for Sergio," I urged her. "Convince your family to hold back because your son loves the heir of their family fortune. These children are innocent in all of this. They don't care about a thousand years of feuding, or old hostilities. All they care about is that they love one another. Just as Sergio is the most important treasure you have, Bianca is his most important treasure. Don't retaliate and force him to choose."

I could tell she was undecided, on the edge of saying either yes or no.

"Let me think of this and discuss with Father. In the

meantime, know that I will give you my assurance that the Montenegro girl can have free access to her villa—the one she inherited from her Uncle Guido. If she ventures outside the boundaries of what the humans would consider her property, toward our section of the lake, then I will do all I can to chase her away, which might involve harming her physically. But she is free to access her treasure."

That was a start. And if Bianca could stay at the villa, then Sergio would, no doubt, find a way to visit her there. Now, if only I could manage to discover a way to keep the two families from continuing, or escalating, this war between them, I'd be happy.

I nodded and followed Daniela as she led me down the winding paths of the garden to the redwoods. There at the base of the Dawn Redwood, the Metasequoia, was Mr. Sommariva.

He looked ancient. His skin was waxen and drawn so tight against the bones of his skull that he seemed to be mummified. He turned to me, his eyes sunken and hollow. There was no hint of that flirtatious man who'd felt me up a few days ago.

"My daughter says that you have magic to grow plants. Are you an elf? Can you help me?" He choked on a sob and reached out a hand to touch the charcoaled bark of the tree. "See what they've done. See what they did to my treasure. This tree…the burns to this tree nearly destroyed me. It's one of the most precious things in my gardens."

I reached out a hand to touch the bark, my fingers next to his. The pain of this tree, the damage…it was almost to the point of being beyond my abilities to heal. How could someone do this to a tree that had been and still was so close to extinction?

"Papa, Amber has agreed to help restore your treasure to the best of her abilities. I know you've felt what she's done in the citrus grove as well as the other areas. She might not be able to heal everything, but she can bring many of our beloved trees and shrubs back to their glory. In return, she has asked that we allow the Montenegro girl to reside in her villa without harassment, and that we not retaliate against this attack."

I heard a subsonic grumble that made me quiver, along with a clicking noise. Mr. Montenegro turned his eyes to mine, the pupils elongated like a reptile's. "I have no grievance against that young girl, no matter what scum she might descend from. But we would appear weak if we let the attack on our home and treasures to go without any action on our part."

I was relieved that both leaders of the Sommariva clan had agreed to allow Bianca access to her inherited villa, but the other demand of mine was key to ending what would become a war.

"Then where does it stop? The Montenegros believe you killed Guido for his trespass in purchasing a villa in what you consider your territory. They were willing to hold back, but when Daniela attacked Bianca and injured her, they were the ones who felt they'd appear weak if they let it go. If you retaliate, then they will, then you will again. Both of your treasures will be destroyed. Your families will be destroyed. The humans who have lived by your side and kept your secret for centuries will be destroyed. Someone needs to be strong enough to stop this chain of events. I'm hoping that's you."

He turned a puzzled glance my way. "Didn't Guido Montenegro die of natural causes?"

"His family is convinced he was murdered, but they put out the story about natural causes to save face and as a way of letting your family know they weren't going to act on you in retribution for his death."

He frowned. "We didn't kill him. *I* didn't kill him, and I

didn't authorize any of my family to do so. In fact, I told everyone to leave him alone. He stayed in his villa most of the time when he was here, and never came near our lands or our treasures. He was a private man who kept to himself when he wasn't off adventuring in Antarctica or someplace else. And he played a darned good game of backgammon, too."

"Father!" Daniela gasped. "You socialized with him? You played board games with a Montenegro?"

He waved a hand at her. "I ran into him one day while drinking Bellinis in a little bar in Milan. It was neutral territory. He bought me a grappa. Turns out we had a lot in common, including a love of backgammon." Mr. Sommariva turned to his daughter. "A thousand years ago our ancestor escaped with his. They were the only black dragons to survive the war. To live in safety among the humans we needed to humble ourselves. We needed to live as humans, to mate with them and have offspring with them, diluting our dragon blood. Our families were not always enemies. And while I want to kill every Montenegro for harming my treasure, I would not have blamed Guido for this had he been alive. And I will not blame that young girl."

I held my breath, wondering if this tired, elderly dragon would be the key to peace.

"Papa, that young girl seduced Sergio. He has bonded to her."

The man shrugged. "Then let them go make love and have dragon babies together. It might do us all a world of good. You're far too protective of him, Daniela. He's a young man, and if he's given his heart, then so be it. Besides, if that girl is at all like Guido said she was, she'll give me some wonderful great-grandchildren. If I live to see them, that is."

Things were looking better for Sergio and Bianca, but I had a bad feeling that a war between their two families might bring this all crashing down, regardless of how much Sergio's grandfather might be willing to allow them to be together.

"I will heal this tree," I announced. "I will restore it to its full glory with no damage at all. And I will come back each day to heal as many of the rare and old-growth plants and trees as possible, but I will only do this if you not only agree to let Bianca reside in her villa in peace, but if you promise not to retaliate against her family for this attack. Those are my terms."

Mr. Montenegro set his jaw. "We had no part in Guido Montenegro's death. Their attack on us was warrantless. And I've been told the girl's injuries were minor. She probably won't even bear a scar from them. We can't sit passively while those gutter rats destroy our treasures and harm our family."

"I'll deal with that," I told him. "And I'm not telling you that you can't defend yourselves. If they come here again, go ahead and burn them. But don't go into their territory to attack them, or steal or harm their treasures. That's what I'm requesting."

He stared out across the waters to the mountains where, for now, no dark, winged shapes lurked. "Okay. If you'll help restore my treasure, I won't go after them. But only this time. If they attack again, then I *will* have my revenge."

That was as good as I was going to get. I'd need to work on the Montenegro side of things, but this was a start. They'd had their own revenge, and I was pretty sure the dragons on the mountains this morning had been a sort of early-warning and defense system.

I was figuring these dragons out. It wasn't war, this thing between them. It was an exchange of blows. One hit, the other returned with a strike of their own. And so on, back and forth until someone found a way to stop the back-and-forth without losing face. I got the feeling no one in the Sommariva family really wanted to see their rivals dead. They just didn't want their treasures stolen or their family attacked.

We'd come to an agreement, so I motioned for the elderly man to move back. Then I placed both hands on the tree and sent myself through the bark, into limbs and leaves, and down through the roots. It was badly damaged. Trees are built so that they can usually come back from traumatic injuries such as this. I'd seen ones split into two from a lightning strike eventually recover and put out new growth. The danger was that a tree this damaged was weak and open to all sorts of parasites and bacteria that would rot and destroy it before it had a chance to recover. Trees grow slowly, where parasites and bacteria are fast. Once they were in, the tree would be fighting a losing battle.

The first thing I did was seal the wounds. Even if I couldn't completely heal this tree, I could give it a better chance if I made sure it wasn't open to infection or infestation. That done, I worked to repair the damage, starting at the burned trunk and working outward and upward. It took time. And when I was done, I was ready to take a nap in the grass.

"I don't think I can do much more than this tree and what I did earlier," I told Daniela and her father. "I've got to head to my seminar now but I'll be back early tomorrow morning. Just let me know which ones I should concentrate on first."

"I'll leave a list of priorities," Daniela told me. "Thank you. Just healing what you've done helps immensely. I feel much better already."

"I do as well." Mr. Sommariva reached out and gave me a hug. "Go to your seminar, then rest, or do whatever you need to do to recharge. I promise you that I'll keep our bargain."

CHAPTER 21

Bianca ran to me as soon as I pulled into the courtyard of Abbondio castle. She was pale, her hair parted so it covered where her head injury was. I noticed she had on a long sleeved shirt as well and she was favoring that left shoulder.

"Oh, Amber." She threw herself into my arms. "Is Sergio okay? Uncle Marcus vowed to kill him and his mother. They took my phone and I've had no news."

I hugged her tight. "I've seen Daniela and her father and they're okay. Sergio wasn't there during the attacks. I thought maybe you'd know where he was. His mother hasn't seen him since what happened in Bellagio."

She pulled away, anxious eyes searching mine. "No! They took my phone away and I'm not allowed to leave." She bit her lip. "I…I think I might know where he is, but I don't want to say when someone might overhear us."

Having recently been a teenager myself, I focused in on one part of her statement. "They took your phone? They probably read your texts. If he tried to contact you, they'll know where he is."

My heart stuttered. There would be no peace between these families if Bianca's uncle killed Sergio. His words might have just been in the heat of anger. There was a big difference between fighting adults and fire-bombing a villa, and murdering a teenager.

She lifted her chin. "They wouldn't. We had a code, and spoofed our numbers so it looked like different people were texting each time. I'm not a fool. I knew very well what would happen if I got in trouble and Grandmother searched my phone."

I let out the breath I'd been holding. "Good. Sergio is most likely safely holed up somewhere away from his mother, then. It's probably best if you didn't try to see him for a while," I told her, worried that she might lead her family to the boy. Maybe I could act as an intermediary, though? There had to be some reassurance she wanted to send to him, and I know she'd rest easier if she knew he was safe and unharmed.

"I'm confined to the castle grounds." She moved back a few steps and lifted her hands with a frustrated sound. "I couldn't stop them. They knew I'd been injured. I told them it was my fault, but they wouldn't listen. Grandmother was furious. She sent Uncle Marcus and the others last night and confined me to my room. And now everything is ruined. My life is ruined. I'll never be able to see Sergio again. I'll never be able to see my villa again. I'll probably go through the Melancholy and die before I'm twenty."

She had very real concerns, but I still bit back a smile at the familiar drama. "I'm trying. I don't know that I can do much to help you and Sergio, but I've come to a deal, a cease fire, with the Sommarivas and I want to talk with your grandmother to see if I can do the same with your family.

Her eyes widened. "A cease fire? How can that be? We

have attacked them, destroyed some of their treasure. They will retaliate."

"They've promised not to." I looked over at the other seminar attendees filing into the dining room. So much for my hopes of getting this apprenticeship. I wouldn't even have a respectable score on the tests at this rate. But peace between these two families was more important than whatever faint chances I'd had at getting this job.

"Will your grandmother see me?"

She smiled. "She most certainly will. I told her last night about how you and Irix came between me and Daniela, and how you sheltered me and kept me safe. One of the reasons I came out is because she is eager to thank you."

Instead of heading into the house, Bianca turned and led me to a tiny chapel in the front courtyard. It was small, a private sanctuary that didn't look big enough to hold more than six or eight worshippers—or one dragon.

Catarina was in human form, seated on a wooden bench at the front of the chapel. She was clearly lost in prayer, but rose when she saw us.

Prayer? They were dragons, yet they had a little Catholic chapel for private devotions, and she was tucking a rosary into her pocket. It reminded me of all the human blood that flowed through their veins, that at this point, they were just as much humans as they were dragons.

They were half-breeds. Like me. We were all learning to deal with conflicting urges and all the different parts of ourselves. Just as I didn't fully fit in with full elves or full demons, these dragon hybrids must feel the same—no longer fully the dragons who had escaped here a thousand years ago, nor fully human enough to feel truly a part of the society they lived in. I'd been so lonely, a weird half-breed surrounded by those not like me. In spite of having their family around them, they must feel the same.

Family. No wonder they clung so closely to each other. They'd adapted from the solitary dragons that Sparky had claimed them to be and developed close-knit family groups. Surely it couldn't be so difficult for them to also let go of grudges. How much larger would their "family" of half-breeds be if they could just accept each other as like themselves.

"You are Amber?" The woman asked as she approached, her hands outstretched.

I placed my hands in hers, noting her cool, soft skin contrasting with the broad metal bands of her rings.

"I wanted to thank you as well as your demon fiancé for helping my granddaughter yesterday," she continued. "Not just by intervening in Bellagio, either. Providing sanctuary for her in your home was brave. I know we are intimidating, and so few humans have the fortitude to confront us. For a human and a demon to defy more than a dozen dragons to protect a girl… You and your fiancé have truly earned a place as friends of the Montenegros."

Bianca hadn't told her. I caught the girl's eye and lifted an eyebrow, wondering why she'd kept my secret.

"We would hardly leave an injured teenage girl naked on the streets of Bellagio," I replied in a lighter tone. "And in spite of her anger and her words, I don't believe Daniela would have seriously harmed Bianca."

"I was to blame, Nonna," Bianca spoke up. "I was in their territory. And she caught me with her son. I hit my head when I fell—that was an accident. But with the pain, I shifted to my dragon form, and I truly believe Sergio's mother saw that as an attack. Her son was there. She moved to protect him."

Catarina made a low noise in her throat. "I do not blame her for impressing on you the folly of trespass, but you are not some seductress enchanting her oh-so-innocent son.

What's done is done as far as your mate-bond. I'm equally unhappy about the situation, but I'd hardly attempt to kill a man my beloved granddaughter now considered her treasure."

"She wasn't trying to kill me," Bianca protested.

The woman's eyes narrowed, her pupils elongating slightly. I was suddenly very aware that my hands were still clasped tightly in her own. "That burst of dragon fire could have killed you had you not moved. You're lucky you only bear superficial burns. Witnesses say she did intend you great harm. I'm sure she was acting rashly out of emotion, but no matter how she might have regretted your death, that shot was meant to kill."

"Grandmother–"

"No." She released one of my hands to waive Bianca's protest away. "And she shoved her son behind her, not because she was afraid you would hurt your beloved—as if that were ever possible—but because she didn't want him to intervene and be hurt in the fight between you two. Your kind heart and your love blinds you, my dear. This boy may be young enough to have retained his innocence, but the other Sommarivas have not. They are our enemies. They are guilty of a murder attempt on one of our young. They are guilty of my son Guido's murder. One I was willing to over-look, in spite of the great pain it caused me. The other I could not. I know you grieve over the loss of your villa and your mate, but you will heal. And you will eventually have my treasure to call your own."

"But they didn't kill Guido," I interjected. "His death was not at their hands. His presence bothered them, but the whole time he lived there, from the moment he bought the villa, they never made a move on him. In fact, the elder Mr. Sommariva claims they had some kind of odd friendship where he would meet up and play backgammon with Guido.

The Sommarivas may be guilty of many things, but not the death of your son."

Catarina blinked down at me, her eyes still in that weird transition phase between human and dragon. "How could you know such a thing? You have only just arrived this week, and do not understand how things are between dragons. They could lie to you and you would not know it."

"Why would they lie to me?" I pressed. "They have no reason to do so. They didn't kill Guido. Daniela bitterly regrets her attack on your daughter. And in spite of the damage you've done to their treasure, they wish to propose a peace. They will allow Bianca to live in peace in her villa and not attack her if she strays into their territory as long as she is respectful and doesn't make any attempts to steal or harm their treasure. They will not retaliate for last night's attack on their villa. All they ask is that you do the same—that you cease all attacks on them, and that if Sergio is found in your territory, you do not harm him."

Catarina hissed. "That boy is not welcome in our territory. He will not come near my treasure."

"Well, he is welcome in *my* territory," Bianca cried out. "My treasure is his. He can stay at Villa Montenegro. And I'll have you know the moment I inherit, Grandmother, he will also be welcome here."

"That, he will not," a deep voice commanded. I pulled my other hand from Catarina's and turned to see Marcus. The chapel suddenly felt suffocatingly small. "You may entertain whom you choose at your own villa," he snarled, "but not here. And I warn you that inheritance rights or not, you will soon find yourself ousted as the matriarch of this family if you insist on ramming a Sommariva down our throats."

"He's right, Bianca," Catarina said in a more soothing tone. "There's a good chance you'll be taking on this family while you're still young and not fully into your own powers.

You'll need the support of these distant cousins as you have no siblings or immediate family of your own. Your Great Uncle Marcus can only do so much to hold them back if you disrespect them so."

"Surely you wouldn't stand by and watch them kill me?" Bianca asked her uncle.

I shivered, seeing something deep in his eyes that I didn't like. Catarina was right. I knew nothing of dragons and their society, but I got the feeling that if Bianca stepped over the line, Uncle Marcus wouldn't have any problems standing by while the others killed her.

"Of course not. But how long do you think the two of us could hold out against all the others? Some night in our sleep, we would find our throats slit, and that boy of yours as well."

Catarina shook her head. "No. That cannot happen." She turned to Bianca. "Darling, I ache for your pain, truly I do, but you must face the reality of your situation. You've given your heart to one who is an enemy of our family. Openly acknowledging your relationship, or bringing him here, isn't possible. I'm not saying to give him up—I know how impossible that is with a life-mate—I'm just telling you that you must be discreet. Over time, everyone will ignore what they must know goes on outside of our territories and in private, but they'll let you both be if neither of you demands your mate be acknowledged as part of our family."

"I won't sneak around, living my life as a spinster because my family are bigoted old fools," Bianca declared hotly.

Catarina waved her protest away and turned to me. "We accept the peace terms that the Sommariva clan proposes. We will not attack them as long as they do not attack us. We will respect their territorial boundaries as long as they respect ours. If Sergio Sommariva is seen in our territory, we will bloody his nose and send him home, but we will not kill him unless he makes a habit of his trespass." She turned to walk out of the chapel, then stopped at the doorway to turn around. "And please tell Daniela that I appreciate her allowing Bianca her treasure. I know that was not an easy concession for her to make, and it shows me that she is truly remorseful about the attack in Bellagio."

"Or she wants Bianca close enough to easily kill her," Marcus added with a growl. "Do not trust them, Catarina. This peace offering is a ruse."

Catarina's shoulders drooped. "Probably, but one of us needs to have faith, and I've decided it will be me. It is *my* treasure that is at risk here, after all."

$\mathcal{I}$ hustled into the seminar room, well aware that every eye turned to watch me make my way to my seat.

"Where were you?" Eva whispered.

"The chapel," I whispered back, not wanting to tell her that the Montenegros had been there as well. Celio was listening in, and I knew he'd immediately think I was somehow trying to schmooze the family into giving me the apprenticeship no matter what my scores on the test were.

"The chapel?" Eva chuckled. "Great idea. I've done everything else to help me win this thing. I'd appreciate some divine intervention right now."

"Prayer won't take the place of study," Celio sneered. "Neither will sleeping with the presenters and judges or trying to ingratiate yourself to the Montenegro family."

"Shhh," Marta hissed with a glare that effectively stopped our conversation.

I sat, fuming, not able to concentrate at all on what the presenter was saying. Celio was such an ass. Gah, I hated that guy. Hated him.

Then I remembered what Irix had said and shot the Spaniard a side-glance. He was ignoring me. Pointedly. So I closed my eyes and opened myself up to his fantasies.

Yikes. All he was thinking about right now was bashing my head against a stone wall until my brains leaked out. So much for Irix's theory, unless Celio were some psychopath who liked having sex with women he was violently murdering, the man wasn't harboring a secret attraction to me.

And now he was thinking of winning the apprenticeship while I failed miserably and was a crying heap on the stairs. In this fantasy, he kicked me as he walked by. Then I reached out and grabbed his leg, begging him to teach me all he knew about wine, to share his superior knowledge, even though I was too stupid to understand any of it.

Pretty, but dumb. Because it would be an unfair world if someone were to be as gorgeous and sexy as I was and smart, too. He'd not lose to the bimbo. And I had to be a bimbo. He'd worked his whole life for these opportunities. What would it say about him if some no-name, inexperienced American with nice tits and a pretty face bounced in and won?

Wait. Now we were getting somewhere. I had nice tits. I was gorgeous. And he needed me to be dumb, needed to hate me, because for someone whose only experience with wine was a summer internship to win over him would mean that he wasn't as smart as he'd hoped, that all his work over the last decade would be for nothing.

It wasn't about me. It was about him. It was about Celio's fears that his hard work wouldn't pay off in the end, that getting ahead was less about dedication and perseverance and more about having a pretty face and a nice set of tits. I hadn't exactly helped with my smug attitude that first day, or by having sex with one of the presenters. Maybe if I tried to be nice to Celio, to acknowledge that his knowledge and experience were far beyond mine, he'd stop fantasizing about bashing my head into a wall.

We broke early to allow us all time for study and tasting as a group. Everyone sat around with their notecards, quizzing each other. After an hour, others moved into the tasting area while Eva, Marta, and I talked about what we were going to suggest for the Muscat grapes. I told them about my sparkling wine. Eva was planning a dry Moscato similar to those DiMarche had been doing. Marta was going to propose a dessert wine, but was concerned she'd lose points since she was planning to add a few other varietals in addition to the grapes grown in the vineyard.

I glanced over at Celio. "I wonder what he's going to suggest?"

"A sweet wine like what I'm planning," Marta said. "He's addressing the sweetness through a different yeast strain and added fructose late in the fermentation. I dislike adding sugars and the yeast strain he's wanting to use will lead to a very light alcohol wine—too light in my opinion." She shrugged, looking very French at the moment. "It is what it is. I'm proposing the addition of Muscat of Alexandria and Orange Muscat and that may throw me out of the running."

Eva nodded. "I wanted to add Zibibbo in with the Muscat Blanc, but decided against it for that very reason. I'm using a different yeast to try to get the wine drier and the alcohol content close to twelve percent."

They made my recipe sound so basic, like I was a hobbyist with a jug of store-bought grape juice and a packet of bread yeast. This was where I was the weakest, since I had no background in winemaking at all. If I were to have any chance at winning this thing, I'd need to make up the difference with a high score on the written test and on the tasting.

And I knew how much I sucked at the tasting portion. Looking down at my notecards, I decided I'd study them later, and do what I could to hone my ability to identify wine by taste.

"Does anyone want to quiz me on tasting?" I asked, hoping I didn't get stuck with Celio again.

Marta smiled. "I'll help you."

She coached me through six wines, gently correcting me, and asking me questions along the way to help me come to the correct answer. Honestly, I learned more in the hour I spent with her than three days of lectures at this seminar. She was patient, kind, and encouraging. Everything that jerk Celio was not.

The room started to clear out as everyone went home, and I thanked Marta for her help, feeling much more confident about tomorrow than I'd been earlier in the day.

"I think you have a good palate, Amber, and you clearly are very smart about detecting wine and grape components," she reassured me. "This is just new to you. Once you start to link what is on your tongue with the terms and information you've just learned you'll be a top-notch sommelier, or enologist, or vintner. You have a natural talent, and I'm impressed by how quickly you've picked all of this up."

I beamed, thanking her again, and looking over to glare at Celio. I wasn't a bimbo. I'd show him, that ass.

Marta chuckled. "Don't pay him any attention. The competition here is very intense, and he sets very high standards for himself. He has had to work very hard for every job, every recognition, and he is frustrated by the ease with which those with natural talent learn what takes him so much more effort to do. I admire Celio. He is dedicated, and not afraid to work very hard for what he wants. He has talent, but not the natural talent that you do. It bothers him to think that you might achieve in a few months what has taken him years."

"I just wish he wasn't such a jerk to me," I complained.

"He will be less of a jerk Friday, once all the testing is over and the apprenticeship has been decided. Right now he is…" she searched for the correct word. "Stressed…."

Yeah, well me, too.

I thanked Marta again and lingered a bit, going through my notecards and writing down a few additional things. As I headed out to my car, I saw a figure seated on the stone bench that overlooked the sprawling vineyard. It was Catarina Montenegro, stylish as always with a perfectly tailored olive jacket across her shoulders. She seemed lost in thought, but looked up and gestured to me with a smile as I headed past her to my car.

She patted the bench and I sat beside her, taking in the deep green of the grapevine leaves against the lighter shade between the rows, all of it contrasting against the bright blue of the late afternoon sky.

"Admiring your treasure?" I teased.

"Beautiful, isn't it? It was my father's before me, and my grandfather's before his, and soon it will be Bianca's."

"Not too soon, I hope."

She smiled. "My granddaughter helps keep the Melancholy at bay. Eventually I will succumb, but she reminds me so much of my beloved Pierre, of her father, and especially of Guido with his innocent faith in everyone, that I find myself at peace around her. She, more so even than my treasure, is a balm on the grief I feel at the loss of my mate so long ago."

"When did he die?"

"Nearly a hundred years ago. He grew old and no money in the world could prolong his life beyond the very mortal flesh he was born to." She sighed. "Our lives have been shortened as we've interbred with humans, but we still outlive them considerably. As much as I hate Daniela, I felt her pain at the loss of her mate. He was too young. They had too short a time together. Perhaps that is why she clings so tightly to her son."

"Bianca need never go through that," I said cautiously. "Sergio is a dragon, as she is. She'll not have to live for decades, or even centuries, mourning the loss of her love, sliding into Melancholy because of his absence."

She turned sharp eyes on me. "My heart aches for her. She is my only grandchild, the last of my line, and I want her to have every joy her heart desires. I want her to feel safe and whole surrounded by her treasure. But just as we all face tragedy with our human mates, she will face it with hers. Even if I were to allow it, the boy's mother would never accept a match between them. The Sommariva clan would overthrow Sergio and give his treasure to another just as my own cousins would do the same to Bianca. Yes, the two lovers would have each other, but they would quickly die, distraught and in pain, without their treasures."

"How do you know that? Maybe both of your families would be more accepting than you believe. And with all the human blood in their veins, maybe Sergio and Bianca would be able to survive without their treasure—without *your* treasure. Perhaps they'd have the strength and ability to find a treasure just as satisfying somewhere else, one that they found and built together."

Catarina shook her head, turning her gaze once more out to the vineyards. "Perhaps. But humans can be just as attached to their treasures as any dragon. I'm not sure their blood has in any way tempered the dragon that runs through us, even after all these generations."

I knew better than to push things further. I'd made huge progress today in bringing these two families to peace. Maybe it was too soon to expect any of them to budge on

Sergio and Bianca. Maybe with time, the two lovers would find a way to be together.

Although, from experience, I knew that teenagers were impatient. Time might not be something that either Bianca or Sergio were willing to give.

’d spent all night holed up in the villa with flashcards and reference books, studying and having Irix quiz me. At midnight I was on the edge of tears and gave up, throwing the index cards across the room and stomping off to cry on my pillow. I didn't want to go out and find sex. I didn't want Irix to hold me. I didn't want anything but to get this over with, fail embarrassingly in front of the other seminar attendees, and have Celio gloat at me.

I was that pretty American girl who wasn't good enough. All I had going for me was my looks and my willingness to put out.

No. I was more than that. I wasn't the dumb Barbie-doll slut Celio thought me to be. I was smart. I'd graduated at the top of my class, scored that internship at DiMarche over thousands of applicants. I'd held New Orleans together when that magical group had tried to destroy it. I'd helped Maui when Pele had been one tantrum from burning it all down. I'd saved countless orchards and vineyards in Northern California from the machinations of an evil elf and a pair of plague demons. And here I was, an intermediary between two dragon families.

I wasn't dumb, I just didn't have the background that all these other people had. I'd study. I'd do the best I could on the exams. And if this was something I really wanted, I'd work my way up through the ranks, and give this another shot in five or ten years. When someone reaches for the stars, stretches for that tough goal, there's no shame in failure, only in failing to try at all.

I'd met Daniela early at the coffee shop before heading out to Bergamo. She listened to all I told her about my meeting with Catarina and Marcus and agreed to the terms we'd discussed yesterday. Once again, she said they'd allow Bianca access to and enjoyment of her villa, as well as the right to come into the other towns across the lake. She could have one member of her family with her at the villa, but no more, and those dragons needed to remain there unless they were going in and out of the territory to return home.

But one thing Daniela would not budge on was Sergio. He was still missing. I could see from the dark shadows under her eyes, the way the coffee cup shook in her hand, how worried she was for him, but she declared that she would never give her blessing to any union between her son and a Montenegro. Like Catarina, she said their family would oust Sergio if he married Bianca.

I thought about the problem the whole way to the castle. Peace. And I had no doubt that Sergio would find a way to sneak in and see Bianca. She'd made it clear guests to her villa were her business and hers alone. But how long could they sneak around before someone decided to take matters into their own hands? Bianca's insistence on seeing Sergio would jeopardize her ability to inherit her grandmother's treasure, and the same with Sergio. I knew it would be just a matter of time before either family decided they needed to do away with the offending lover.

And then the peace would crumble. The only thing that

would hold this together long-term was if Bianca and Sergio separated forever. Or if they ran away. And I got the impression that neither option was a viable one.

As I pulled up the road to the castle, the smell seeped in through the car. Someone must have been burning garbage or debris or something. It made me tense up, reminding me of the way everything had smelled after the dragon attack on Villa Sommariva.

Then the vineyards came into view and I felt as though I'd been punched in the chest. Long strips of black, where vines had been burned to charcoal from what looked like an aerial attack. I put the pedal down, nearly dropping the bottom out of my little rental car when I hit the stones of the driveway at speed.

The house looked undamaged, as did the tower and the winery out back. It seemed that the destruction had been contained to the vineyard. Had it been the Sommarivas? Of course it had! Who else would have flown in to attack the Montenegro treasure? But the question in my mind, beyond the safety of the family, was who had done this? Had Daniela lied to me and retaliated for the attack on her treasure? I remembered her sitting across from me this morning, and just knew she hadn't been involved in this. There had been no hint in her face that she even knew about this.

But if it wasn't her, then who? Was there a rebel in her family, someone acting alone against the orders of their family patriarch? And if so, was that person also responsible for Guido's murder?

It wasn't until I entered the dining room that I realized I was the only one here. We had exams today. The place should have been full of attendees frantically studying and waiting their turn to take the written portion of the test, as well as the presentation of our wine recipes. Instead the room was completely empty.

"Oh! Did no one call you and tell you?"

I turned to see a woman I didn't recognize. She was twisting her hands together, gathering the hem of her shirt up in a knot. Her eyes were rimmed with red.

"No. Is today cancelled?" I asked.

She nodded then shook her head. "Postponed. Until tomorrow. Thankfully we did not suffer too much damage. Only to the vineyards, and then only the oldest vines, the ones we'd already harvested. Minimal losses, and easily replanted next year, but Catarina is devastated. She was not fit...not in a good place to be entertaining humans right now."

I got the subtext through her heavily accented English. "Is everyone okay? Was anyone injured fighting them off?"

They must be formidable indeed to have repelled an attack before much of anything had been damaged.

"They fled before us," she scoffed. "Two swipes of the field, and the moment we flew out to launch a counterattack, they were off into the night. Cowards. Weaklings. We will crush them. They will not live to see tomorrow. In truth, they will not live to see the sunset."

I ran from the castle in a panic for my car. Were they flying right now toward Lake Como? No. They'd want to surprise their foes and attack either under the cover of night, or to come close as humans and switch to their dragon form later. Either way I had to warn Daniela. I was positive she didn't know about this attack.

And something about the attack was weird. Whoever had done this hadn't been able to pull together enough supporters to do more than burn a few rows of vines in something that was more approaching vandalism. And this was supported by the fact that they'd fled before they actually had to fight.

I couldn't let Daniela and her family pay the price for what one or two rogues had done.

Jumping in my car, I navigated the bumpy driveway as fast as I could, speeding up once I'd hit asphalt. It wasn't until I was half an hour away from the castle that I heard a rustling noise from the back seat and saw a dark head rise up in my rear view mirror.

I screamed and swerved, nearly crashing the car.

"Fuck! Bianca! What are you doing here?"

She was a stowaway in my car. I knew very well what she was doing here.

"I need you to help me." Her voice hitched on a sob. "They locked me in my room so I couldn't go. They're going to attack. They'll kill all of Sergio's family and him as well. I need to warn them."

"I'll warn them," I told her. "You need to go back home where it's safe."

She did need to go home, but I had no time to turn around and take her there. If I dropped her off along the way could she get home? I was reluctant to leave the girl by the side of the road where she'd be alone and vulnerable if there was an attack. I could call, send Irix over to talk to Daniela, but I was the one that had forged a relationship with the woman and her father. I was the one who had bargained my elven skills for this peace. I wasn't sure Irix could do more than warn them and put them on the defensive.

Would they go on the defensive? Would they wait in their villa for the Montenegros to rain fire down upon them, or would they fly out to meet them halfway, in the mountains on the other side of the lake? I wasn't sure if asking Irix to warn them would do more harm than good.

"I can't go back to the castle. Can you take me to my villa? I'll be safe there. And it's mine. It's my treasure. Take me there."

She was rambling, her words breathless.

"Bianca, did you see what happened last night? Who attacked, because I met with Daniela this morning and I'm positive it wasn't her, nor was it done with her knowledge. The only hope I have to defusing this situation is if I can go to her with some way to identify the attackers."

She climbed through into the front seat beside me. "Two, maybe three at the most. It was dark and moonless last night, so all I saw was the shape of dragons outlined against their fire. They swept the vineyard, doubled back for another strike, then fled before us."

"Why not attack the castle?" I asked.

She shook her head slowly. "I don't know. Maybe if there were only a few, they were scared to come that close?"

"They still could have firebombed then ran," I insisted. "Hit the castle with their initial strike, with surprise on their side, then take out a strip of vineyard on their way out."

She frowned. "You're right. It's what I would have done. And if they had done that, then Grandmother wouldn't be preparing for war right now. She would have secured and repaired her treasure before venturing out."

"So maybe someone wanted to lure her out, to have her treasure unattended, or have her among those fighting?"

Bianca shuddered. "I can't imagine the Sommarivas would want Grandmother fighting against them. She is fierce and strong. You're right though. Why *wouldn't* they attack the castle? The damage they did was to the least valuable part of the vineyard. We actually were getting ready to replace those vines anyway. It's almost as if they knew what could be sacrificed, the least important and replaceable part of our treasure, and deliberately targeted those."

I frowned, concentrating on my driving. It was as though they'd smacked the hornet's nest and ran, as if the goal was to manufacture a situation, an excuse, to get back at the

Sommarivas for their attack. It was as though the goal was to get the Montenegros to declare war and annihilate their foes.

"Bianca, do you think it's possible that it was a member of your family who burned the vineyards last night?"

Her eyes grew huge. "No! Who would do such a thing? Our holdings might not be my cousins' treasure, but they still have bonded to it. It would cause them pain to harm our family treasure. It would be like cutting off a limb."

"But if they thought it would serve a greater good? If they thought by getting your grandmother to walk away from the peace table and kill the Sommarivas? And possibly kill Sergio as well?"

She sucked in a breath, then slowly shook her head. "But why? My cousins would be risking their own lives if we go to war. And killing Sergio does none of them good. Whether he lives or dies, I'll continue to inherit. And I'll remain childless and unmated. Uncle Marcus's children will inherit after I'm gone."

"Will you, though?" I pressed. "Remain childless and unmated?"

She shot me a sharp glance. "What do you mean? I told you that we only mate once and we mate for life. I cannot be with my mate, so I will remain alone. And I will suffer the Melancholy early."

"That's not what I mean." I watched her carefully out of the corner of my eye. "If there is peace, then you will be able to live at Villa Montenegro. You'll be able to walk the streets of the towns around Lake Como without fear. You can't tell me that you haven't thought of this. If you and Sergio are discreet, there is no reason you can't continue to see each other. He can sneak into your villa, and once you're an adult, he won't even need to use the secret passageways anymore. You'll live there alone, an eccentric dragon hoarding her treasure."

She sighed. "Yes, but it will be short-lived. When Grandmother dies, I'll be expected to live at the castle. It will be my treasure as well, and I'll be expected to live there as part of the family holdings. You heard her yesterday. If I bring Sergio to the castle, my family will drive both of us out."

"But even then, you'll still be able to see him now and again. You won't need to be at the castle every hour of every day. You could still regularly visit your villa and see him there," I continued.

Bianca nodded. "Yes. I'll admit that was my plan."

A plan with a flaw. "Daniela told me that some dragons don't have children, and that most have only one. She said that having two is rare. But when she told me all of that, she was talking about the pairing of a dragon and a human mate. You and Sergio are two dragons. You'll become pregnant. And there will be no hiding that from your family, or hiding the fact that the baby is Sergio's."

She bit her lip. "They know I'm mate-bonded. If I'm pregnant, they will know it is Sergio's as it could be no other's. But you're wrong about the chances of that happening. I'm not a full dragon, and neither is Sergio, no matter what our families like to claim. There is a chance that we will have a child, but equally a chance that we won't. And we'll be careful to make sure that doesn't happen."

"You'll be careful until you're not. Bianca, I know what it's like to love someone with all of your heart and soul. You ache to be with them. You want to build a life together with them. And for many of us, that longing includes the desire to have children. You don't seem like someone who would be happy to remain childless. Eventually you'd become careless, either on purpose or just from chance, and you'd be pregnant. Then what would happen?"

Sorrow filled her eyes. "We'd be denied our family's treasure. We'd be kicked out of both of our territories, if not killed outright. Our child as well."

"Someone knows that, Bianca. I think someone in your family staged the attack in hopes that your grandmother would declare war. And if Sergio isn't killed in the fighting, he'll be hunted down and killed later."

"No!" Tears glistened on her lashes. "I just want to live in peace with Sergio and our treasures. I want to love him, to be with him, to have his hatchling. They'll never let that happen, will they? Neither my family, nor his."

"No," I told her softly. "They probably won't. I had hopes that with peace between your families, in time tensions would lessen to the point where you might be able to be together."

"Right." Her laugh was bitter. "Perhaps in three or four centuries. By then both of us would have withered away from the Melancholy."

We drove in silence for a while, my heart heavy. Eventually she gave me directions to the villa. I'd had her text Irix for me, telling him to warn Daniela and her family for me, but urge them *not* to go on the attack. With his help, I didn't need to be in quite in the tearing hurry that I'd been before. I could take the time to get Bianca settled into her villa, to make sure she was safe there with Ilaria before I left.

Irix and I had approached the villa from the lake, so I was completely lost and reliant on Bianca for her directions down the twisting and turning roads through the steep mountainside that the villa backed onto.

Finally there, we approached a huge black metal gate, ornate flying dragons along the top. Bianca leaned out and typed in the code and the gate swung inward, closing right after we passed through. I parked in a carport, then followed her down a gravel path that opened to the view that had taken my breath away earlier this week. We were up high, looking down at the roof of the stepped villa and the lake beyond. I felt like I could see forever. There was no way dragons could sneak up on this place in their winged form, at least with this vantage point.

"I used to shift up here and fly down, swooping along the lake to land on the lawn out front." She smiled fondly. "Uncle Guido would always scold, saying that we should not be in dragon form unless it was an emergency. He was worried that the humans might one day decide they didn't want to live next to creatures such as us, and in our complacency, we'd be vulnerable. He was also worried about pushing the fact of our presence too much into the Sommarivas' face. But I like to fly. I wish we could all fly without fear."

I did, too.

We went down the narrow steep steps, past the path to the grotto where I'd first seen Bianca and Sergio together, past the two rooms separated by the arches with the wide lawn where Irix proposed, and into the villa.

"Ilaria!" Bianca called out, but there was no answer.

Just as I'd been reluctant to drop Bianca at the gates and drive off, I didn't want to leave her here until we'd located Ilaria. There was a war brewing, and for all I knew, someone would sneak in here and do her harm. I believed Daniela's promise, but if there was a renegade in the Sommariva clan, they may seek to assassinate Bianca. And if, as I was beginning to wonder, there were someone in the Montenegro clan who was using the war as a pretext to kill Sergio, then they might search here, thinking he'd taken refuge in the one place his family wouldn't look.

There were no dragons in the skies yet. Irix was delivering my early warning. No matter how much I itched to be where I could hold these two warring families off before they wreaked havoc on the lakeside towns, I couldn't leave Bianca alone.

We searched but still couldn't find the woman.

"Maybe she's with the others preparing to fight?" I asked Bianca.

She shook her head. "She'd fight from here. If they wanted her to join in, then she'd meet them here, close to the villa. She wouldn't go back to the castle only to return with the others. First, she can keep an eye on things and let the others know what to expect in terms of Sommariva readiness. Secondly, she's very bonded with the villa. It's her treasure. She aches when she has to leave here. In some ways, she's more bonded to the villa than I am."

"Because of her age?" I asked, making myself at home and plopping on a sofa. If the woman didn't turn up soon, I'd need to text Irix and let him know I was staying here for the foreseeable future…and hope that he could hold Daniela back from any action that might be construed as being on the offensive.

"It's not just that. Some of us bond more tightly to our possessions than others. Some of us are more dragon than human. Others more human than dragon."

She sat as well, but perched on the edge of a sofa, her eyes continually straying toward the desk. And I was pretty sure I knew why.

"So Sergio is here? Hidden in one of the secret passageways in the house?" I asked casually.

She shot me a nervous glance. "No. Why would you say that? It wouldn't be safe for him to hide here, with Ilaria in residence. She'd find him and attack him, chase him away from our treasure. She knows the passageways as well as I do."

"Not all the passageways." I watched her pick at the hem of her sleeve and fidget at my words. "Your Uncle Guido showed all of them to you because he was planning to let you have this treasure upon his death. He would have kept some of that back from Ilaria. A man doesn't build a labyrinth of secret passageways in and around his home for protection from his enemies, then tell everyone about it."

She sighed, looking again toward the desk. "It was the safest place, the one place his family would not dare step foot on to search for him. Our sense of smell was one of the first things to be blunted when we started inter-breeding with humans. As long as he stayed hidden and quiet, Ilaria would never know he was here. It's how I planned to sneak him in and out once our families came to an agreement on territories. It's how we were going to continue to see each other if we couldn't get married and live openly together."

"His mother is very worried about him," I told her.

"Sergio believes if he stays away until there is an agreement for peace, his absence will give greater incentive." She glanced again toward the desk. "He's deep in a passageway that leads to a neighboring home on the other side of the mountain—a sympathetic human who was a friend of Uncle Guido's. When it is safe, I'll go get him. Until then, it's best if he stays hidden from all except me and our human friend."

I heard a door slam, and a breathless Ilaria burst into the room, her purse on her arm.

"Bianca! You should be at the castle where you'd be safe. Does your grandmother know you're here?"

Bianca jumped up and ran to Ilaria, hugging her tightly. "No. They locked me in my room, and are busy with their plans. I'm sure none of them has checked on me yet. Even if they do, my car is still in the driveway, and I obviously didn't fly out. They'll think I'm still there."

Ilaria smiled. "Clever naughty girl. Your human friend here smuggled you out, didn't she?"

"Yes. I had to be here, to protect my treasure in the coming battle. Ilaria, Amber thinks the Sommarivas didn't attack our vineyard, that maybe this is a ploy by one of our own to have Sergio killed in battle."

The woman shot me a quick look. "That seems like a lot of work to go to when patience and a knife in the back would do the job just as well."

Bianca pulled away from her. "I love him, Ilaria. I would never forgive a kinsman who killed my mate. I'd make sure any dragon that harmed him suffered the same fate."

"Calm down little one. I was only pointing out the absurdity of your friend's idea." She smoothed a hand down Bianca's hair, still smiling. "I have nothing against that boy. In fact, I'd be thrilled if you both were able to be together forever, to never spend a moment apart."

Bianca beamed. I knew she was thinking that the future would be so much easier if Ilaria could be a coconspirator in sneaking Sergio in and out. If the woman was as bonded to the villa as she said, then she'd be unlikely to leave it and give the lovers a chance to be together.

But something bothered me. Her casual dismissal of my theory, the lack of fretting over Bianca's presence in what was about to become a war zone. Maybe Ilaria thought to lure Sergio out with her neutral stance, only to be the one plunging a knife into his back.

"You're free to go now, Amber," Bianca told me. "Thank you for giving me a lift, and for keeping me company until Ilaria returned. I'll be safe now."

"You won't leave the villa?" I insisted. "If the fighting comes too close, you'll escape through the passageways?"

She nodded and I saw a shadow pass in the distance—the shape of a huge black dragon against the snowy cap of a mountain. I glanced out and saw other shapes on the horizon. It was about to begin. And I really did need to get back to Irix before I was stuck right in the middle of the battle.

CHAPTER 24

I said my goodbyes, gave Bianca a hug and those air-kisses that these Italians did, and headed out. It wasn't until I reached my car that I got that weird sense of something wrong. My car hood was still warm from the drive here, parked right outside the carport. There was only one other car there—a blue Fiat. It had been there when we'd arrived. Bianca had left her car at the castle.

Ilaria's car. And it had been here when we arrived. Where had she gone with her purse on her arm that she hadn't taken her car? It would have been ridiculous for her to shift into her dragon form and fly somewhere, as she'd be naked and without her purse when she arrived. And the villa was on the side of a mountain, inaccessible aside from the lake or this access road. She'd hardly have gone hiking around the mountain dressed as she was with a four-hundred-dollar designer purse on her arm. And with the open windows, we would have heard her come in by boat.

Ilaria had been in or around the villa the whole time, either on the grounds or in one of the secret passageways. She'd grabbed her purse and slammed that door shut on purpose, to make us think she'd just come back from some trip to town.

I ran back. Had the woman hoped to eavesdrop and find out where Sergio was hidden? Did she now hope to gain Bianca's confidence and get her to reveal her lover's whereabouts?

I burst through the door and came upon a scene from a crime show. There was blood splattered on the silk wallpaper, blood soaking the rug. The desk had been shoved aside, revealing an opening in the floor. And there, standing over a body was Sergio.

Terror warred with relief. Sergio was unhurt by the look of him, even though he was covered with blood, but as his odd dragon eyes turned to mine, I saw shock and horror in them.

The body…it was a woman by the legs and shoes. I caught my breath.

Bianca rose from behind the desk and I nearly passed out in relief. She was covered in blood, holding a knife, her face ashen.

"Did she try to kill Sergio?" I came around the desk to see that the woman on the ground, was, in fact, Ilaria. And she was dead.

"No." Bianca's voice shook. "She tried to kill *me*. I've known her my whole life. I trusted her. Uncle Guido trusted her.

That was about when I realized that some of the blood on Bianca was her own. "Are you okay?"

She nodded, her eyes welling up with tears. "She cut my arm and I got the desk between us before she could strike again. She said… she said that if I was dead, the villa would be hers."

"I heard her scream and came running, but couldn't get

out of the tunnel." Sergio gestured at the desk. "Bianca let me in."

"He startled Ilaria pounding on the tunnel door, and I jumped her when she was distracted. I didn't mean to kill her."

Bianca started to sob and Sergio gathered her in his arms, bloody clothing, knife and all.

Had Ilaria been the one who had killed Guido? Had she planned on using the battle as cover for assassinating Bianca? And the big question…

"Would she have inherited Villa Montenegro if you'd died?" I asked.

"There was no clause in Uncle Guido's will naming her so, and I have no will." Bianca looked down at her cousin through her tears, still in Sergio's arms. "The villa would have gone to Grandmother and been part of her family holding. Ilaria wouldn't have gotten it unless Grandmother gave it to her."

I was starting to get a bad feeling about all this. "And if your grandmother died? With you gone?"

"Where are you going with all this?" Sergio demanded.

I ignored him. "Bianca? Who would inherit?"

She took a deep breath, putting a few inches between herself and Sergio, but still keeping her arms around him. "With all her children and only grandchild deceased, the family treasure would go to my great-uncle, Marcus. And so would the villa."

"And does your uncle have any particular attachment to this villa?"

She shook her head. "No…not really. He'd probably sell it if he ended up with it. The castle and the vineyards and the tower and the winery he loves as if it is his own, but this villa means nothing to him."

"So it wouldn't be a big deal for him to give it to someone, say a cousin, who served him well? Who helped him inherit the treasure he really does want?"

Sergio growled and looked down at Ilaria's body. "*Someone* promised her the villa if she killed you, and Marcus would be the only one in the position to do that if you died, Bianca."

"Aside from your mother," she snapped back. "The villa is in your family's territory, after all. She's already threatened to kill me. It would be easy for her to promise Ilaria she'd seize the villa upon my death and allow her to purchase it on the sly."

"My mother wouldn't do such a thing," Sergio retorted.

"She tried to burn me," Bianca snapped back. "She'd be getting rid of her son's unsavory choice in a mate, throwing her clan's enemies into chaos and most likely hastening my grandmother's death with my murder. And it would be easy for her to go back on her promise to Ilaria or kill the woman after it all was done."

The other dragon snarled. "She wouldn't do that, Bianca. Besides, then she would need to face Marcus, who is *not* in his Melancholy and wouldn't hesitate to burn us to the ground. Even if she were so cruel as to plot in cold blood to kill my mate, she wouldn't be so foolish as to trade an enemy who only wants to be left alone in her sorrow for one who is quite eager and capable of killing us all."

"He's right," I told her. "Daniela and her family weren't responsible for the lame attack on your family's treasures last night, and they're not behind this. It's Marcus."

Bianca caught her breath. "He's not so stupid. He'd never get away with it. Grandmother would kill him for plotting my murder."

"Not if your Grandmother thought the Sommarivas killed you. You snuck out. You were here, in their territory at your villa in the middle of a battle. She'd think that one of them—probably Daniela since she threatened you—snuck in and killed you."

"No." She shook her head. "He wouldn't do that. He wouldn't."

"Yes, he would."

I froze at the deep masculine voice, turning to see Marcus standing in the doorway.

"And now I don't have to worry about Ilaria blackmailing me." He walked over to look down at the body and the rest of us edged around the desk. "How convenient."

Crap. I knew, without him saying another word, that none of us were to leave this room alive. Even me. He might have spared me as someone he thought human, but not after I'd made a big deal about brokering peace between them, and made it clear that I was very much involved in matters between these two families. I knew he'd never let me out of here alive. I'd end up a casualty of this battle, just like Bianca and Sergio.

A long, thin knife appeared in his hand, a duplicate to the one Bianca had taken from Ilaria. "Let's do this easy, shall we? Quick and painless, just like Guido. We don't want to destroy your pretty treasure now do we Bianca? I'll even let you name which cousin you want me to give this wretched place to."

We all shuffled a few steps around the desk, and I saw that our movements weren't just to keep the furniture between us and Marcus. There was a tunnel under this desk, an escape route. And every step we took brought us closer to it.

"I won't let you kill her," Sergio vowed.

I felt the same, but I was holding my speeches, waiting to see how this played out before I made my move.

"It would be a shame for you to resist." Marcus took another step. "If you fight me, we'll do it as dragons, and a reptile my size is going to seriously damage this room and the priceless valuables inside it. Afterward I'll make sure to burn as much of it to ash as I can. You'll both still die, but Bianca will die in agony, knowing that her treasure has been destroyed."

"I'd rather die fighting," she vowed. "If the villa is damaged in the process…well, that's the price I'll pay for not laying down and letting you slit my throat."

We continued our slow dance around the desk. Marcus made a tsk noise, but before he could say another word, Bianca stepped over the opening and dropped straight down.

Marcus shouted and lunged, but just as Bianca vanished, Sergio transformed, ripping his clothes and knocking everything aside, including me, as he became a black dragon.

By the time I'd rolled to my feet, Marcus was a dragon as well, and I could do nothing but dive and duck, hugging the edges of the room as the pair of them lashed into each other.

Well, there was one thing I could do. Huddling in a corner, I pulled out my phone and texted Irix.

I could hardly tell which dragon was which. They were grappling, intertwined as their mouths bit down on shoulders and torsos. Wings flailed, talons at the very edges slashing and tearing through the leathery membranes. Powerful legs kicked and scraped as they tried to dig claws into the hard scales covering their flesh. It was all I could do to keep from being trampled or concussed by swinging wings and tails. The noise was deafening—roars and the sound of smashing furniture and broken glass as shelves crashed and the desk and chairs were stomped on and knocked into walls. The silk wallpaper was torn and shredded, the stone underneath dented from the repeated blows. Marcus kicked out a back leg as he lunged forward, and sunlight streamed through the hole he knocked through the thick wall.

I cowered and ducked, wondering what I could do. There wasn't a plant in the house for me to speed-grow. That was my one big trick, aside from a few things with water that I'd done in Maui, and there was none of that nearby either. The only thing left in my lame half-breed arsenal was lightning, and I was reluctant to unleash that in such close confines. Looking around, I saw something that might be of use and ran across the room, jumping over a swinging tail and climbing up a low, splintered shelving unit to yank a sword out of a decorative teak holder.

It was one of those Japanese-looking swords the Samurai use. I had no idea what to do with it, but as I pulled it from the scabbard, I realized it was sharp and sturdy, and would have to do. I'd seen guys on TV cut through wooden dummies with these things. Hopefully that meant they'd be able to penetrate dragon scales. If not, I was going to have to go for Marcus's wings or the eyes.

Or just lightning-bolt the crap out of him. They might breathe fire, but I was pretty sure that as lethal as Marcus was, he wouldn't enjoy being electrocuted.

Another tail swung, barely missing my head. A spray of blood decorated the torn wallpaper, and I realized that one dragon was significantly more injured than the other. Sergio. The slightly smaller one. It was difficult to keep them separate with the speed of their attacks, but I held the sword like a baseball bat and waited, ducking the smaller tail that swished my way and lunging forward.

Chopping a tree, I thought as the sword bit through scales and into flesh, jarring me as it came to an abrupt stop against what I assumed was bone. The dragon roared and pivoted, with me still holding the sword. It was like a childhood game of crack-the-whip—the sword firmly lodged in the dragon's leg, me gripping with hands slippery with blood and sweat as I tried to yank it free. My feet went airborne as the dragon kicked out. My hands slipped and I flew across the room to smack against the wall and slide to the floor.

Everything blurred, and my chest ached as I took tiny little breaths to get much-needed air into my lungs. I saw jaws open wide, sharp white teeth. I heard a click and rolled trying to get out of the way. Another set of jaws clamped down on the larger dragon's neck, pulling him aside and reclaiming his attention just as the burst of flame poured forth, missing me but melting clear through the stone where I'd just been sitting.

It felt like I walked through the inside of a kiln, like a thousand needles in my skin. The air was so hot it scorched my lungs and I turned my head, hoping that my distraction had been enough to give Sergio the upper hand.

And then I heard it. Far away, but approaching with the speed of a jet was a high-pitched shriek. I looked up and saw a golden-red blur, then covered my head as the outer wall of the room exploded inward.

Irix.

Marcus turned and blasted him with fire. I hunched down low, covering my head and fearing the worst. Sex demons weren't particularly high on the power-scale of Hel, and I was terrified about what dragon fire might do to my beloved. When I peeked up, what I saw made me cry out. Irix's leathery wings were nothing but bones and bits of glowing, smoldering flesh where the membranes had been. The skin and muscle had melted from his body, making him look like something from a horror movie. I readied my lightning, prepared to bring the entire villa down on our heads in retribution. But then something jolted the fury from me— Irix was still upright, his eyes like golden coals, his double-row of teeth sharp as he opened his beak wide and lunged forward to close on Marcus's scaled snout.

I gulped, thinking how much more terrifying Irix was as

this half-melted, undead prehistoric monster. Not bothering to fix his injuries, the demon went on full attack against Marcus, clawing and biting. The dragon kicked out and snapped one of the demon's wings backward, but beyond a squeal of pain, the damage didn't seem to bother Irix.

Sergio had stumbled free of the melee, shifting back into his human form to better stay out of the way. I saw the burns down his abdomen and along the side of his leg, saw the slashes and blood still dripping from his head and arm. He shot me a look that said a thousand words and dove for the desk, vanishing through the passage with an agility that someone with those burns shouldn't have been capable of.

Marcus roared to see his prey vanish and spun around, blowing a blast of dragon fire down the tunnel. Irix grabbed him from behind, digging his claws deep into the dragon's hard scales and using his skeletal wings to pull Marcus backward. The dragon pulled himself up to full height, lifting the demon from the ground, and threw himself backward.

They went out what had once been the outside wall, crashing into an enormous tree before bouncing off and hitting the ground. The tree cracked, smashing into the roof of the room next to me and raining down on my head with leaves, branches, and little acorn-like nuts. There was a rush of air and Marcus flew into the room, transforming just as he went down the passageway after Sergio and Bianca.

Irix was seconds behind him, crashing on the floor and skidding across it into the wall next to me, his wings useless, his flesh completely melted from his body. All that remained of the demon was blackened bones and those eerie, glowing, golden eyes.

In a flash he was in his human form in front of me, reaching out to help me to my feet. "Are you okay?" He gathered me close, and I tried to push him off.

"Yes. Get him. Go. He'll kill Sergio and Bianca. Go."

He ignored me, his hands roaming over my arms and down my waist. "Did he burn you? I will tear him apart and Own his soul, torturing him for all of eternity if he so much as bruised you."

I shivered, hearing the truth in Irix's words. He was a demon. Yes, he'd developed fondness and some compassion for others, but when it came down to it, I came first in his very short list of priorities. It warmed my heart to know I meant so much to an amoral demon, but I was fine. There were others who were about to be very much *not* fine.

"Irix, if you don't go help Bianca and Sergio I will never give you a blow job again."

He pulled away from me, his golden eyes searching mine. Then he chuckled. "Darling, your wish is my command."

Then he hopped on top of the splintered desk in all his naked glory and saluted, shifting into a much smaller version of his demon self before vanishing down the passageway.

CHAPTER 25

I hesitated at the entrance to the passageway, assailed with doubts. I was the weak link here—a feeling that was becoming irritatingly too familiar this trip. Yes I had talents, and in the past I'd been able to do amazing things with them, but always with the help of someone else fueling me. In New Orleans, I'd needed Irix's energy. In Maui, I'd needed Pele's. And in Napa Valley, I would have been dead had Irix and Harkel not been there to help.

It stung. I was too young, too weak, too inexperienced—both when it came to the enologist seminars and in this fight against dragons. There was a limit to what a twenty-two-year-old half-elf/half-succubus could do, and it chafed.

As I looked down the tunnel, I saw that it dropped about six feet down before heading off horizontally. Those before me had just dropped down, but I was relieved to see metal rungs in the stone side, just as there had been in the dungeon at the castle tower. I listened but heard nothing, which made me realize how far these tunnels went and how many twists and turns there must be to muffle the sound.

I couldn't stay here and wait, watching the inevitable

dragon battle that was probably right now squaring up across the lake and hoping that Irix, Bianca, and Sergio came out of this alive. I couldn't just wait to see what, or who, came out of this passageway at the end of the day. But what good could I do? It looked to be solid rock down there—an environment where I wouldn't have access to any plant life to use either for offense or defense. And I doubted letting lightning bolts loose in tight quarters would help either. I turned around, looking to see if that sword was here and usable, and nearly fell over something that felt like marbles under my feet.

A dozen of them rolled into the passageway, clattering on the stone below. I looked down and realized that the floor was covered with acorns—not marbles. The gigantic green oak had come crashing down on the villa, and hundreds of the unripened acorns had broken free.

I dropped to my knees, grabbing them and shoving them into every pocket, into my waistband, down my shirt, even into my bra. Then I climbed down the iron rungs, closed my eyes and stretched out my senses to catch the whiff of sulfur and brimstone in the distance, then took off.

I ran as fast as my half-elven legs could carry me, through the narrow passageways, ducking down, and jumping up when a ledge blocked my path. Acorns fell from my clothing as I ran, leaving a trail that reminded me of the breadcrumbs Hansel and Gretel had dropped behind them. Remembering their fate, I hoped I didn't end up in a witch's, or dragon's, oven.

A blast shook the tunnel, raining dust and bits of rock down on my head. I speeded up, beginning to sweat. Was the tunnel growing hotter? Yes, it most definitely was. And that realization prepared me for the scene that greeted me as I rounded a sharp corner.

There was a large cavern area with rock walls that glowed

red and orange. It was so hot I could hardly breathe. Three dragons and one prehistoric bird-like demon stood in the room.

One dragon stood hovering over another that looked seriously injured, guarding it and baring its huge teeth to the other dragon. Irix was behind them, trying to kick through where the tunnel had caved in, cutting off their exit. Marcus had them trapped, and without much room to maneuver and fight, he had the advantage. All he needed was a few blasts of his dragon fire, and he could kill them all.

And he knew it. He was letting them think about their situation, letting the futility of it all sink in before he killed them.

It was so hot that I wasn't sure my plan would work, but it was better than no plan at all. I emptied my pockets and yanked my shirt from my pants, shaking out the hundreds of acorns I'd carried down the tunnels.

Grow. I poured my energy into the acorns, fighting against the heat that threatened to sear and burn my little saplings before I could bring them to a big enough size to do any damage. Marcus turned to see me, and laughed, the sound odd coming out of a dragon's mouth, then he swung his tail and knocked down my trees.

The other dragon, Bianca I decided, roared and shot fire at her uncle, but she was clearly tired and it did nothing more than turn his scales a brighter, deeper black. Irix kept kicking, a thin beam of light coming through the rubble showing me that he was close to getting through. If I could just buy him enough time, he could get through, and once outside they'd have room to fight. If they could get outside. Sergio didn't look like he was moving.

I scooped acorns up off the stone floor and threw them at Marcus, growing them in mid-air, but they just bounced off his hide. I got lucky with one and poked him in the eye. It didn't do much more than make him mad.

Real mad. He reared back and snarled, that clicking sound deep within his throat. I squeaked in panic and grabbed more acorns from the ground. Irix let out an earsplitting shriek when he saw what was going on and tried to launch himself over Sergio and Bianca to protect me, but there was nothing he could do.

It seemed like time slowed. Bianca trying to engage her uncle and draw his attention from me. Irix, clawing around the others blocking his path. Marcus opening his mouth wide—so wide I could see the fire gathering in his throat. I threw the acorns, because I didn't know what else to do, and moved to duck—futile though that might be.

Before I could drop down, I saw the acorns go into Marcus' mouth and down his throat. He choked, coughing.

Grow. I threw every last bit of myself into the command, reaching out and connecting with Irix, yanking energy from him without any reservation.

It was a desperate act, but I was desperate. I wasn't sure if any of those acorns had survived the dragon fire in his throat. Probably not, given that I'd seen dragon fire melt stone and metal. But if there had been one acorn that hadn't burned to ash...

Nothing happened. Then suddenly everything happened. Marcus inhaled on a cough, extinguishing the fire in his throat. Of all those I'd thrown, one acorn burst into life, slamming its branches and trunk down through the lower half of Marcus's jaw, dropping him to the ground and pinning him to the floor as the roots slammed their way through the stone. He clawed the ground, trying to get up, then clawed his face, making that clicking noise in his throat to summon his fire and burn this tree.

Grow.

I felt my knees hit stone, my hands shaking as they touched the floor. The tree trunk thickened, branches sprouting and lifting, punching through the dragon's skull and reaching upward, slamming into the ceiling of the tunnel and knocking their way through to the sky above. Rock and dirt rained down on us, and when it finally settled enough for me to see, I started to laugh.

Probably not the most appropriate thing to do when I'd just impaled a dragon through the head with an oak tree, but sometimes humor takes a dark path.

"Amber?"

I looked up and laughed even harder. Irix was in his human form, naked, looking like he'd dropped fifty pounds. His skin was dotted with blood, his face haggard. Dirt and stone dust covered him.

"I pulled so much energy from you, threw so much at him. I thought I'd killed us both." My laugh turned to a sob and I covered my face, smearing dirt into my tears. Irix's arms came around me and lifted me, cradling me against him.

"It's a good thing I've been storing up." He rocked me gently. "Somehow I knew you were going to need a bunch of energy, but this wasn't exactly what I was envisioning."

"I killed a dragon," I hiccupped. "All by myself I killed a dragon. That's pretty fucking amazing."

"Yes." He chuckled, kissing the top of my head. "Yes, it is."

"Bianca? Sergio? Are they?" I squirmed a bit in his grasp, trying to look over his shoulder to see if the other two dragons were okay. It would be horrible if I killed Marcus, only to have the tunnel ceiling collapse and do in the two dragons I was trying to save.

"We're okay," Bianca called out. "Sergio's hurt, but he'll be fine."

I remembered the burns on the boy's abdomen and leg

and thought about the scars his grandfather bore. But he was alive. That was what mattered. And the dragon who'd started all this was dead. Marcus had killed Guido. He'd tried to start a war. He'd tried to assassinate his great-niece. And now he was dead. I'd killed him. Me. A twenty-two-year-old half-elf/half-succubus.

"I killed a dragon with an acorn." I giggled, drawing a look of concern from Irix. I was weak. I could barely stand upright, I was so weak, but I'd killed a dragon. With an acorn.

CHAPTER 26

Sergio shifted back into his human form and leaned heavily on Bianca as we all walked through the tunnel back to the villa. Me and three naked people, walking through a dark underground passageway. It just added to the entire surreal feeling.

Bianca cried when she saw the damage to her treasure, but then she straightened her spine, and turned to me.

"I need to fly out to see Grandmother and let her know what her brother has done—and what he was intending on doing. That should get her to hold back her attack."

"Me, too," Sergio said. He was leaning against one of the few walls that hadn't been smashed, pale and obviously in pain. "If Mother agreed to a peace, she'll want to uphold that. She won't fight unless the others attack."

"And I'll make sure they won't attack," Bianca assured him.

I was so impressed by these two. They were teenagers, and yet they already were showing the leadership and thoughtfulness they would need to lead their clans. Or clan. Because I had renewed hopes that now the two families would be able to put their differences aside and let the pair of them heal wounds that had festered for centuries.

"Is there someplace neutral where both Daniela and Catarina can meet?" Irix asked. "I think it would be best if the two of them sat down together and faced each other for this, rather than deal with go-betweens. It's harder to claim misunderstanding when you've made assurances in person."

Sergio and Bianca turned to each other.

"Here?" the girl asked.

Sergio nodded. "It's in our territory, yet it's your treasure. If you would consent to having Mother here after what she did…"

Bianca nodded. "Absolutely. I'm the one she injured. If I welcome her here, it will show Grandmother that I don't harbor any grudge toward Daniela. And that I don't fear having her so close to my treasure."

There was a tremble in her voice at the last sentence that told me how much it bothered her to have anyone near her treasure—especially someone she'd always considered an enemy. Again it struck me how mature she was to force down that instinctual response and offer her home in a gesture of good faith.

"And if they don't agree?" I asked, because that was still a possibility. "What happens if at the end of all this, both women decide on a cease fire, but still refuse to acknowledge your relationship?"

Bianca's jaw firmed, her eyes narrowed. "Then I will give up my treasure. I'll leave with Sergio, if he still wants to elope. I'll leave and I won't look back. I might die young. And it will pain me terribly to leave my family and my home behind, never to see them again. But I'll do it to be with Sergio. I won't sneak around and hide with him, denying to my family that he is my mate. I want to be with him openly, for the rest of my life. And if I can't do that here, I'll do it somewhere else."

"And me as well." As she'd spoken, Sergio had moved closer, taking her hands in his. "Bianca," he said, lowering himself painfully down to one knee. "Darling, I'm naked and dirty and will forever bear these horrible scars. There's a good chance I'll be completely broke and we'll be homeless somewhere in Europe. I don't even have a ring for you yet. But will you marry me, Bianca?"

Her eyes shone and she dropped down to her knees level with him. "I will marry you, Sergio. Yes, I will marry you."

And that had to be the most romantic proposal I'd ever witnessed. Well, besides Irix's, that is.

"Then we should hurry," Irix reminded them gently. "Before your families begin to actually fight."

That got them moving. Bianca jumped up and helped Sergio to his feet, exclaiming over his wounds as he shifted into his dragon form. She made sure he could take flight, then shifted as well, flying toward the opposite mountain. Irix came up beside me, wrapping one of his arms around my waist and pulling me close.

It wasn't long before four winged shapes approached over the lake, two from the north, and two from the east. Irix helped me through the hole in the side of the villa and down onto the lawn where we watched the dragons circle and come in for a landing next to the broken tree.

All four of them shifted into their human form. And were naked. I'd never get used to this. It was like being at a nude beach where I was the only one with my clothing on.

It didn't seem to bother the dragons. Daniela and Sergio walked forward, then sat on a pair of stone benches. Catarina and Bianca did the same.

"First, please allow me to extend my apologies toward losing my temper and injuring Bianca," Daniela spoke first. "I can promise you that will never happen again. And as I told Amber, I'm willing to allow Bianca and a family member of her choosing access to the villa without any harassment on my family's part. She is free to walk anywhere in our territory aside from Villa Sommariva as long as her intentions are peaceful, and we will not bother her."

Catarina gave a stately nod. "And I apologize for our attack on your treasure. Our retaliation was excessive."

Daniela smiled wanly. "I'm a mother. I understand a knee-jerk overreaction when it comes to our children. Or grandchildren."

I held my breath. Hoping that things would continue to move forward without any intervention on mine or Irix's part.

"Bianca has told me that your family had nothing to do with Guido's death, or the damage to our holdings last night." Catarina reached out a hand to smooth her granddaughter's hair. "And I owe a debt of gratitude toward your son for protecting her from an assassin."

I noticed that she hadn't named Marcus. It must hurt to know that her own brother murdered her son, and would have killed her granddaughter. She had pride, and clearly some painful truths were best kept private.

Daniela nodded. "Do you accept our offer of peace?"

Catarina hesitated. "A cease fire, perhaps. I cannot see there ever being peace between our families, and what is between your son and my granddaughter will have to end. That pains me greatly, but I see no other way."

"Yes," Daniela quickly replied. "Our family would never accept a mate-bond between a Sommariva and a Montenegro, especially with our heir."

"Then they will lose their heir," Sergio snapped. "Mother, I have asked Bianca to marry me and she has accepted. We will leave, and you will never see us again if you don't accept our mate-bond and acknowledge it."

"Me, too," Bianca told her grandmother. "Either the family accepts us, or we will leave."

I suddenly saw a sliver of common ground, because we happened to be standing right on it. Bianca had welcomed the enemy into her home, made it a neutral spot. The villa was hers, but was in Sergio's territory. It was both of theirs. It was where both families overlapped, and hopefully where they could come together.

"Wait just a moment," I told them all. "Here's where we are so far. Both of you agree that Bianca gets access to her villa without any hindrance or threat. There will be no retaliation for previous attacks. Neither of you will do harm either to each other or to the other's property."

I waited for both women to nod.

"Sergio and Bianca have stated that they are mate-bonded and will be married. That's not up for discussion. It's happening. Done. No argument. What is open for discussion is where they will live and if either of them will continue to be the heir."

I could practically hear the sharp, pointy dragon teeth grinding.

"If Bianca is no longer the heir, my treasure will go to a distant cousin from my great-uncle's line," Catarina ground out, as if the very idea caused her pain.

Daniela sighed. "Mine as well upon my death. I don't want my son to vanish, never to see him again, but I don't want him a target for assassination from his very own family."

"Sergio is welcome within my villa," Bianca spoke up as if

she was reading my mind. "This villa is my treasure. We will both abdicate and live here. My treasure is his treasure."

There was a moment of ominous silence. "That is not wise, Bianca," Catarina told her firmly.

"But–"

"No," the older woman said. "I know you love him, child, but establishing your treasure as a neutral territory opens up all sorts of other problems. You'll never be safe here. Your treasure will never be safe."

"*He* is my treasure," Bianca insisted. "He is my mate. We will be married. Then what is his is mine."

"Perhaps…" Daniela tapped a finger against her lips. "They are young. Let us declare a peace—not a cease-fire, but a peace. Villa Montenegro will be neutral ground, if Bianca consents to allow her treasure to be called such. I will designate a few of the towns around the villa likewise to be neutral territory. We will arrange meetings, non-confrontational events where both of our families in small numbers can be present and can grow used to each other's presence. Perhaps in time this peace will be strong enough for our families to unite through a formal announcement of Bianca and Sergio's mating."

Catarina thought for a moment. "Very small numbers at first, and we should be present during these events to ensure that no blows are exchanged. Do you truly think it will work?"

Daniela smiled. "I've recently discovered that my father was meeting your son Guido in local taverns to play backgammon. If the two of them can manage to build a friendship, then I'm hopeful others in our family can as well."

"Can you wait?" Irix asked the two teenagers. "You'll need to continue to hide your romance for a while, maybe slowly bring it into the open as tensions between your two families decrease."

Bianca and Sergio's eyes met. The boy grinned. "Sure. As long as I'm not grounded and have the freedom to come and go as I please, to visit friends and possibly even spend the weekend away. With friends."

Bianca blushed. "The one passageway will need extensive repairs, but the others will always be open to you, Sergio. I meant what I said. My treasure is your treasure. This is your home. And I hope you plan to spend as much time here as you can."

Catarina sighed. "I see a million things that can go wrong with this, but I'll do it for my granddaughter. I remember what it was like to lose your heart. And I remember what it feels like to have your life-mate gone forever. I don't want her to suffer that pain."

Understanding flashed across Daniela's face, because she too had lost her mate just as Catarina had lost hers.

"Peace? And shall we pray that soon that peace may lead to friendship?" Daniela put out her hand.

Catarina reached across and took it in her own, shaking the woman's hand firmly. "To peace. And future friendship."

I let out a breath. It seemed that for once, this Romeo and Juliet story wouldn't end in tragedy after all.

CHAPTER 27

Our tests had been rescheduled for the next morning. I'm sure the other attendees appreciated the extra time to study, but the delay wouldn't benefit me. By the time Daniela and Catarina had hammered out all the details of their peace, and we'd helped Bianca put up tarps and section off the portion of her villa that was now in serious need of repair, it was late afternoon.

Irix and I were hungry. And I'm not just talking about missing lunch either. I was shaking like I'd run a marathon, and my fiancé looked positively haggard. I wasn't sure what we'd be able to attract right now, but taking care of our demon needs was paramount.

Irix was so exhausted that he didn't even protest my climbing into the driver's seat of the Panda. Bianca had given him some of her Uncle Guido's clothing from a bedroom closet, and surprisingly it all fit reasonably well. None of it was cheap, so of the pair of us, Irix was far more appealing. I was filthy, sweaty, with a blistered burn on my left arm that wouldn't heal until I got laid. Bianca had also generously offered me some of her attire, but the girl was barely five feet tall and about thirty pounds lighter. I took one look at the slacks and light-weight sweater and knew I'd look ridiculous, even if I managed to get it all on without ripping it apart at the seams.

Miraculously, Irix and I had scored. Repeatedly. And although I knew I needed to study, some things took priority, so I ended up not hitting my books until well after sunset. And I was pretty sure it was evident in my test scores.

By noon I had a raging headache. An essay exam. A verbal exam. A tasting of three white and three red wines, and then the presentation of my recipe.

The recipe had been the most nerve-racking. They'd asked me all sorts of questions about how I planned on enhancing the orange blossom aromas, or balancing the something with the something else. I had no idea. I was an elf. I just stuck my finger into things and manipulated the structure through my non-human skills. I knew that wouldn't fly here, and they'd probably be appalled at the idea of me sticking my finger in vats of wine anyway. Originally we were supposed to do our testing, then leave at noon and come back the next day for results, but now it was all squished into Friday, so we sat in the courtyard overlooking the vineyard with the few scorched rows and waited for the others to complete their tests and everything to be tallied up.

"How did you call those reds?" Eva asked me in between bites of ham and cheese. It was her third sandwich. I'd learned over the last week that my new friend was a nervous eater.

"2014 New Zealand Red Zin, 2015 Italian Cab, and 2012 French Cab."

She grimaced, stuffing the rest of the sandwich in her mouth.

"What? Did I blow it? How did you call them?" I was

panicking. I'd been panicking since last night, but now I was really panicking.

"I had the Red Zin a California."

"It was a California," Celio told us, his voice full of smug confidence. "Did you guys call the Gewürztraminer?"

I muttered something unintelligible. Gewürztraminer. I'd totally screwed that one up.

"It's okay," Eva told me. "I'm sure you killed it on the written exam."

That one had been less nerve-racking. Actually I had some confidence that I might actually have scored reasonably well on that one. There had been a lot of viticulture and botany questions, and I'd been able to memorize enough of the chemistry stuff that I was fairly certain I at least passed. The oral exam hadn't been as horrible as I'd feared either.

"They're calling us back in," Marta said. She stood, smoothed her hands down her pants, and gave me a nervous smile.

We all followed her in, Eva grabbing another sandwich from the table in the hall.

We sat. They passed out our scores. I paged through mine, relieved that I hadn't done as poorly as I'd feared. Then as one of the presenters went on and on about how well we'd all done, and that each of us had promise and a brilliant future, Catarina and Bianca came in.

My stomach turned into a gigantic chunk of lead. Eva frantically ate her sandwich. Celio clenched his teeth, staring straight ahead. Marta twisted her hands together and bit her lip. Every one of the attendees looked like they were all on the verge of a heart attack.

Catarina took the stage. I saw Bianca wink at me and smile.

No. No. Please don't let me get this for the wrong reasons. I glanced over at Celio and knew how much he'd hate me if I won because of the friendship I'd developed with Bianca, because of how I'd helped her and Sergio.

Catarina repeated all the praise the presenters had just heaped on us, then looked down at the sheet of paper she held.

"Our new apprentice enologist is…Marta Lefebvre."

Everyone let out a breath. The room applauded as Marta cried and laughed at the same time. Catarina finished her speech, thanking us all for attending and wishing us luck in our professional careers. We all took turns hugging and congratulating Marta, and the room slowly began to clear.

It felt so anticlimactic. There were still ham sandwiches on the table in the hall. Notecards and papers were scattered around where attendees had abandoned them as they walked out of the castle to their cars. I watched as they headed back to their lives, feeling as if I'd just turned a corner in my own.

"I wanted you to win."

I turned around and saw Bianca behind me.

"I really hoped you win because I would love to have you here with me for the next two years. You did well. Everyone did well."

"Marta deserved it," I told her. "She's really good. Not just as an enologist either. She's good with people. She'll be great at teaching and mentoring others. I think you've got one of the best."

Bianca gave me a quick hug. "I know, but I still wish you'd won. Will you and Irix be able to come out to the wedding? Sergio is thinking next fall. It might be a small, private ceremony depending on how this peace is progressing between our families."

I looked down at her hands and saw the big honking diamond on her finger. She wiggled it at me with a happy grin.

"It was Sergio's grandmother's. I met his grandfather last

night. He's…he's really scary, but he gave us his blessing once he realized that I wasn't there to steal his treasure, and that Sergio would be calling the Montenegro treasures his own." She blushed. "And he grabbed my butt when he hugged me."

I shook my head. "He grabbed mine, too. Don't let him get away with that. He doesn't get a pass on groping his granddaughter-in-law just because he's old and in his Melancholy."

She laughed. "I won't. Although I don't think he'll do it again. Sergio told him next time he groped me, he'd find himself with a stump instead of a hand. Can you and Irix make it to the wedding? Please say yes!"

"I'm pretty sure I'll be able to make it," I told her, thinking of what I'd be doing in the fall. Irix and I would be in New Orleans, with me working with Jordan. I was confident that I could get a week off to fly to Italy. "Do you think you and Sergio could come to our wedding? We're tentatively planning for early May."

She bit her lip. "It's scary to think of being so far from our treasure, but…yes. Yes, we will come. We need to trust our families to guard our treasures without us, and I truly want Sergio and I to see some of the world before we become too bonded to our villas and castle. Yes, we will definitely come."

"We're leaving Sunday," I told her. "One more day in Italy. Will we see you before, or is this goodbye?"

She grinned. "I think Sergio was hoping to take you and Irix around to the parties on the lake Saturday night, so I'll see you then."

Good, because this trip suddenly seemed to be winding down too fast. Yesterday Irix and I were facing a dragon, and not twenty-four hours later I was saying goodbye to new friends, and putting away any hopes I'd had about a career in the wine industry and two years in Italy.

I lingered a bit in the hall, then headed out to the parking area where my car and a red Fiat were the only two still in the lot. Sitting over on the short stone fence where Eva and I had been earlier was Celio. I don't know why I didn't just get in my car and head back to Lake Como, but instead I headed over and sat next to him.

"I'm sorry you didn't win," I told him.

His laugh had an edge of bitterness to it. "Don't you mean you're sorry you didn't win?"

"I knew the afternoon of day one I wasn't going to win. I don't have the background or experience that the rest of you do. I'm glad I came. I learned a lot and met some really cool people, but Sunday I'll head back to the States and put my botany talents to use in a different way."

He turned to me in surprise. "You're giving up? Don't give up. You've got loads of natural talent. You just need to work in the industry for a few years and get some experience. In five years, you could be teaching at this thing if you stick with it."

Wow. Celio had actually said something nice to me. Color me shocked.

"I was kinda at a crossroads when I came here. A friend of mine had offered me a job down in Louisiana studying the bayous. She works for the park service down there now, and is forming her own non-profit. She's already been awarded a grant for the work and is starting this spring. My fiancé has a house down there. I've got friends there. The job is really interesting, and I know I could make a difference…."

"Then why spend a week here, studying like crazy for an enology apprenticeship?" he asked.

I sighed. "When I applied for the internship at DiMarche, it was a total long shot. It sounded cool, and I was a bit shocked when I got it. And I loved working in the vineyards. I thought… I guess I just wanted to see where this would take me. I knew this would be a long shot as well, but if I'd gotten it, I would have thrown myself into it one hundred percent. It's weird, thinking how very different my life would have been if you all had suddenly gotten the flu and I'd been the only one who showed up today for the testing," I teased.

"Yes, well that's the only way you would have won, Bimbo," he laughed. "I still think you're foolish for not pursuing this. You've got talent, and you're really good with people."

"Yes, I am. Especially presenters who are interested in lunchtime hanky-panky," I drawled, remembering that he'd seen me sneak out with Leo.

He snorted. "Not just that. I saw how you built up a friendship with the Montenegros. You're good with people. But I guess that will be just as useful a skill working on your bayous."

"Maybe." I swung my feet and looked out over the vineyard. "So what are you going to do now?"

He shrugged. "I still have my sommelier position in Paris, but I think I might see if I can get something with one of the wineries in Spain next year. As much as I love pairing the right wine with the right food, I really want to work more on the creative side."

I climbed off the wall to stand, brushing the dirt off my slacks. "Well, best of luck to you, Eurotrash Snob."

He stood as well and extended his hand. "You too, American Bimbo. Keep in touch? Now that you're not in competition with me, I'd love to hear how things are going with those bayous."

I shook his hand, and felt something between us. Not sexual at all—which was confusing the heck out of my succubus self. Friendship. A completely platonic friendship. Yeah. That would be cool.

"I will keep in touch," I promised.

Maybe he could recommend a good wine for my

wedding. Maybe we'd honeymoon in Paris and eat at the restaurant where he worked. Maybe someday he'd head across the Atlantic and visit us in New Orleans. I hoped so, but for now I was putting this chapter of my life behind me, leaving this castle and winery to drive back to Lake Como where I'd party with Irix, celebrate our last few days in Italy, then fly back to the States where I'd give Jordan the good news and plan my wedding.

My wedding. Closing one chapter of my life, and opening another. I was so excited.

EPILOGUE

It was early Saturday night. I was packed and ready to leave, feeling that odd sense of sorrow and excitement that comes when a vacation ends. Irix and I were restless, so the pair of us headed out to a little tavern that had outdoor seating, and Irix immediately headed out after a patron who had been giving him the eye ever since we'd arrived, leaving me with half of a bottle of wine and a yummy charcuterie tray that I wasn't about to let go uneaten.

I'd just poured myself a second glass of wine when I felt something. Actually I felt someone—a presence that sent a shiver down my back. It was an angel. He appeared from nowhere, materializing over near the boat rental dock and walking over toward me. Without a word, he sat down next to me, eyeing my wine.

"Hi." What does one say to an angel? Should I offer him a glass of wine? Some cheese?

"Elf. Merry meet. How does your human fermented fruit drink compared to those from your homeland?"

I'd never had elven wine, but I remembered how Hallwyn had described it. "There is more of an alcohol bite even among similar types and strengths, and the flavors are less complex and rougher, but I find it quite acceptable." I hoped Irix had snuck out the back, and was far, far away from this angel.

Wait. There was no need for Irix to run.

"He's got immunity, you know." I lifted my chin in a challenge to the angel.

He laughed softly, taking a drink of my wine and contemplating it a moment before nodding in approval.

"Yes, I know. I'm with the Grigori and we've all been told. I recognized his energy signature a few days ago and have quite enjoyed the show the two of you have put on here. An elf and a demon—a sex demon at that. I never thought that would happen. Be careful, elf. Others might not be as open-minded as you and might see your affections as a betrayal."

That betrayal had happened with my mother. I hoped I didn't meet her end. But the world was a different place. *This* world was a different place than the elven kingdom in Hel that had sentenced my mother to death for daring to bear a half-breed child.

"I'll be careful," I told the angel, knowing that I'd already been far from careful in the last year.

The angel looked in the direction Irix had gone. "Tell him to take care as well. There are angels here who are not Grigori and who won't acknowledge his immunity. Both of you should be on your guard."

"Thank you."

He stood, then eyeing my wine picked up the glass and drained it. "I needed to shave this morning. Shave. And the beverage affects me, calming me, making me want to slumber. We angels can no longer easily resist the call of the flesh. This world is a different place than it was just a few short years ago."

I nodded, not sure where he was going with all of this.

"Chaos." His eyes met mine. "We try to hold it back. We try to mold and shape it to suit our needs, but in the end it destroys everything."

"There is no such thing as destruction, only change," I told him, repeating something Sam had once told me.

A ghost of a smile hinted at the edge of his mouth and the wine glass shattered in his hand.

"Change such as this? But what remains no longer serves, no longer is suitable to its intended purpose." Bits of glass tinted pink with faint blood rained down upon the table-cloth. "Be ready, elf. For the apocalypse is upon us."

Although the individuals in this book are fictional, the settings are based on real villas and locations you can visit if you find yourself in the Lake Como area.

Villa Sommariva is based on the famous Villa Carlotta in Cadenabbia, complete with paintings, statuary, and amazing gardens. There's even the wet grotto that Daniela likes so much.

Villa Montenegro is based on Villa Balbianello, built in the 12th century. It's been used in several big budget movies (and it's the perfect place for an incubus to propose).

Castle Abbondio is based on the Castle of Grumello near Bergamo. http://www.castellodigrumello.it/ Yes, it does have a winery, vineyards, and a tower with a really cool dungeon. (No, I did not have sex in the dungeon.) Cristina Kettlitz, whose family has owned the castle for generations, was an amazing and gracious hostess. She was amused that I'd be using elements from her family's castle in my novel, and that the fictional version would be a dragon clan's "treasure".

If you'd like to rent a villa for your vacation like Irix and Amber did, check out Love Como (LoveComo.com), where Vittoria Solano will help you find the perfect spot for your holiday. There's even a recipe for Pizzocheri on their blog!

And lastly, many thanks to Daniela Stephanz Anderson, who organized the tour I tagged along with this past spring. She's a whirlwind of energy and if there's something she doesn't know, give her five minutes and she will. Daniela asked if I could name a character after her in this book, so *poof*, she's a dragon!

I had no idea what the fantasy plot for City of Lust would be until we were heading in to Lake Como on our bus from the airport, and I looked across the lake into the snow-capped jagged mountains and envisioned dragons circling their peaks, diving down across the waters. It's a gorgeous spot, and I highly recommend Lake Como as a vacation destination, as well as New Orleans, Maui, and Napa Valley.

Hel…well, I don't recommend vacationing there!

I hope you've enjoyed Amber and Irix's exploits in the Half-breed series. Although City of Lust is the final book in this series, look for a short story in 2018 on the wedding, and the occasional cameo in other Imp World books.

ACKNOWLEDGMENTS

A huge thanks to my copyeditors Kimberly Cannon and Jennifer Cosham whose eagle eyes catch all my typos and keep my comma problem in line, and to Damonza, for cover design.

Most of all, thanks to my children, who have suffered many nights of microwaved chicken nuggets and take-out pizza so that Mommy can follow her dream.

ABOUT THE AUTHOR

Debra lives in a little house in the woods of Maryland with her sons and two slobbery bloodhounds. On a good day, she jogs and horseback rides, hopefully managing to keep the horse between herself and the ground. Her only known super power is 'Identify Roadkill'.

debradunbar.com

<u>The Templar Series</u>

Dead Rising

Last Breath

Bare Bones

Famine's Feast

Dark Crossroads (2018)

* * *

<u>The Imp Series</u>

A Demon Bound

Satan's Sword

Elven Blood

Devil's Paw

Imp Forsaken

Angel of Chaos

Kingdom of Lies

Exodus

Queen of the Damned

* * *

<u>Half-breed Series</u>

Demons of Desire

Sins of the Flesh

Cornucopia

Unholy Pleasures

City of Lust

* * *

<u>Imp World Novels</u>

No Man's Land

Stolen Souls

Three Wishes

Northern Lights

Far From Center

* * *

<u>Northern Wolves</u>

Juneau to Kenai

Rogue

Winter Fae

Bad Seed